Browse the critics' glowing praise for *US...*
author RHONDA POLLERO and her "t...
Finley Anderson Tanner novels

"Witty, upbeat, all-around entertaining. . . . A great read with plenty of attitude!"

—Janet Evanovich

"A fun, fascinating journey you won't want to miss."

—Nora Roberts

"A good blend of laughter and mystery. . . . Perfect for a little escape."

—*Fallen Angel Reviews*

"Amusingly entertaining and filled with fascinatingly appealing characters."

—*Single Titles*

"Will make readers eager for an encore."

—*Kirkus Reviews* (starred review)

"Bright, breezily written. . . . Full of humor and quirky characters."

—*Sun-Sentinel*

"Stylishly entertaining. . . . Certain to be a runway hit."

—*Booklist*

"A great book to curl up with on the beach."

—*Fresh Fiction**

"Fun."

—*Publishers Weekly*

"Rhonda Pollero's humor and compelling mystery will keep you turning pages."

—Tess Gerritsen

"An amazing talent. . . . Murder has never been this much fun!"

—Cherry Adair

BARGAIN
HUNTING

Rhonda Pollero

GALLERY BOOKS

New York   London   Toronto   Sydney   New Delhi

Gallery Books
A Division of Simon & Schuster, Inc.
1230 Avenue of the Americas
New York, NY 10020

First Gallery Books trade paperback edition October 2012

GALLERY BOOKS and colophon are registered trademarks of Simon & Schuster, Inc.

For information about special discounts for bulk purchases, please contact Simon & Schuster Special Sales at 1-866-506-1949 or business@simonandschuster.com.

The Simon & Schuster Speakers Bureau can bring authors to your live event. For more information or to book an event contact the Simon & Schuster Speakers Bureau at 1-866-248-3049 or visit our website at www.simonspeakers.com.

Designed by Jaime Putorti

Manufactured in the United States of America

10 9 8 7 6 5 4 3 2 1

Library of Congress Cataloging-in-Publication Data

Pollero, Rhonda
  Bargain hunting / Rhona Pollero
    p.   cm.
1. Women lawyers—Fiction. 2. Florida—Fiction. I. Title.
  PS3616.O5684B37   2012
  813'.6—dc23   2012015019

ISBN 978-1-4165-9082-8
ISBN 978-1-4391-0100-1 (ebook)

For Shirley,
you finally get your wish.

BARGAIN HUNTING

Some mothers are nurturing,
others eat their own young.

one

"You have god-awful taste in men, Finley."

This, I mused, from the woman currently trolling for husband number five. Or was it six? I would have fired that shot over the bow, but I knew I was outgunned. My mother was a formidable foe, and for some reason, when I was being called on the carpet, I morphed from a capable twenty-nine-year-old into a timid seventeen-year-old.

"And to think you brought that man to your sister's wedding. I raised you better than that."

I nearly choked on my Cobb salad. Raised me? She'd been too busy being Mrs. Somebody-or-Another to bother raising me. I used to tell my friends that I'd been raised by wolves until one of them pointed out that at least wolves show affection by licking their young. My mother wasn't hardwired for affection. Well, not unless you were my perfect younger sister, Lisa. She'd been perfect as a pediatric oncologist and now she was perfectly married to the perfect Dr. David Huntington-St. John IV, one of the richest men in Atlanta. Without even trying, Lisa has elevated perfect to the next stratosphere.

Me? I'm a paralegal. My mother sees this as a menial job and never understood why I took my LSATs but never bothered applying to law schools. She doesn't get that I want a life, not an eighty-hour-a-week job chained to a desk.

"Tony would have been a much more appropriate choice," she insisted as she chased a bit of grilled mahimahi around on her plate.

"Tony has a fourteen-year-old daughter *and* he's my boss," I said, defending myself as I dabbed at the corners of my mouth with my linen napkin. I'd barely eaten a third of my salad, but my churning stomach couldn't handle another bite.

"You of all people should know that isn't a problem," my mother said as she smoothed her perfectly lacquered brown hair. As usual, everything about her was proper and in its right place. She had on a pale yellow Chanel suit with lime green pumps and, unlike every other woman in Florida, stockings. She wore a pretty lime-and-yellow brooch up high on her collarbone. Very Jackie O., which made sense, since my mother fashioned herself after the American icon.

Cassidy Presley Tanner Browning Johnstone Rossi—or whatever the order is—is a stunning woman in her early fifties, though she looks more like forty thanks to early intervention plastic surgery. She was barely twenty-two when I was born. At the time, she was a single mother, a fact I only found out when I was thirteen. Until then, I'd been told that my name was a combination of family names. What went unsaid was that Finley and Anderson were the surnames of the two men my mother was sleeping with when she got pregnant with me. And yes, that does mean my initials are FAT; and no, there isn't a joke I haven't already heard and disliked.

My mother likes to blame me for the premature end to her career as an opera singer at the Met in New York, but in all honesty, she developed nodules on her throat and once they were removed, her voice never fully recovered. Just as she hadn't fully recovered from my transgression at my sister's recent society wedding in Atlanta. Only it wasn't my transgression. Liam McGarrity was the sinner in question. He'd gone out of his way to take potshots at my mother, and while it had been fun at the time, the hour had come for me to shed my pound of flesh.

At least I was shedding in a good place. Sunday lunch at Ironhorse Country Club was lovely. The small restaurant had floor-to-ceiling glass overlooking the manicured golf course beyond. I didn't give a flaming fig about golf; I just loved the stunning flowers and meticulously kept grassy knolls. Not that we were there for the view—at least not *that* view. My mother had her eye on a cardiologist from the neighborhood, so we'd been lunching at Ironhorse for a while now. Guess it was lucky for Mom that she'd gotten the club membership in one of her lucrative divorce settlements.

"At least do me the courtesy of listening when I speak to you," she chastised in the quiet but threatening tone I hear mothers use on toddlers at grocery stores.

"I am listening." Kinda. "But what more can I do than apologize? Which I have done a gazillion times already."

Her brown eyes narrowed. "You're sorry I'm upset, but you aren't sorry for doing what you did. That is the crux of the problem."

I wanted to throw Liam under the bus. After all, it was his idea to get frisky at the wedding for all to see. It was his idea to exchange verbal barbs with my mother. I was an innocent bystander. Albeit an amused one. "Great-aunt Susan liked Liam," I offered weakly. My great-aunt didn't just like him. I think she had a serious crush on him, especially after he'd spirited her around the dance floor a time or two.

"Aunt Susan likes every man."

Then no wonder you were named for her. Oh, right, back to the name thing. My mother was born Susan Presley but thought Cassidy was a better stage name so she had it legally changed.

"Would it have killed you to bring Tony Caprelli on the most important day in our family's life since Lisa graduated, *with honors,* from medical school? And what did you do to your back?"

"Nothing, my back is fine, why?"

"I just assumed there was a medical reason for the way you're slouching."

Out of habit I snapped into position. "Tony had an emergency that weekend, Mom. Liam or no Liam, he still would have missed the wedding."

"*That* we could have explained away. But that vulgar man. He made you a spectacle."

"Since half the bridesmaids were lit and practically giving lap dances by the third hour, I think my one dance paled in comparison."

"Not in my mind, it didn't."

Thankfully Philippe came over and asked, "May I take your plates?"

"Yes, thank you," we said in unison.

Philippe took both plates and balanced them in one hand and on his forearm. "Shall I bring a dessert menu?"

"Yes."

"No," my mother countered. Poor Philippe's face showed he didn't care for being west of the rock and east of the hard place.

"Just coffee," I relented.

"Tea for me," my mother corrected.

"When did you start drinking tea?" I asked.

"It's much better for you. You drink far too much coffee. All that caffeine will eat through your stomach lining."

"Tea has caffeine."

My mother slowly shook her head as her collagened lips pursed so she could make some sort of tsking sound. "Must you argue with me over every little thing? One would think you'd be grateful being treated to a nice lunch."

I noticed that as she criticized me, her attention was drawn over my left shoulder. Discreetly, I dropped my napkin on the floor and as I bent to pick it up, I glanced backward. "I am grateful," I lied. It wasn't like she'd invited me to lunch. It was more of a command performance. I could have one foot in the grave and would still jump if she said jump. God, I am such a wuss. "Isn't that Dr. Chambers who just arrived?"

"Did he?" she asked coyly. "I barely noticed."

Yeah, right. "I thought you were hot for him."

"Finley Tanner!" she gasped, one hand going to the ever-present strand of pearls at her throat. "I can't believe you'd be so crass."

"Sorry. How about, I thought you were intrigued by him."

"He's a lovely gentleman. Cardiologist. Widower."

"Then he's right up your alley," I said into my water glass. Thankfully my mother was busy waving demurely.

"He's coming over here. Behave."

What did she think I was going to do? Strip naked and dance on the table?

"Cassidy," the doctor greeted, taking her hand and gallantly kissing her ring. No wonder she liked him. Rich, single, and a suck-up. "And let me guess, this is your sister."

I couldn't help but smile at the twinkle in his blue eyes as he played out the game.

"Heavens no," my mother answered. "This is my daughter Finley. Sisters," she fairly gushed. "Seriously, Burt." She was practically cooing.

He took my hand and gave it a gentle squeeze. "Honest mistake. I should have guessed that this lovely girl is your daughter."

I didn't know why. My mother, like my sister, is dark haired with brown eyes. I, on the other hand, am a fair-skinned blonde with blue eyes and a completely different bone structure. I wondered if I should tell the good doctor that I got my looks from either Mr. Finley or Mr. Anderson. No, that would send my mother into a rage the minute we were alone.

"Please excuse me," I said as I rose from my chair holding my new-to-me fuchsia Prada clutch. Just one of the items I'd treated myself to with my Ellen bonus.

I'd done well with the Ellen bonus. Turns out it paid to save your boss from a lunatic. The fact that I'd spent the bonus twice already was irrelevant. After what I'd gone through, I deserved a little splurge. Okay, so it wasn't so little—but seriously, it wasn't as if the law firm of Dane, Lieberman, and Caprelli was going to rain money on me on a regular basis. Especially since the firm had officially changed its name. I missed Mr. Zarnowski, but with his sudden demise from a heart attack, Vain Victor Dane wasted no time having the doors repainted and new stationery ordered. As the managing partner, he held a lot of power. He also got manicures more often than I did and, unlike Ellen Lieberman and Tony Caprelli, he simply tolerated me.

". . . wasn't it, Finley?"

Oh God, I'd zoned out during the flirtation stage. I took the safe route. "Definitely." Please, *please* let that be an appropriate response.

When I didn't get the infamous Cassidy glare, I felt the muscles between my shoulder blades relax. As nice as the promise of strong coffee was, I could use a mojito. Or two.

As Philippe arrived with my coffee and my mother's tea, I asked the doctor, "Are you waiting for someone?"

"My golf partner. Thanks to his eagle on fourteen, we won this morning."

"Congratulations," my mother said.

I gulped down my coffee, a faux pas not lost on my mother. "Look at the time," I said. "I feel terrible but," to quote Liam, "I have a thing and if I don't leave now, I'll be late. Dr. Chambers, perhaps you could keep my mother company while she has her tea?"

"Of course," he said when he stood. "It would be my pleasure."

"Thank you again for lunch," I said to my mother. She was busy staring at the good doctor. "I'll call you," I lied.

"Mmm-hmm," she managed as she glanced up at me. It was the first time in ages I'd seen approval in her eyes.

I wasn't sure when I'd become my mother's wingman, but I didn't care. It got me out of post-lunch chitchat and out of the club, and it wasn't quite two P.M. If I had a singing voice, which I don't, I might have belted out the hallelujah chorus as I made my way to my champagne pink convertible. Technically it belonged to the Mercedes Leasing Corporation, but I thought of it as mine.

Slipping behind the wheel and turning over the ignition, I tuned into WILD 95.9 for a recoup of the Kevin, Jason, and Virginia show, and then happily pointed my car in the direction of I-95 south. Going home made me happy. And why wouldn't it? I had a small but lovely cottage on Palm Beach proper, with my very own little strip of beach. It hadn't always been so lovely. In fact, when my mother first sold me the cottage, which was supposed to be part of my inheritance from Jonathan Tanner, the only father I'd ever known, it was a dilapidated mess. With a partial mummy in the closet. Thanks to my darling, dear friend Sam, who also happened to be my former neighbor, using his magical interior design skills turned the cottage into a showplace. It was done in whites, teals, and corals and was very, very Florida.

If I took the long way home, I'd pass right by the Gardens Mall. As much as I wanted to, I had to restrain myself. Between my mortgage, my credit cards, and my car lease, I really needed to control my spending. For me that was like trying to hold my breath for thirty minutes. Underwater. With my mouth open. Now I had my friend Jane, the accountant, sitting on my shoulder and making me feel guilty about every penny I spent.

Jane and I had been friends since the day we'd lied our way into a gym two-for-one promotion. Five years later, Jane still worked out regularly, while I considered a brisk walk to the coffeepot cardio. Jane wasn't your typical accountant/financial planner. She looked more like one of the Pussycat Dolls than a bean counter. And she was quite fond of corsets and leather, but somehow managed not to look like a dominatrix. Maybe it was her perfect body. Or the pretty way her brown hair framed her face. She had big brown eyes that always mirrored her smile, and Jane smiled most of the time. Unless she was reviewing my monthly spending with me. Then she'd get frown lines between her eyebrows. If I won my next eBay auction, she'd probably need Botox for those lines.

I was willing to go as high as two thousand for a diamond bezel for my Rolex. Well, I technically don't have a Rolex. Yet. I'm buying the parts on eBay, and then I'll have a jeweler assemble it and voilà, my very own pink oyster-face Lady-DateJust. The two thousand was supposed to come out of the twenty-five hundred I'd gotten as a bonus from Ellen. I'd already bought twenty-two hundred dollars' worth of clothing, shoes, purses, and other accessories. I couldn't help myself. It was just so much fun to shop like the old days, even if it was only temporary. Now it was time for me to turn back into a financial pumpkin.

Thanks to my mother, I no longer had access to my trust fund, so I was forced to live on my own salary. She thought she was building my character. In reality, she'd just forced me underground, into the world of thrift shops and outlet malls. And eBay, of course. As long as I had a dry cleaner, I was able to work around my financial precariousness. Kinda.

Exercising a great deal of self-restraint, I made my way to Chilean Avenue and parked in the center of the horseshoe-shaped drive made from crushed shells and cut the engine. It was a truly stunning day—a clear, blue, cloudless sky with temperatures in the low eighties and a nice breeze coming off the ocean.

"Take the rest of the day off," I told myself as I locked my car and went inside.

The first thing I did was kick off my heels, then I began to unzip my vintage Lilly Pulitzer shift-style dress as I walked toward my bedroom. Thanks to Sam and my contractor, Harold the ex-convict, the three-bedroom home was down to two bedrooms with spacious bathrooms and large closets. Hey, a girl's got to have her priorities. The guest room was very girlie. Lots of floral arrangements and colorful sculptural elements to cut the starkness of the white spread on the double bed. My bedroom is a thing of beauty. My room is teal, coral, and white. Again, I have a white comforter, but Sam knew just how to accessorize the room to make it look homey and not sterile. And my bathroom, well, it is drool worthy. I have one of those fancy spill tubs and a beautiful view of the ocean. In fact, every window in my room has a stunning view of the beach.

I changed into a bathing suit and sarong, and padded barefoot into the kitchen. The room was all polished stainless steel with pure white counters and teal and chrome stools. Taking out some mint leaves from the fridge, I placed them in a tall glass. Next I squeezed some fresh lime juice in with the mint. I added powdered sugar—easier than making simple syrup—and mashed all the stuff together with the back of a long iced tea spoon. Some crushed ice from the spout on the front of the fridge door, a little rum, and some club soda and I was in business. Still, I sipped the mojito for quality control before heading outside.

Taking my laptop, I went out to the small cabana off to the left of the pool. I wanted to check my e-mail and my auction status before I went down to the beach to veg out on my teak lounge chair in the sand near the water's edge.

It only took about ten minutes of salt air, and possibly the alcohol, to completely relax me—an amazing feat since it usually took me several hours to regain my sanity after spending time with my mother. Checking my status, I discovered that I was still the high bidder on the bezel auction, but that didn't mean much. I was holding at fifteen hundred but I wouldn't add the other five hundred until a few seconds before the end of the auction. Bidding on eBay isn't a hobby, it is an art. One I am quite good at.

My e-mail was pretty light, just some social stuff from friends. I scrolled down and found one from Izzy. She was Tony's fourteen-year-old daughter and we had this bonding thing going on. With Tony being widowed since his daughter was an infant, Izzy seemed to like having a female presence in her life. It had totally backfired on me. Since Izzy liked me, Tony felt he couldn't pursue a relationship with me in case we ever broke up. He didn't want anything to get in the way of Izzy's happiness.

I lounged on the cushions, my computer within easy reach. Sipping my mojito, I thought about Tony Caprelli and could feel my pulse quicken. He was a criminal attorney from New York and hot. Not just handsome hot, but wicked, smoking hot. He had dark hair and eyes the color of rich coffee. He was the perfect guy for me, at least on paper. He was polished, educated, articulate, and *honest,* an important quality after the whole cheating-Patrick debacle. And did I mention he was hot? He had that kind of commanding presence that pulled at me. Worse still, he'd admitted that he was attracted to me. It was like handing me a Rolex box, only to open it and find it empty. Totally unfair.

If Tony was perfect for me, Liam couldn't be more wrong. Yet just thinking his name left my Tony thoughts in the dust. He was one of those guys who just screamed, "Love me and you can fix me!" with one look into those crystal blue, bedroom eyes. Trust me, I know better. You can't ever love a guy enough to fix him. And Liam McGarrity needed a lot of fixing. He was secretive, still close to his ex-wife, and the sexiest man I'd ever met. Every time I saw him it took all my willpower to keep from jumping his bones. Even though the intelligent part of me knew he was Mr. Wrong, my libido didn't give a damn. I wanted him. Especially after dancing with him at my sister's wedding. I almost moaned at the memory of being pressed against his rock-solid body.

"Stop it!" I snapped.

Opening Izzy's e-mail, I saw that she was reminding me about her next school dance, which was only two weeks away. This one was more important than the last because she had her first date. Only I'd been sworn to silence. Tony would never go for his little girl having a date, so I was her cover. Great, I thought. My mother and a fourteen-year-old were both getting more dating action than I was.

Izzy still needed shoes and I'd promised to take her to the mall this weekend. With my mother's command, I explained that it would have to wait until next weekend. I sent her an e-mail to that effect even though it was still early afternoon and I'm usually up for any kind of shopping.

I was too relaxed to go through the motions of showering, dressing, and all the paint and bodywork associated with going out in public. Besides, I was tired. I was in my third week of fighting the Sleepy and Wanda Jean relocation battle. They were squatting on land that belonged to the lone heir of the Egghardt estate, entrusted to me by my firm. Lenora, the heir, was willing to let them stay; she just wanted them to move their trailer to the far edge of the property so she could build a lucrative equestrian center on the rest of the land. To date, Sleepy and Wanda Jean were not cooperating. Sleepy swore up and down that the late Mr. Egghardt had promised him that piece of land for life. Only he had nothing to back up his claim. It was the kind of estate that made me crazy. Usually I loved being an estates and trusts paralegal, but lately that had changed. Dane-Lieberman had sent me back to school to be better trained to support Tony's criminal practice. I was still doing estates and trusts, I just had more duties. So the last thing I needed was a couple of hicks screwing up an estate.

Another e-mail was from my friend Liv, who wanted to know if I'd like to go out on a blind date. Her boy toy had a friend in town and she wanted to know if I'd round out the foursome. Liv is so stunning she could have any man on the planet. Said boy toy lived in a room above his parents' garage. I could not understand the attraction. I wrote her back:

Not just no, but hell no. Have a good time.

I begged off dinner with Becky as well. I just felt like playing homebody. Finished with e-mail, I put my computer away, made another drink, and went down to the beach. I stayed there until the sun was blocked by my neighbor's privacy fence.

Not one to cook, I called my favorite Chinese place and had some moo shu delivered. I even splurged on some remaki. I ate way too much, then lay on the sofa and channel-surfed for a while before I settled on an old Meg Ryan–Tom Hanks movie. Maybe watching happily-ever-after hadn't been the smartest move. When the credits rolled, I felt more like a loser than ever.

Around midnight, I decided to go to bed. Sun, three drinks, and a full belly had me yawning like a newborn. I drifted off without incident. No, the incident happened in my subconscious. I was in the middle of a rather vivid dream about a man with black hair and blue eyes when my sleepy brain processed some banging. In my dream state, I started looking around for the source. Coming awake, I realized the sound was in the real world.

The dead of night means just that. Dead. As in dead quiet. So why, I wondered as I shrugged into my robe, was I hurrying toward the front door at o'-dark-thirty? Well, because someone was pounding on my door while alternately laying on the doorbell. All the ringing and banging was making my head pound.

My mood didn't improve when I spotted the Mustang parked behind my car. "Liam McGarrity! You'd better have a freaking stellar goddamn reason for—"

As soon as I'd opened the door, Liam slumped inside, falling to his knees. I blinked twice, trying to wrap my sleep-addled brain around the sight before me.

The right side of Liam's shirt was stained a deep scarlet from just below the armpit to the hem. His skin was ashen. He had one arm draped around the former Mrs. McGarrity, but Ashley was having trouble supporting his weight.

"Here," I said as I worked my way under his arm and got him back up off the floor. "What the hell happened?"

"I got shot," Liam said, his voice steadier than his body.

"We need to have him lie down," Ashley said.

"No." I pivoted on my bare foot and tried to steer his weight back toward the door. "We need to get him to a hospital."

"No hospital," Liam insisted. "Just some sleep and a Band-Aid."

"You think a Band-Aid will help remove a bullet?"

"Through-and-through," he said.

"Save your breath, honey," Ashley insisted. "I've already tried. He won't go."

Honey? I glanced at the bleached blonde. Had she actually called me honey? "Then why bring him here?"

"Nice to see you, too," Liam said with a weak smile.

"Can we take him to lie down and then talk?" Ashley asked, exasperated. She started for the sofa. The *white* sofa.

"Let's get him to the guest room." Where he can bleed on my white sheets. Which, unlike the sofa, I can easily throw away.

Being one of Liam's crutches was cumbersome, especially when we started down the hallway. We did a sort of crab step, and then maneuvered him into the virgin room. Never dawned on me that my first houseguest would be a private detective with a hole in his side. As I choked on the unappealing smell of gunpowder, blood, and Ashley's ungodly strong rose perfume, I yanked back the crisp white comforter and tugged the corner of the sheets free. My tongue was coated with the metallic taste of adrenaline as I deposited Liam on the edge of the bed.

Ashley was immediately on her knees—and yes, I thought something unkind—and slipped off his shoes and helped raise his legs up on the bed.

Liam winced. "We're gonna need some towels and some Steri-Strips."

"Towels I have," I said as I started out the door. "Steri-Strips I don't."

"You can get them at the store, then we can take the Mustang . . . oh . . . somewhere."

"Take his car where?" I asked Ashley, who seemed to be the one with the plan.

Liam shook his head. "We've got to talk about this first, Ash."

"You called me for help," Ashley snapped. "You don't get to complain about how I provide the help. I was the one who thought to bring you here, wasn't I? It isn't like anyone will come looking for you in Swankyville."

I glared at Ashley. "You woke me up from a dead sleep just to diss my address?"

"No," she said as she undid Liam's belt.

This was getting awkward. Here I was in my house watching some other woman undress Liam. "Is that really necessary?" I asked when she began to unbutton his shirt.

"I've got to see how bad it is. Could you get those towels now?"

I decided fetching towels was better than watching Ashley and Liam interact. Yeah, so he was bleeding, but that hardly explained why he was so cooperative with her. If that had been me, he would have been arguing or complaining, or both.

Obviously three mojitos weren't enough.

When trouble shows up on my doorstep,
its ex-wife comes, too.

two

I gathered together a stack of my less-loved towels and took them to Ashley. I brought along my first-aid stuff too, though I wasn't exactly stocked like a *M*A*S*H* unit. Neosporin, aloe, and some invisible Band-Aids were about it.

When I walked into the bedroom, I really wanted to hurl. Ashley was pressing a bloody rag against the wound but not before I got a look at the two small holes where love handles would eventually grow. "We really should get him to a hospital," I argued.

"No hospitals," Liam insisted firmly. "It looks worse than it is."

"Honey, run to the store for those Steri-Strips, 'kay?"

"I'll get several packs," I replied, wondering how Ashley would look with the strips taped to her mouth. She knows my name, and it isn't Honey.

I yanked on a pair of yoga pants, a shirt and shoes, twisted my hair into a messy bun, and headed out the door. There was a twenty-four-hour Walgreens just over the bridge, so I went there and with some help from the pharmacist, I found what I needed, paid, and left. My nerves were a little frazzled to say the least. I had no idea how or why Liam had been shot. Or why he'd called Ashley to the rescue. I had to admit, I was a touch jealous. Okay, so maybe more than a touch.

By the time I returned, the bleeding had slowed. "Got any Super Glue?" Ashley asked when I placed the pharmacy bag on the bed.

"Sure." I went into my emergency clothing-repair Baggie and grabbed the tube.

Liam winced when she used the glue to rejoin the edges and perspiration beaded on his forehead. "Got a beer?" he asked through gritted teeth.

I went to the kitchen and retrieved a cold one from my re-frigerator. I lingered a tad, not wanting to witness part two of the glue-Liam-back-together project. I handed him the open bottle just as Ashley was finishing with the Steri-Strips. "That should hold," she said, admiring her handiwork, then she wrapped the gauze I'd bought as an afterthought around his torso.

"Wouldn't stitches have been a better choice?" I suggested.

"Less painful," Liam agreed. "But gunshot wounds have to be reported."

"C'mon, honey. You and I need to go get my car."

"Sorry, honey," I returned. "I'm not in the mood for a road trip. Take a cab."

"That's probably a good idea," Liam said. "Even though your car is six blocks from the scene, if the cops are out canvassing, you don't want to get caught."

Ashley shrugged. "You want me to park the Mustang behind the house?"

"Um, hello? My backyard is all pool and no parking."

"Put it behind the Dumpster for now," Liam instructed.

"On the new sod?" I asked.

Liam offered me a weak smile. "I'll replace it."

"You take care of him, hon—Finley."

She flipped open her cell and called a taxi while I tried not to notice that Liam wore boxers. It was like trying not to notice the sun. Flustered, I started gathering up bloody towels and clothing and twisted them into a ball. "I'll wash this stuff."

"I don't suppose you have anything I can put on?" he asked as he gingerly sat up.

I opened the closet door and took out a shopping bag. "The pants will probably be too short but everything else should be fine." I started to leave when he called my name. "Yes?"

"Can you toss these in there, too?"

Liam was shielded by the fold of the comforter but my throat nearly closed when he flipped me his boxers. There was some blood on the waistband. A fact I discovered as I struggled to keep from peeking at his nakedness. Shot or not, he still had the ability to make my breath hitch in my throat.

Before I had the machine going, Liam came out of the bedroom with deep frown lines between his eyebrows. "Which way to the bathroom? I need to wash my hands," he asked in a clipped tone.

"Is there a reason you're being all snotty to me?"

"I don't like being lied to."

"And just what is it you think I lied about?"

"Bathroom?"

I pointed down the hall and to the right. "I wasn't lying, it actually is a bathroom." I was actually getting pissed that he was pissed. After all, it was now nearing dawn and I'd abandoned sleep and reason to deal with his gunshot. I shook my head and muttered, "Gunshot," as I went in to assess the damage to my guest bed. What the hell had I gotten myself into?

There were only a few drops of blood on the sheets. I grudgingly thanked Ashley for that but it didn't change the fact that Liam had gone from gratitude to attitude in seconds.

I heard the water turn off and expected Liam to return to bed. Instead he walked down the hallway toward the living room. I turned and followed.

"Shouldn't you go back to bed?"

The khaki slacks were about two inches too short and the shirt was unbuttoned. Hard to stay mad at a guy when he was flaunting his bare chest in your direction. "What?" I asked, irritated.

"These are Tony's clothes, right?"

I nodded. "He left them here."

"I thought the two of you had decided not to . . . ya know."

I rolled my eyes. "He and Izzy came over for a swim and since he didn't go in the water, he accidentally left his change of clothes here. Would you feel better wearing a sheet, like a toga?"

He raked his hand through his mussed hair. "So you didn't . . ."

"So what if I did? Last time I checked I was a single woman with a perfectly healthy sex drive."

Liam winced. I wasn't sure if it was from pain or embarrassment but I hoped it was the latter. I wanted him to be thinking about my sex drive because lord knew my mind was wondering about his most of the time. A matte of dark hair formed a V that tapered into the waistband of his pants. Kinda like a GPS directing me to the good parts. I should have been thinking about the gauze holding his wound closed, but for the life of me I couldn't clear the lust fog from my brain.

I am a horrible person.

"Do you need anything?" I asked.

"Depends on what you're offering."

"Coffee, water, flight-attendant basics."

"I'll take another beer."

"Self-medicating?"

"Yep."

I settled on the opposite end of the sofa from him and glanced at the clock. It was nearly 4 A.M. and it didn't look like sleep was part of the agenda. "Want to tell me what happened?"

"I found a body."

"So you had Ashley bring you here? A body shot you? Shouldn't you call the sheriff's office or *Unsolved Mysteries* or something?"

"The deceased *was* a member of the sheriff's office. He was shot with my gun."

My brain was spinning, trying to fit the pieces of his conversation into place. "Back up. What happened to make you kill a deputy?"

"I didn't kill him."

"But you said it was your gun."

"It was. But I haven't seen that weapon for five years. I don't know how José Lopez was shot with it."

"How can you be sure it was yours?"

"Serial number."

"Did you lose the gun?"

"In a manner of speaking. Look, I know this is asking a lot, but can I hang here for a while? If anyone saw my car at the scene, I'm sure the cops will go looking for me at my place. I doubt they'd come here."

"Am I aiding and abetting?"

His eyes met mine. "Probably. But if it comes to that, I'll swear you knew nothing about José or the gun."

"But if you didn't do anything—"

"It won't play like that. Trust me."

The thing was, I did trust him. Liam had saved my life on more than one occasion. "Is there blood on your shoes?"

"Probably. I'll take them out back, rinse them, and then hit the soles with some bleach."

I nodded. "To screw up any presumptive test for blood."

He offered a half smile. "Very good. I see Tony has taught you a lot."

"Stay put. The last thing I want to happen is have that glue and those Steri-Strips come loose. I don't have Ashley's stomach." *Or her bond with you.* I took Liam's shoes out back and took care of them, leaving them on the lanai to dry.

I couldn't get over how different he looked in a blue oxford shirt that did magical things for his eyes. It was quite a change from his cargo shorts or jeans and Tommy Bahama shirts. As attractive as he looked, it just didn't feel like Liam. He wasn't the preppy-casual type. Other than my sister's wedding, I'd only seen Liam in his signature attire. He'd looked magnificent in the tux for the wedding, but this ensemble made him look like a Ken doll.

When I returned I said, "There's a comb in the guest basket in the bathroom."

"No need," Liam replied as he raked his fingers through his hair again. All that did was give him a tousled, just-out-of-bed look that made my stomach clench. Even in the midst of a crisis I couldn't control my hormones. God, am I ever lame.

"Give me the bleach so I can rinse the traps in your bathroom."

I handed him the bottle. As he walked away I got a sinking feeling. While I was happy to give Liam aid and comfort, and probably more than that, I felt as if I was getting in over my head. Liam didn't need the help of a paralegal who had worked exclusively in estates and trusts for eight years before adding criminal defense work to her repertoire. He needed a lawyer. He'd probably get pissed, but it seemed prudent to call Tony. He'd know the best course of action. Besides, the two men had a friendship that went back more than a decade.

I reached for the phone and dialed Tony's cell. I didn't want to call the house phone in case Izzy was sleeping.

"Caprelli." His voice was deeper than normal and a little scratchy. And a lot sexy.

Obviously my brain was consumed with sex.

"It's Finley. I'm sorry to bother you this early but something has come up. Liam was—"

"Who the hell are you calling?" Liam demanded.

I placed my hand over the mouthpiece. "Tony. You need him."

"No, I just need a couple of hours. Then I'll be out of your hair."

"Finley?" Tony asked into my ear.

I looked at Liam, tilting my head to one side. "Please?"

"Gimme the phone."

I handed Liam my cell.

I didn't hear the words Liam was saying because his eyes surveyed my bare neck, then dropped lower, to the snug fabric of my workout top. A shiver tickled my spine.

The buzzer from the washer dragged me back to reality and while he spoke to Tony, I went in and switched the laundry over. When I returned, Liam was off the phone and on the sofa. The hum of the dryer just off the kitchen echoed in the quiet of the room. The placement of the laundry area had been the brainchild of my friend Sam. Every design element made sure that nothing obstructed the views of the ocean. Including the triple sliders leading out to a stunning piece of beach I considered all my own. In reality, it wasn't mine. Florida doesn't allow individuals to own private beaches. But Palm Beach got around that rule by building a succession of seawalls that took claw hooks and a hefty amount of rope to scale.

Liam's large frame made the room feel smaller. I sat at the opposite end of the sofa with my legs tucked under me and one elbow resting on the padded top. "Going to tell me the whole story?"

"Not much to tell," Liam said.

I went to the fridge and got him another beer, then made myself a cup of hazelnut coffee. I opened a plastic bottle, added cream to my coffee, then rejoined him.

"Someone was killed with your gun. Seems to me there's a story in there somewhere."

Liam shrugged. The action caused a strain on the ripple of ab muscle peeking above the gauze and pulled taut the seams of Tony's shirt. Apparently he was more broad shouldered than Tony. I really needed to stop making these comparisons. Attraction or not, Liam really was the wrong man for me. For any woman. Well, except for his not-so-ex-wife Ashley. As far as I could tell, she was the only woman who was a constant in his life and I'd often seen the two of them out at restaurants or clubs in downtown West Palm. It bugged me that he still had some sort of relationship with his ex, but I was in no position to challenge him on that one. Plus there was the issue of me always picking the wrong man. A habit I'm trying really hard to break.

"What did Tony tell you to do?" I asked.

"We worked out a thing."

God that infuriated me. Always with the *thing*. "Do I need to drive you to the sheriff's office?"

"Not yet."

"Was Tony pissed that we destroyed evidence?"

"He didn't say anything," Liam answered nonchalantly.

"You're not giving me a lot to work with here," I commented, growing frustrated. "You're the one who involved me. Doesn't that at least earn me the right to know what happened? Who was José Lopez and how did you get shot?"

"I got shot with a gun and José Lopez was my partner when I was still on the job."

Since he'd been a police officer, I assumed they made you turn in your gun and badge when you left. At least they did on television. "Is that how he got your gun?" I asked.

"The last time I saw that gun was just before it was put in the evidence locker. That was five years ago."

I fiddled with a strand of hair that had come loose from my messy coif. "I'm assuming things don't normally go missing from the police evidence lockup?"

"Not usually, no."

"Why would José take it out now? And who shot you?"

Again he shrugged. "I didn't see the shooter. As for the gun, maybe he was taking a second look at the case."

"What case?"

Liam took a long pull on the bottle. "A closed case from five years ago. Though I can't think of a valid reason why he'd be wasting his time on it. Besides, he was transferred to traffic division after the incident."

"What is this *incident*?"

"Let it go, Finley."

"You brought me into this," I reminded him, irritated. "I think the least you can do is fill in the gaps so I'll know why I'm bleaching shoes at dawn."

"I've done questionable things for you."

That was true. Liam had helped me break and enter, and even destroy evidence on one occasion. "I know that. But you've always known why I was in trouble. Now the proverbial shoe is on the other foot."

"They took my gun five years ago."

"Why?"

"Because I shot and killed a kid."

My road to happiness is under construction.

three

When I emerged from my bedroom, Liam was asleep in the guest room, so I tiptoed down the hall, folded his clothes, and left them in the doorway to his room, then headed off to work.

I had mixed emotions. What if the glue didn't hold? What if the police discovered him in my house? But mainly, why and how was he responsible for shooting a kid? He'd refused to answer my battery of questions, so I was left to wonder. I was sure there was a good reason, but Liam wasn't going to share.

As I arrived at the office, Margaret Ford, firm receptionist with a quarter-century of service, was just getting settled behind the horseshoe-shaped desk in the lobby. Glancing up, her face registered shock when she saw it was me entering the building before nine.

"Do I have any messages?" I asked her even though I already knew the answer.

"I haven't checked with the service yet. Try back later."

"And a cheery good morning to you, too," I muttered, appropriately loud enough as I went to the elevator.

The firm took up the entire four-story building and my office was on the second floor. In my tenure at the firm, I'd gone from a shared cubicle in the bullpen to a private office with an almost-view of the Intracoastal. Now I got to hand assignments to the bullpen, which made my life a lot easier. It was no longer my responsibility to have exhibits prepped, or make copies, though I did have the freedom to walk the two short blocks to the courthouse to file documents as needed, a task I normally scheduled to coincide with lunchtime and/or the end of the day. This allowed me two-hour lunches and the chance to leave earlier than the required five o'clock. But today I'd come in early so I could catch Tony before the actual start of business. I knew he came in early after dropping Izzy off at the pricey Palm Beach Day Academy, my alma mater. And his car was in the parking lot.

After preparing my office by turning on the computer and the coffeepot, I went up to the fourth floor. The executive offices were in the shape of a wagon wheel. The partners' private receptionist wasn't in yet, so I was able to walk into Tony's office without being announced.

He greeted me with a warm smile as he shrugged off his jacket. "What's up? Wait. Is Izzy becoming a pain?"

I waved my hand. "Of course not. I just thought we should talk about my early morning call for help."

"Don't give it a thought. Liam explained it all to me."

"Are you going to help him?"

Tony got a blank look on his face. "Help him buy a new tire?"

I blinked twice. "What?"

"He said he'd call AAA and it was a good thing he was near your house."

I felt a little like I'd fallen down the rabbit hole. Plus I was distracted by his cologne. "What tire?"

Little lines appeared on Tony's forehead. "Liam said he didn't have a spare. He walked to your place and then you called me. Bad choice by the way, I hate changing tires."

That sneaky bastard. Liam hadn't told Tony the truth. Should I, or not? I decided not since I'd run the risk of suffering Tony's ire if he found out I'd spent the night aiding and abetting. Between screwing with my mother's mind and lying to my boss, Liam was working his way to the top of my shit list.

"Okay, then." I started to back out of the doorway. "Sorry I called. Hope it wasn't a bother."

"What's wrong?" Tony asked.

"Long night. Sleep deprivation." I hurried out. Well, I hurried as much as you can hurry in four-and-a-half-inch Coach Bethanie heels.

Back in my office, I tried Liam's cell. No answer. Then I tried my house phone and got the same result. I was torn between concern and irritation. He could have left or he could be lying on my floor in a puddle of blood. I checked my functional-but-not-Rolex watch. I had a meeting with Ellen and then an hour to drive out to Indiantown for round seven with Sleepy and Wanda Jean. Ellen would freak if I blew off the meeting, so I needed a plan.

I called Liv, since she had the most fluid schedule.

"Hi, Fin."

I'd ease into the favor. "Hi. How was your date?"

"We ended up at the Blue Martini. The third wheel hooked up with some girl at the bar, so it worked out."

"Did you pay?"

"I can't believe you're asking me that."

I smiled. "That would be a yes. Any chance you could do me a favor?"

"After you blew me off yesterday?"

"I blew you off because I didn't want to have dinner with a friend of garage boy. A date with an unemployed young-twenty-ish guy isn't a date. It's more like babysitting."

"FYI, Kevin has a job."

"Doing what?"

"He's a waiter."

"Sounds like my dream man."

"I didn't ask you to marry him. It was just dinner."

"With a twenty-year-old? More like dinner and a grope."

"And you called for a favor?" Liv asked with amusement in her tone.

"Any chance you can swing by my house and check on things?"

"Check on what?"

"Liam came over last night and he was . . . sick. I just want to know he's okay."

"The man you swear you don't want to date came over for chicken soup. Which, by the way, you don't know how to make."

I sighed. "Could you just do it, please? There's a key taped to the potted palm out back by the sliders."

"That's a safe system. What about the alarm?"

"Don't worry. I didn't turn it on."

"Another brilliant safety feature. Especially when your contractor has a criminal record as long as my arm."

"He has two arrests," I said, defending him. "Please?"

"Sure. I'll go now, then I'll call you in a bit."

"Thank you."

I tried Liam's cell and my home phone and still nothing. I had a sinking feeling in my stomach, but I was stuck. Hopefully Liv would call me back before my meeting with Ellen. Liv was a pretty take-charge kind of person, which is how she'd turned her small party-planning business into the premier event organizer for all the movers and shakers on Palm Beach and the surrounding areas. A major plus for me and my friends. She often slipped us into parties to mingle with the famous, rich, and *über*rich.

I gathered up my ever-growing Egghardt file and pulled on a sweater to cover my bare arms. My St. John's blue crepe dress with a wide scooped neck was no match for the billowing cold of the air conditioner.

Ellen Lieberman had done a one-eighty on me after I'd basically saved her from the clutches of a killer. Along the way I'd learned her deepest, darkest secret, and to my credit, I'd kept her confidence. Well, mostly. My BFF Becky knew because she'd been part of the kidnapping, but I did share the info with Liv and Jane just because it was such good dish. The only other person who knew was Liam, who I was still thinking might be passed out and bleeding profusely in my house. I flirted with the idea of calling an ambulance, but I wanted to respect Liam's desire not to have the gunshot reported. Something more had to be going on and I didn't want to screw things up before I had the whole story.

I went back up to the fourth floor, only this time the executive secretary was planted at her desk. She glanced up at me and asked, "How may I help you?"

"I'm here to see Ellen."

She used the intercom to announce me, then gave me a nod of her head before I ventured down the hallway to Ellen's office and conference room, hefty file tucked under my arm. I had hoped Liv would call me back, but no word yet.

Ellen Lieberman was a senior partner along with Vain Victor Dane and Tony Caprelli. I liked her well enough, though like my mother, she thought I should have higher aspirations than being a paralegal. At least now she'd lightened up a little.

I stuck my head in Becky's door on the way.

"Hi," she greeted me, looking up from the thick deposition open on her desk.

She had on a really nice nubby silk suit in a deep persimmon, with a strand of chunky amber nuggets and matching earrings. She was sporting amber bangles on her wrists and, as always, her auburn hair was simply but professionally styled. Becky and I had been roommates at Emory. Becky had gone on to law school, while I'd returned to South Florida. Upon graduation, she'd joined the firm with a singular goal, becoming the youngest female partner. I know she was secretly disappointed that they'd brought Tony in after Mr. Zarnowski's death, but that hadn't dulled her ambition in the least. She worked long hours at Ellen's side and Ellen was truly a mentor to her.

"I have serious dish," I whispered.

Becky placed her pen in the crease of the deposition and gave me her full attention. "Go ahead."

"I can't. I've got a meeting, but can you do lunch?"

She nodded.

"Will you call Liv and Jane? Maybe we can all meet at Cheesecake Factory. Say one?"

"Works for me."

"If you get hold of Liv, tell her to call me on the main line and to tell Margaret it's urgent."

"Why?"

"I'll explain later," I promised.

I went to Ellen's office and found the door ajar. I knocked twice, then grabbed the handle and pushed my way in. "Good morning."

Ellen was seated behind her desk, the top covered with piles of varying heights. Her very curly red, gray-streaked hair was secured with two pencils and her face was devoid of any makeup. Even fresh faced, she was attractive, in spite of the fact that she did everything possible to hide it. She smiled and nodded her head in the direction of one of the two chairs opposite her desk. "Hi, Finley," she said as she continued to sign her name to a small stack of papers. "You look tired."

"Last night was a nightmare," I mumbled.

"You're having nightmares?" she asked, giving me her full attention as she slipped her reading glasses up like a headband. "I hope it wasn't related to the kidnapping."

I shook my head. "No. No. I'm fine. You?"

She shrugged. "I'm glad that mess is behind me. And thank

you for not broadcasting what you found out. Word travels fast in this place."

"Don't I know it," I agreed as I took my seat, cleared a small space for my file folder, and met the gaze from her bright green eyes. "Lucky for you she got Baker-acted, so there's no need for your secret to come out in open court."

"And if she ever gets out of the institution, she'll face a parole violation." Ellen waved her hand. "Enough of this. Where do we stand with the Egghardt matter?"

I opened my file and took out the memo and the letter. "This is a recap of my last two meetings with Sleepy and Wanda Jean." I passed her the paper. "In a nutshell, they're refusing to relocate."

"You passed on to them the information that Mrs. Egghardt is willing to allow them to stay at the new location at a rental rate of one dollar per year?"

"Didn't faze them."

Ellen stood and went to her coffeepot and poured two cups. Her footfalls were silent thanks to the cork-soled Birkenstocks she wore with her shapeless but colorful muumuu. She let out a long sigh as she passed me my cup and sat back down. "You know what has to be done then, right?"

I handed her the second piece of paper. "I've already drawn up this letter."

Ellen pulled down her readers. I watched quietly as she scanned the letter, then asked, "How do you think they'll take this?"

"Not well."

"Have it sent FedEx with a delivery confirmation."

I drummed my manicured nails on the arm of the chair one time. "I'd like to deliver it in person."

Ellen's eyebrows drew taut. "I don't think that's a good idea. Didn't you say the man was armed to the gills?"

I nodded. "But I have a rapport. I'd like to take one more shot at getting them to move the trailer to the edge of the property. That letter might be all the ammunition I need."

"I think his ammunition trumps yours. At least take Liam with you."

"Will do, so long as he's available." And not bleeding or passed out in my house. Why hadn't Liv called?

"Go ahead, then," she said as she signed the letter and handed it back to me.

I toted the file back to my office. I'd given one of the interns the letter to copy, one for the file, one for Leona Egghardt, and one for me. I always kept copies so I could fill out my time sheets each week. Vain Victor Dane was a stickler when it came to accounting for billable hours. While his hourly rate was nearly four hundred, mine was a more affordable one seventy-five. And Vain Dane was happiest when he could bill a client, even at my reduced rate.

After dumping the file on my desk, I quickly grabbed the phone and called Liv.

"Hello?"

"Well?" I asked impatiently.

"Sorry, Finley, something came up at work. I'll go by after lunch."

He could be dead after lunch. "That's okay, forget it." I was already packing up my new Coach briefcase.

"You sound mad," she said, her tone slightly somber.

I took a breath. "I'm not mad. Really."

"Are we still on for lunch?" she asked.

"Sure, I should be back by then."

"Back from where?"

I was digging my keys out of my purse. "I have to go to Indiantown. I'll stop by my house on the way out there."

"Your house isn't on the way. It's the *opposite* way."

"That can be our little secret."

I made it home in record time, praying Liam was safe and that I hadn't gotten caught by the red-light camera on Okeechobee. I wasn't sure if I'd slipped through the light while it was still yellow, and the last thing I needed was a traffic fine. I added that to the list of things pissing me off that I ascribed to Liam.

His Mustang wasn't parked behind the Dumpster. My heart raced. Maybe the police had found him and had the car towed as evidence. Or maybe he'd gone out for a late breakfast. My hand was shaking as I shoved the key in the lock. "Liam?" I called as I entered. "Liam? Are you here?"

I went from room to room, but there was no Liam. Save for the few droplets on the guest room bed, there was no blood. My worry rolled into irritation. If he'd only answered his phone, I wouldn't have been so panicked. *Selfish bastard.*

After setting the alarm, I left and went to Indiantown. This was my seventh or eighth trip out to the trailer on Collier Road. Each time I got a less than warm welcome.

Collier Lane was nothing more than a dirt road marked by a slanted mailbox with plastic spinners and red reflector dots on the leaning post. At the base of the post was a faded ceramic thing with a man in a sombrero pulling a cart filled with plastic flowers. Not exactly PC. I made the right and slowly crept up the road, driving in a slalom fashion to avoid the deep potholes. It took about three minutes before a structure came into view.

Calling it a home was a stretch. It was a trailer with a curled and dented aluminum skirt. Twelve dogs came rushing toward my car, some barking, some growling, all scary. There were two cars on the side of the house. Both had weeds jutting up through them. On the opposite side was an older-model truck with as much rust as paint under a crudely constructed carport. Well, it wasn't a carport so much as it was four metal poles with a worn and torn tarp across the top. There was a kiddy pool in the front yard, flanked by two Barcaloungers with springs popping through the fabric. The sofa on the porch could have been part of a matched set. As I brought my car to a slow stop, Cujo and company continued to bark and growl. When the screen door opened, I saw that Sleepy wasn't alone. His companion was a really large shotgun.

Needless to say, I wasn't feeling wrapped in the warmth of his welcome. The armed bozo wore a stained wife-beater shirt and had a potbelly testifying to a serious beer-drinking hobby. What little hair he had was swept over to one side. It was gray and as dull as his washed-out brown eyes.

The dogs continued their attack on my car while the man on the porch cradled the gun like an infant. I could hear more dogs in the distance and wondered if they were the understudies for the Hounds of the Baskervilles. Great. Dogs with a side order of more dogs.

Just behind Sleepy I could make out a shape in the shadows behind the tattered screen door. I was ready to slam my car into reverse and head back the way I'd come when Sleepy placed his thumb and forefinger in his mouth and whistled loud enough to be heard over the hum of my car engine.

The pack of matted, mangy dogs instantly raced toward him. The unseen pack in the distance still barked and snarled but even after a scan of my surroundings, I couldn't seem to locate them. With the visible dogs heeled, I felt comfortable enough to depress the button, opening my window little more than a crack. "Mr. Bollan?" I called politely.

He nodded as the ears on two of the hounds lifted alertly.

"Miz Tanner."

He rested the gun against the aluminum home and started walking toward me. Wanda Jean stepped out from inside the trailer and followed closely on his heels. She always appeared far friendlier, quite a feat given that what I could see of her gray hair was up in pink foam curlers and her attire consisted of a faded paisley housedress and slippers that scuffed the dusty ground with each step.

I so didn't want to leave the relative safety of my car. Reluctantly I opened the door, my eyes fixed on the six dogs watching my every move. I have a history with dogs and it isn't good.

Mr. and Mrs. Bollan walked past the garden of fake flowers and weathered lawn ornaments until we met on neutral ground.

"Nice to see you again," he said, offering me a sun-leathered hand with dirt and God only knew what else crusted beneath his nails.

I quelled the urge to reach for the Purell in my purse after we briefly shook hands.

"Remember, call me Sleepy and her here Wanda Jean."

"Miss," she said as she reached around her husband's girth.

I reached back and pulled out my briefcase.

I think Sleepy scowled. Hard to tell since he had a serious overbite, so the two yellowed teeth on top made him look like a perplexed beaver. Then he explained, "We still ain't changed our minds."

"Sleepy," Wanda interrupted with a smidge of irritation. "Let's go inside where we'll all be more comfortable."

I didn't have high hopes for that option, but I followed along and pretended I didn't smell the stench of sweaty dog and grease.

The smell of the cooking grease was stronger in the trailer, and once I spied the pots on the stove, I figured I'd taken Wanda away from preparing the midday meal. Two flies zipped around the room, occasionally stopping long enough to visit the flour-dusted chicken thighs sitting out on the chipped Formica counter. Some sort of greens that looked more like they belonged on the shoulder of I-95 sat in a colander near the sink. A thick, yellowish cloud of smoke hung in the air.

"Have a seat," Wanda said, pointing to an animal-hair-covered chair near the window air-conditioning unit that had dripped condensation down the wall. "Let me get you some iced tea."

Just to be polite, I said thank you even though I would have preferred coffee. At least with a hot beverage I had the possibility of boiling off some cooties. I perched myself on the very edge of the dirty chair and began taking out the letter Ellen had signed earlier in the day.

After handing me a plastic cup of tea, Wanda and Sleepy sat down, swiveling their seats away from the small television balanced on an old orange crate. A cable box teetered atop the machine. Grabbing a remote off the armrest, Sleepy muted *Judge Judy*.

"It seems we've come to an impasse," I began.

"I don't know about no impasse, I just know we ain't leaving here," Sleepy said, his tone defensive. "Walter and me was in 'Nam together. That's when he offered to let me live on this land. We got pinned down in Dak To in '67. Walter got hit, and after I carried him to the aid station, we, well, we was friends from then on." Sleepy shrugged and scratched his sizable belly as he took a long pull on a can of generic beer.

"There may not have been no blood bond, but we belong here," Wanda added. "Mr. Walter was always good to us." She reached behind her on the windowsill and took a framed photograph down and handed it to me. "Raised all eight of our children right here."

I tried to imagine the trailer holding ten people.

"This is L.D., short for Little Donald."

I glanced at the picture and "little" would have been the last adjective I'd use to describe the rotund, balding man in the back row.

Wanda continued, "Then Walt, after Walter. Next is Homer, he works as a firefighter in Montana. Lorraine, she's a nurse, Mary-Claire is raising her own family. This pretty one"— Wanda stopped and stroked the cheek of the girl in the shot— "that's my Penny." Wanda's eyes seemed to inexplicably mist over. "Got us five grandbabies so far. Duane is in the navy, and last is Mitzi. She's the baby and we're real proud of her. Mitzi just finished her third year at the community college."

"As I've said, you have a lovely family," I fudged as I returned the photo. "I'm not sure what more I can do to explain this, but Walter dying has changed things."

"I don't understand. Me and Walter had an arrangement," Sleepy said, his eyes narrowed to beads.

I sighed heavily and again said, "Mr. Egghardt died without a will, so his niece inherited all of his estate, including this parcel of land."

Wanda looked at me with bulging, alienesque eyes while sleepy just looked really pissed. Red blotches rose from his neck to his face and I was very, *very* glad the shotgun was out on the porch.

"Walter wouldn't have wanted to put us out of our home," Sleepy insisted. "I don't see how him dying changes that."

Now I could hear a stereo chorus of barking and growling dogs. Acoustically, I realized some were in the backyard and others were mere feet away with their snouts pressed against the screen door. Obviously they'd picked up on their master's displeasure. I was growing uneasy, wondering if the animals were plotting to attack.

Again Sleepy whistled and the porch hounds fell silent. The backyard dogs just kept on yelping, growling, and barking. It was hard for me to concentrate, especially when a cat came from out of nowhere and snaked its way around my ankles. It had harsh, brittle hair and a jagged scar down its face, leaving it with only one eye and part of one ear.

Wanda made a clicking sound with her tongue. "Come here, Lucky," she coaxed.

"Lucky?" I asked as I watched the cat cross the three or four feet separating us. The thing had more scars on its body and its tail was little more than a calico nub.

Wanda smiled. "She was a stray. A few years back she got into the kennels. Of course, we hurried out and got her when we heard the ruckus."

"Of course," I murmured as Lucky, now occupying Wanda's lap, gave me a cycloptic glare.

"We fixed her up best we could but didn't think she would make it. But she's tough," Wanda said, scratching the cat between the ear and a half. "That's why we call her Lucky."

I'd clearly been there too long because the explanation made perfect sense. Of course these people wouldn't do vets. From the décor, early 1970s greens, browns, and avocados, and the antiquated appliances—who doesn't have a microwave?—and all the other knickknacks, I guessed the Bollans had little if any substantial income.

"What happens with the proceeds from our sugarcane?" Sleepy asked. "We've lived here since the late sixties. Raised all them kids here. You trying to tell me some woman we've never met can toss us out? Just like that?"

"We've done everything possible to bring this to an amicable resolution."

"Load of crap if you ask me," Sleepy grumbled.

I reached into my briefcase, took out the letter, and passed it to Wanda Jean. I thought that was the safest way to handle it. Turned out not to matter. Sleepy snatched it away from her before she could so much as read the letterhead.

Sleepy's face burned red. "This is bullshit!"

"Sleepy, mind yourself. This young lady is only doing her job."

"I'm sorry it's come to this Mr.—Sleepy. Miss Egghardt's offer still stands. She'd be happy to set you up on the southwest corner of the property."

"What's it say?" Wanda asked, her face pinched with concern.

"Says we gotta be outta here in ten days."

"That isn't what it says," I corrected. "It requests that you move to the assigned parcel of land within ten days or we'll have no option but to begin the eviction process. If that happens, you'll end up with nothing. Is that what you want?"

"'Course not," Wanda Jean answered.

"Then please take Miss Egghardt up on her offer. It's more than generous." I stood and moved to the door, then reluctantly stepped onto the porch, fully prepared to pick up the shotgun and start picking off the herd of vicious dogs. I was spared that unpleasant task by Wanda Jean, who also had perfected the two-fingered, piercing whistle.

"We'll think on it," Wanda Jean said as I went to my car.

"Not a damned thing to think on," Sleepy growled.

The dogs chased me halfway back to the main road.

A secret is often followed by a lie.

four

I was the last one shown to our table at Cheesecake Factory. The place was loud and crowded with workers from in and around City Place. I wove my way through the labyrinth of tables, then slid in next to Becky in the booth.

"Bad morning?" Liv asked.

"Bad everything," I replied with a weak smile. "Sorry I'm late."

A waiter came by and handed me the tome they called a menu. I didn't need it. A bad day meant only one thing—high-caloric sweet corn tamale cakes. I placed the menu down in front of me.

"So what's the dish?" Becky asked.

Liv's aquamarine eyes lit up and Jane leaned forward.

"Liam got shot."

"By whom?"

"How?"

"When?"

I held up my hand. "Ashley brought him to my house at four A.M.," I began, then told them the full story. Or as much of it as Liam had shared with me.

Jane shook her head, a mass of brunette hair brushing against her shoulders with each movement. "I don't believe it. Liam wouldn't just shoot a kid."

"I agree," Liv seconded. "There has to be more to the story."

"But that doesn't explain the dead ex-partner or getting shot five years after the kid got killed," Becky said in her usual analytical style. "Did he give you a hint as to why he thinks the two things are related?"

"He said something about a serial number, but then he pretty much just blew me off."

"Did you seriously use Super Glue?" Jane asked.

I nodded. "Well, not me. Beer Barbie, I mean *Ashley*, did the actual gluing."

Liv tapped her chin with one pink-tipped fingernail. "How come he called Beer Barbie and not you? I thought after the wedding that you two were . . . ya know."

"Apparently not," I said on a long breath. "He must trust her more than he trusts me. Probably takes her calls, too."

"That was kind of rude to leave your place without so much as jotting you a note."

"Jotting?" Becky teased Jane. "What man do you know who jots?"

I reached into my purse. "I think it's time for a Google search."

The waiter returned for our orders, then I went right back to my smartphone hunt into Liam's past. "The print is so damned small," I grumbled.

Becky laughed. "Or maybe you're getting so old you need glasses to see fine print."

I glared at her for a second. "There's a ton of hits. I'm going to have to do this back at the office." I slipped my phone back into my purse.

Becky frowned. "What happened to the no-Googling-friends rule?"

"Liam and I aren't friends," I insisted.

"Then what are you?"

That was a good question. One that followed me back to my office, my belly full of fried carbs. My gut was telling me to go to Tony and come clean but something was stopping me. Loyalty to Liam? Fear of losing my job for getting involved—even peripherally—in Liam's shooting? Maybe both.

I listened to my voice mail. My heart sank into my shoes when I got the message from Tony to meet with him at three o'clock. Did he know? *Shit.*

That gave me an hour to research Liam and check my bid on eBay. I opted to do the latter first. It was quick and easy.

Settling into my comfy leather chair, I wiggled my mouse to bring my computer out of hibernate. I found an additional e-mail from Tony reiterating his need to see me. That didn't bode well. Great, I was up to my eyelashes in debt. The last thing I needed was to lose my job. There was also an e-mail from Tony's daughter, Izzy, reminding me again of our Saturday shoe-shopping date.

I poured myself some coffee, then logged into eBay. I was still the high bidder, but that didn't mean much. The auction didn't end for another two days. Plenty of time for someone to swoop in and steal the coveted bezel away. I set my account for hourly updates so I could stay on top of the action.

Tony's summons caused a knot to form in my stomach. I couldn't concentrate on anything but my possible dismissal. Not known for my patience, I decided the best defense was a proactive offense. I carefully crafted an e-mail response:

Tony: What case, so I can prepare? Thanks, Finley

In a flash I got my answer:

New case. Murder. See you at three. Tony

That wasn't exactly helpful, but he didn't mention termination. Or Liam. Maybe I was just suffering from my guilty conscience. Or maybe it was wishful thinking. What were the chances of Tony getting two new homicide cases in one day?

I had two choices: I could sit and obsess for an hour or I could keep my brain occupied by researching Liam. Again, I opted for the latter. I'd be just as fired in an hour as I was right this second.

I started with a simple Google search but that brought up enough hits to be unmanageable. I narrowed the search to just his name and the word "shooting." Now my results were culled enough for me to work with. What I gathered from news clippings was that Liam and six other officers were executing a warrant on a known gang hangout when a gunfight ensued, leaving one Fernàndo Peña, age fifteen, dead. After further searching, I found two more articles. One was an article about state's attor-

ney Alberto Garza's inability to get indictments against any offi-
cers. The second was a few column inches about Detective Liam
McGarrity deciding to leave the Palm Beach County Sheriff's
Office. No definitive reason was given.

Not a ton of information but more than I'd had an hour ago.
And now it was time for me to walk the employment plank.

Tony's office was much like his home. The décor was midcentury modern and about as un-Florida as you could get. I
knew a decorator had redone the office but I also guessed Tony
had something to say about the chrome, teak, and clean lines.
The pops of color, in my humble opinion, looked more like
they belonged in a loft in New York than a water-view office in
South Florida.

The man behind the desk was a different story. I was practically shaking until he greeted me with a smile.

"Afternoon."

"Hi," I returned as I took a seat, pad and pen in hand.
"What's up?"

Tony tossed a thin folder across his messy desk. "New client.
Travis Johnson. Murderer."

Yeah, my transgressions were still a secret. I opened the file and
scanned the booking sheet. "He's thirteen," I fairly gasped.

Reading Tony's hastily scribbled notes, I found myself shaking my head. "What would make a thirteen-year-old stab his
foster father to death?"

"That's our job," Tony answered. "The kid is a basket case
and not much help. They're holding him at juvie pending his
arraignment before the judge day after tomorrow."

"Will the case stay in family court?"

Tony shook his head. "They'll probably try him as an adult and I'm guessing they'll go for the death penalty."

I felt my eyes grow wide. "But he's thirteen!"

"Which is why I need you to pull *Thompson v. Oklahoma* and *Roper v. Simmons. Thompson* sets the minimum age at sixteen and *Simmons* prohibits the execution of anyone under eighteen. I think we can avoid a death sentence, but it's more important that we win at trial."

I wrote quickly. "But your notes say he did it."

"Travis called 911 after the stabbing. Then waited patiently for the police and paramedics. Spilled his guts to the responding officers. That's going to be a problem, by the way. I need you to find me Florida case law on the admissibility of statements by juveniles outside the presence of a parent or guardian."

Noted and underlined. "Anything else?"

He ticked items off on his fingers. "Travis's school records, medical records, and get in touch with a shrink at University of Florida. His name is Reubins. He specializes in battered children and I want him to sit down with Travis."

"Travis was beaten?"

"Just a hunch," Tony said with a shrug of his impressive shoulders.

That simple motion was just enough to send a hint of his cologne in my direction. He smelled delicious. Too bad he'd played the single-father card, taking me out of the running.

"You're taking Izzy shopping this weekend?"

I nodded. "She needs shoes for her fall formal."

He sighed. "What's wrong with the shoes she wore to homecoming?"

I smiled. "They're the shoes she wore to homecoming. It's a girl thing."

"It's an expensive thing."

"If you don't want me to take her . . ."

"No, no. Get her what she wants. And thank you for handling this so I don't have to."

♦

I'd tried Liam's number several times during the rest of my workday to no avail. I even considered calling Ashley to see if she knew where he was, but that just felt too desperate. The more often I called him, the more my annoyance level skyrocketed. By the time five o'clock rolled around, I was considering calling Crime Stoppers and turning him in myself.

I stopped by the store and grabbed a salad on my way home. Though I was pretty sure my attempt at eating healthy would be waylaid by a few handfuls of Lucky Charms, maybe I could be strong. And maybe hell would freeze over.

Salad in hand, I unlocked the front door and went inside. That's when I saw him and let out a startled scream. "You scared the crap out of me!"

Liam just smiled and shrugged. Then he winced slightly. Good, karma is a bitch.

"Welcome home."

My alarm was beeping so I automatically went to the keypad and reset the system. "How did you get in here without tripping the alarm and why is the alarm back on? That requires a code."

"Safety first," he said.

His voice was deep and seemed to resonate inside me. Tiny goose bumps tingled my skin, making it hard to concentrate.

"How did you set the alarm?"

"With the code."

"You don't know the code."

He rose from the sofa. "Most people use easy to remember codes. It didn't take a genius to figure out that you used your birthday."

I felt my cheeks warm with a blush. "Okay." I made a mental note to change the code. "How did you get in? I locked the house after I came back here to check . . . when I came back here."

"The key taped to the palm out back. You've really got to learn to be less obvious. So," he said as he moved close to me. "You came back to check on me?"

He smelled deliciously male and looked sexy as all get out. He was back to wearing jeans and a faded shirt that did wonders for his already wonderful physique. A single lock of his black hair fell across his forehead and I had to struggle from reaching up to brush it away from his brilliant blue eyes. Truth be told, if he didn't have a hole in his side from a gunshot, I might have jumped his bones in a heartbeat. I remembered vividly how glorious it felt to be pressed against his muscular frame.

God, I needed to put some space between us before I did something stupid to a wounded man. "Want some coffee?" I asked as I quickly put the countertop between us.

"Sure."

"Sit down before you fall down."

He laughed. "Stop acting like I'm on death's door. It's no big deal. I've had worse."

"Where were you all day?"

"Here, mostly."

"You didn't answer your phone."

"I turned it off. I didn't want the cops to be able to track the GPS chip to find me."

"They can do that?" I asked as I filled the filter with a hazelnut blend.

Liam returned to the sofa. "Sure. I bought a disposable when I went out. I wrote the number on that piece of paper," he said as he pointed to a scrap on my counter.

"Where's your car?"

"In a friend's garage."

"How did you get back here?"

"She dropped me off."

She? The joy drained out of my libido. I kept my back to him. "So where did you go today?" God, I sounded like a 1950s housewife.

"The police station."

I twirled around. "You turned yourself in?"

He rolled his eyes. "Of course not. I'm going to find out who killed José."

"So, what? You sat in the parking lot waiting to see if a guy wearing an I'M GUILTY banner waltzed in?"

"It was more like a covert operation."

"To find out what, exactly?"

He shoved his hair off his forehead while I poured the coffee. I joined him in the living room, making a point of keeping as much space as possible between us.

"Had to find out how my gun ended up at José's place."

"Did you?"

He frowned. Deep lines formed at the corners of his eyes. "According to the property clerk, José signed the gun out and swore he was returning it to me."

"Was he?"

Liam took a sip of coffee. "Maybe. I went to his house because he called and told me he wanted to talk. First I've heard from him in nearly five years."

"Around the time Fernàndo was shot?"

Shock registered on his face for a split second, then it was replaced by irritation. "I see you've been doing some research."

"You weren't exactly forthcoming."

"I don't need you digging into my past."

"Oh," I shot back. "You just need me to help you destroy evidence and to harbor your fugitive ass. Sorry I crossed the line."

"Technically, I'm not a fugitive," he corrected. "I'm simply a person of interest."

"Whatever."

Liam placed his mug on the coffee table—without a coaster—and stood, pacing in the space in front of me. I tried. I really tried not to notice the way his jeans fit snugly to his thighs. Or the way his broad shoulders filled out his shirt. I tried. And failed.

"I guess you do deserve an explanation," he said grudgingly.

"It would be nice."

"Deal. If you'll do me one favor."

"You mean *another* favor, right?"

He smiled at me and my bones melted. "Point taken. I need one of your girlfriends to rent me a car."

"Why can't I do that?"

He shook his head, then raked his hair off his forehead. "You and I have a connection. It would be safer if the car was rented by someone other than you."

"So you want me to drag one of my friends into your mess?"

"I was thinking Becky. I did just help you save her from a sicko."

"I won't lie to my friends. I'll rent the car, and if anyone asks, I'll say I was trying to keep the mileage low on my leased car."

"Okay, but you may be biting off more than you can chew. You could get dragged into a mess."

"I think that ship sailed when I bleached your shoes last night. Please fill me in."

"I don't know where to start," he said.

"How about the beginning?"

Liam kept pacing. I took off my shoes and tucked my feet beneath me as I sipped my coffee and waited. And waited. And waited. When I couldn't stand the silence any longer I prodded, "Well?"

"My team got a tip about some guns for sale by a local gang called the Latin Bandits. They were using the gun money to buy and distribute drugs. So we get to the house and before SWAT even parked their van, the shooting started."

"You were shooting?"

"We were all returning fire. It was a residential area and the Latin Bandits weren't going to give it up without a fight. They aren't the kind to back down from a fight.

"So this goes on for about fifteen minutes, then SWAT floods the house with flash bangs and Latin Bandits come running out like lemmings. But there are still guys in the house firing, so we yelled for everyone to get on the ground while we continued to return fire. Eventually things quieted down and we scattered as we entered the house. We cuffed the gang members, and while we were doing that, a shot rang out. So I take cover and nothing happens. Then when I leave the house I see the paramedics working on one of the gang members, on the ground.

"The kid didn't make it. He was fifteen but he was a hard fifteen. Still, too young to be dead."

"I don't understand why you resigned then."

"Internal Affairs did a routine investigation on the shooting and determined that the fatal shot came from my weapon."

"Well, you were in the middle of a gun battle with a gang."

"Except for two things."

"Which are?"

"The kid's hands were negative for gunshot residue, meaning he wasn't one of our shooters. And the weapon identified as the gun that fired the fatal shot was ballistically matched to mine."

"Isn't collateral damage part of police work?"

"It wasn't my service weapon. It was my off-duty gun and I didn't have it at the scene."

"I don't understand."

"I never did either. The last time I saw that gun it was locked in the gun cage at headquarters. I have no idea how it ended up at the scene."

Emptying my mug, I then asked, "So why did you get in trouble?"

"Of the six guys there, only one, Stan Cain, told IA that I used only one weapon at the scene." He raked his hand through his hair again. "It didn't look good for the department for a white cop to kill an unarmed Hispanic kid. They brought me up on charges and even insisted that the state's attorney convene a grand jury."

"What happened with the grand jury?"

"Garza, he was the riding ASA, had my back. I don't think he gave the case his all. He's known as a friend of law enforcement, so he didn't press as hard as he could have. Besides, when I told him my side and Stan backed me, he must have believed there was enough reasonable doubt to make a trial irrelevant. In the end it all shook out with me being given an opportunity to retire quietly or be fired publicly."

"Well, that sucks."

Liam rejoined me on the sofa. "I never did figure out how my off-duty gun found its way to the scene, and after the IA investigation, I was pretty much a pariah. Even José turned on me. He was my partner and he gave a sworn statement that he saw me draw my off-duty weapon from an ankle holster. Which was total bullshit."

"Wasn't there some way to trace how your gun left the locker at the sheriff's office?"

"Yeah, my name on a sign-out sheet and no record of me signing it back in. Which I did."

"Couldn't the gun clerk support your story?"

Liam shook his head. "He said he had no recollection of that happening."

"Then someone framed you. Just like now."

He shrugged. "Do you have any idea how many people would have to have been involved to carry out such an elaborate plan?"

"No, but I suggest we find out."

Bad decisions make good stories.

five

"*You need to get* in touch with Tony," I practically begged. "He can help you make things right with the police."

"How? He's a great lawyer, but he's not a magician. I have a history with the department, and my gun killed José. It isn't like I can walk in and clear this up with a chat over some bad cop coffee."

"But you need legal representation. At the very least, Tony is your friend. You should bring him into the loop."

"Speaking of loops, make a U-turn here and park in the vacant lot," Liam said as I cruised up Federal Highway in Martin County. "You can walk the rest of the way."

"Gee, thanks," I replied. Obviously he had no idea how difficult it was to hike up the street in four-and-a-half-inch heels.

"Sorry, but I don't want to risk getting caught on security tape. Just rent the car and meet me back here."

"What are you going to do once you have a car?" I asked.

"After I swing by Ashley's place, I'm going to start tracking down the officers in my former unit."

"And Ashley can help with that?" *Please don't let that have come out as snarky as it sounded in my head.*

"No, but I have some clothes at her place."

Clothes? As in he kept a drawer at his ex's house? That was bad. A drawer is a serious type of commitment. During the two years I was with Patrick, we never traded drawers. A drawer was a big step. Not that I'm sorry I didn't do the drawer swap with him in light of how badly things ended, I was just stunned to hear Liam admit that he still had dresser privileges with Ashley. God, I sure could pick 'em.

The drawer thing rendered me mute as I exited my car and hiked to Enterprise, where out of pure spite, I rented him the smallest compact they had available. Let him squeeze his six-three frame into that while he was visiting his clothing at Beer Barbie's house. I knew I was being petty but sometimes petty is the appropriate response.

I drove back to the lot and hated the grin on Liam's handsome face when he saw his minimobile. As usual, he was amused by my rebellion. Nothing seemed to irritate him except talking about himself.

"Thanks for the help."

I shrugged. "Please reconsider talking to Tony."

"I'll take it under advisement," he said.

Suddenly his arm snaked around my back and he was pulling me close to him. In spite of my irritation, the feel of his hand splayed at the small of my back seemed to chase reason right out of my head. I placed my hands on his chest fully intending to push him away. Then I felt corded muscle and all rational thought drained out of me.

Liam tilted his head down. I could feel his warm, minty breath wash over my face. His free hand came up and cupped my cheek. His touch was warm. His thumb started to brush my skin, moving lower until he rubbed the pad of his thumb over my slightly parted lips. It was more sensual than any kiss. Well, except for the kiss I wanted so desperately.

I stepped closer while grabbing fistfuls of his shirt, pulling him to me. My fantasy became a reality as his mouth covered mine. Tentative at first, then more urgent and needy. I was fairly certain that my knees would buckle at any moment. Then I felt him wince against my lips.

Duh, gunshot.

I immediately let go of his shirt and took an unsteady step back. His hand slowly slipped away and I was left slightly dazed and a lot confused. Why was I melting in his arms when he had just informed me that he was leaving me to go to Ashley? I'd just moved to the head of the jerk class. Where was my dignity? When did I turn into the kind of person who shared? I am an idiot.

"You should get going," I said, my tone blissfully even.

"Thanks for everything."

"Not a problem." I'd started to walk around the car when he spoke to me in a low, sexy tone of voice.

"We'll pick this up again, Finley."

◆

By the time I got back home it was nearly ten and I was tired thanks to my middle-of-the-night escapades. I was followed inside by the memory of Liam's brief kiss. Like so many of my past relationships—not that Liam and I had a relationship per se—I was wading into dark, swirling waters. Well, not wading so much as drowning.

"Why can't I find a nice, uncomplicated man?" I muttered as I changed into my pj's while the coffeemaker brewed a fresh pot. Maybe there were no complicated men, just complicated relationships. I was definitely no expert. With the exception of her twelve-year marriage to Jonathan Tanner, I'd spent my life with men flitting in and out of our world while my mother indulged her need for serial marriage. My sister seemed to have overcome the family curse, so what was wrong with me? Why was I always attracted to the wrong guy? Worse, even when I know the guy is wrong I *still* want him.

I gave the salad a fleeting glance before going to the pantry and grabbing the Lucky Charms. Lord knew I needed some hearts, stars, moons, and clovers about now. Box in one hand and mug in the other, I went to the sofa and reclined on the pillows so I could turn on the plasma television mounted on the wall. I set the box down long enough to pull my hair back in a ponytail, get up and grab my laptop, return to the sofa, and then settle in for some much-needed me time.

The television was a secondary distraction for the moment. I was looking forward to checking my eBay bid and surfing around for some more parts for my build-it-from-scratch Rolex project.

Yes! I was still in the running for the bezel. After about five minutes, I'd started to look at some watchband links when the newscaster's voice cut through my concentration.

Liam's photo from years ago filled all fifty-two inches of the screen.

". . . Liam Rory McGarrity is being sought by the Palm Beach Sheriff's Office in relation to a shooting in the Riviera Beach area of the county. Anyone with information on Liam Rory McGarrity should contact the sheriff's department immediately. The public is being warned not to approach Mr. McGarrity but rather to call the number currently on your screen."

God, please don't let anyone be watching the early news.

No such luck. My iPhone belted out my Aretha Franklin ringtone. "Hello?"

"Want to tell me what the hell is going on?"

I cringed at Tony's angry tone. "Going on with what?" Stall tactic number one.

"Don't play me, Finley. I just caught the news. Why was Liam at your house last night?"

"Technically it was this morning, not last night." Stall tactic number two.

"Goddammit! Stop screwing around."

"I . . . um . . . think I need . . . Maybe I need an attorney."

I heard him let out a long breath. "Meet me in my office in an hour."

The line went dead. A lot like my career, I feared.

Finding the right outfit for a reaming was a challenge. I decided demure was the best course of action. I went with a gabardine sheath dress in a bold shade of cobalt with an asymmetrical neckline and V-shaped seaming in the back. I'd gotten the dress at the Vero Beach outlets for a fraction of its normal retail because the slender belt was missing. Replacing the belt was simple. I paired it with my brand-new Jimmy Choo Luna peep-toe platform pumps in nude.

Next I carefully reapplied my makeup, going a little heavy on the concealer since I was definitely sleep deprived. A quick run-through with a flat iron and I was as good as I was going to get. I grabbed a pashmina, my purse, a travel mug of coffee, and Liam's disposable-cell number, then drove back to Dane-Lieberman.

I was kind of relieved to see only Tony's car in the lot. I'd been afraid that he might bring Ellen and Vain Dane in on the problem.

Said problem being me.

I didn't *exactly* race up to the fourth floor, mainly because I didn't know *exactly* what I was going to say. The offices were like a ghost town, the hallways lit only by the reddish glow of the exit signs at the stairwells. It was gloomy, which seemed appropriate given my predicament.

When I stepped into Tony's doorway, I heard the muffled voice of the eleven o'clock newscast coming from the credenza on the far wall. Usually the TV was hidden inside the cabinet, but Tony obviously wanted to keep a keen eye on what was unfolding.

He looked up at me and definitely wasn't happy. "Sit."

Stay, heel. Liver treat. I perched on the edge of the seat, my toes tapping soundlessly against the plush carpeting. My mind was racing, as was my heart. I wished he'd stop glaring at me and say whatever it was he wanted to say. Like *"You're fired."*

"Start at the beginning. How did Liam come to be at your house?"

"Ashley brought him over." I obviously had no qualms about throwing her under the bus.

"Ash is in on this, too?"

Ash? It never dawned on me that Tony might have a history with Beer Barbie. Of course he did. Liam and Ashley would have been married when Tony and Liam first became friends. I spent the next thirty minutes recapping my involvement with Liam, all the while Tony's frown deepening.

"You rented him a car?" he asked in a harsh tone.

"He's very determined to find out what happened to José Lopez. Am I going to be charged with a crime?"

"You could."

My toes tapped faster. "What will happen to me?"

"For right now, nothing. But down the road the ASA could charge you with aiding and abetting, harboring a fugitive, and destroying evidence."

"But he wasn't a fugitive when I did any of those things. He was just a guy who was spooked when he discovered his former friend was dead and someone took a shot at him. If anything, Liam is a victim."

"Give me a dollar."

"Excuse me?"

"Give me a dollar. It's your retainer. Now, whatever isn't covered by attorney work product will be covered by attorney-client privilege."

I fished a dollar out of my wallet. "Thank God."

"This only works if Liam comes in and becomes my client. Tell me how to reach him."

"He bought a disposable cell," I said as I took the scrap of paper from my bag. "This is the number."

"Where is he now?"

"He was going to Ashley's to pick up some clothes. I have no idea what he planned after that."

Tony grabbed up the receiver and pressed a series of buttons. I could only hear Tony's side of the conversation and it wasn't pretty. Well, unless you count pretty colorful. The call ended with Tony slamming the phone on the cradle. He held the slip of paper up with Liam's number on it and said, "I'll hang on to this right now. I don't want the two of you putting your heads together until I have a chance to hear Liam's version of events."

"You think I'm lying?" I asked, offended.

"I think you'd go above and beyond to help Liam. Admirable but not helpful. He'll be here at seven tomorrow morning. I want you here at eight."

"Okay, then what?"

"Then we go see the cops and try to straighten this out before it becomes a bigger mess."

My cell phone rang and I was half afraid it was Liam calling to scream at me for talking to Tony. I looked at the caller ID. It was worse, it was my mother, who I'd bet my last dollar—the one I'd just given Tony—had seen the evening news and wanted to gloat.

"Don't discuss this with anyone," he warned.

I twirled a lock of hair around my finger. "I kinda have."

Tony sighed. "Who, and what did you say?"

I told him about my lunch with Becky, Liv, and Jane. "But I didn't give them any details because I didn't have any. I just told them about Liam being shot."

"From now on, keep your mouth shut. You talk only to me, understand?"

"Yes."

"Then I'll see you at eight."

I stood and walked to the doorway, then turned back. "Tony?"

"Yes?"

"I'm really sorry."

"Save your apologies for Victor Dane. If the shit hits the fan, he'll want your head on a pike."

◆

It was 7:05 and I was already dressed for work and sitting at my counter sipping coffee and listening to Roxanne Stein on the morning news. The photo of Liam in his uniform was in a small box off to the right of the news anchor. The story seemed to be the highlight of the early morning newscast. They were still asking for the public's help, only now they included a description and the license plate number of his Mustang.

I was reminded of his remark about a woman hiding the car in her garage and giving him a lift to my place. Ashley, maybe, but that was an awfully big risk. Questioning the ex-wife was almost a given under these circumstances. It wouldn't have been a very prudent idea to stash his car at her place.

The outside lights automatically came on and I heard a car in the driveway. It couldn't be Liam, he was supposed to be meeting Tony. It wouldn't be my mother, she didn't do mornings. I got up and peeked out the window. It was a white sedan with blackwall tires. A cop car. Great.

I answered the doorbell with an anxious smile on my face. Two men stood on my porch, their expressions blank and stern at the same time.

"Miss Tanner? Finley Tanner? I'm Detective Metcalf and this is Detective Wells," he said as they simultaneously flashed their IDs in my direction. "We have a few questions about Liam McGarrity. May we come in?"

I tried to dawn an air of innocence as I pulled the door open and invited them in. "Would you like some coffee?" I asked.

"Sure."

I waved my hand to the sofa and said, "Please sit. Black, cream, sugar?"

"Black," Metcalf said.

"Cream for me, ma'am."

I hated being called ma'am, especially by a guy who looked to be about my age. Wells was the younger of the two. Thirty-ish, with auburn hair and a very pale complexion that included a row of freckles across his nose and cheeks. Metcalf was the more senior of the two. I put him somewhere in his fifties, with a bald head and piercing green eyes that followed me like a tractor beam as I moved around the kitchen.

I refreshed my own coffee, then carried all three mugs to the living room. "Sorry I don't have any pastries or doughnuts. I'm not a breakfast eater."

"Not all cops crave doughnuts," Wells said with a fairly genuine smile.

My cheeks warmed slightly at the stereotype and I giggled nervously. Lucky for me they didn't know me, so I didn't think they would be able to tell that nervous was my new middle name.

Metcalf spoke while Wells took notes.

"I understand you know Liam McGarrity?"

"Yes. For about two years. He does PI work for my firm."

"Dane, Lieberman, and Caprelli?"

"Yes. I'm a paralegal there. I've worked for them for eight years." It dawned on me that I was not following Tony's instructions to speak to no one. Only I couldn't think of a more obvious way to look guilty than to invoke my right to have counsel present during questioning. Did I want the wrath of Tony or the wrath of the cops? I decided the cops were worse.

"Have you had contact with Mr. McGarrity in the last twenty-four hours?"

Shit.

"As far as I know, he hasn't contacted my firm." *Not a lie, Tony called him.*

"We have information that your relationship with Mr. McGarrity is of a more personal nature. Didn't the two of you recently take a trip out of town?"

"May I ask who told you that?"

"Mr. McGarrity's ex-wife. Could you answer the question, please?"

Beer Barbie was such a traitor. I took a sip of coffee, glad that my hands weren't shaking. "Yes, but it isn't what you think.

I needed an escort for my sister's wedding. Tony Caprelli was supposed to accompany me but something came up at the last minute, so Liam was kind enough to stand in."

Wells was writing furiously in a small notepad.

"You stayed at a hotel in Atlanta?"

Beer Barbie had a big mouth. "Yes, but not together. We had separate rooms." *Separate* adjoining rooms. Time to go on the offensive. "There wasn't any sex, if that's what you're suggesting." *Not for lack of trying.* "I have a mother who is very big on etiquette. Liam was simply my escort."

"Did you pay him for his time?"

"Not that *kind* of escort," I said indignantly.

"We have information that you and Mr. McGarrity have worked closely on several cases. Is that true?"

"Yes. But that's part of my job. It often falls to me to hire outside contractors on cases."

"What kind of cases?"

"I do estates and trusts, which involves tracking down heirs and other pertinent information regarding assets and things, and I also do litigation support for Mr. Caprelli when needed."

"He's a criminal specialist, right?"

"Yes." I glanced down at my Swatch watch and stood. "In fact I have a meeting with Mr. Caprelli in a half hour, so if we could wrap this up I'd be very grateful."

"Does the meeting have anything to do with Mr. McGarrity?"

Think! "The last case Tony brought me in on was the defense of a juvenile who is currently incarcerated. I really can't say any more than that without betraying privilege."

Wells flipped his notebook closed and downed his coffee. "Thank you, Miss Tanner."

Metcalf seemed a tad more reluctant to end the interview but he grudgingly got off my sofa. "I'm sure we'll be in touch again," he said as he reached inside the breast pocket of his jacket. "Here's my card. If you see or hear from Mr. McGarrity, I'll expect a phone call."

"Not a problem." *Or an option.*

*MapQuest should really start at direction
number three. I'm pretty sure I know how to get
out of my own driveway.*

six

"Change in plans," Tony said.

I was negotiating a modest amount of traffic over the bridge
that separates West Palm Beach from Palm Beach proper. It's the
unofficial dividing line between the haves and the have-nots.
I lived on the have side. Granted, my little house was smaller
than most of the servants' quarters attached to the mansions
that dotted the island, but I didn't care. I loved my little piece
of heaven.

I put my cell on speaker and placed it in the cup holder.
"What's the new plan?"

"Meet me at the sheriff's office in Riviera Beach at nine.
Bring a pad of paper."

"Okay."

Tony didn't bother saying good-bye, the line just clicked and
went silent. I had a good forty-five minutes, but I couldn't think
of any way to kill the time, so I headed for the office. Marga-

ret wasn't yet at her perch but one of her minions was seated behind the horseshoe-shaped desk. Her name was Wendy or Cindy or something like that. I only knew the petite redhead from the file room and the few snarky remarks I'd heard her say under her breath. Like Margaret, she resented my private office and my salary. Too freaking bad. I resented being called FAT behind my back, so I figured we were even.

"Do I have any messages?"

Wordlessly she passed a few pink slips toward me.

"Is Margaret out for the day?" No one sat behind the sacred sentry desk unless Margaret was at death's door.

"She had an appointment. Is there anything else I can do for you?"

Spill that healthy little bottle of V8 juice on yourself? "No, thank you."

There was a small amount of activity buzzing around the second floor. Mostly interns trying to keep up with their duties and a couple of administrative assistants prepping various projects for the partners. I said hello to the ones I knew as I turned left and went to my office.

I still had the messages in my hand but it wasn't until I sat down at my desk that I bothered to read them. They were all from Jane, and all were urgent. Something was weird. Why hadn't she called my cell? Or my house? Why leave messages at the office instead of on my voice mail?

It was only a few minutes before eight, so I knew she'd be at the gym. I'd return her call on my drive to the PBSO since her workouts ended promptly at eight forty-five. I checked my voice mail while my computer booted. Nothing of consequence except for an angry message from Sleepy Bollan telling me he was going to hire "a legal aide" to fight the eviction. "Great," I sighed, wondering how long this problem would drag out. Maybe talking to his own attorney would convince him to take the deal. I could only hope.

My e-mail was about as disinteresting. A new estate assigned by Victor Dane, along with an edict to contact the client so I could begin the process. I dashed off a quick e-mail to Ellen, letting her know Sleepy's intentions.

The last item was an e-mail from Izzy with a photo attached. She'd looked online and found what she thought were the perfect shoes to go with her outfit. I was impressed. The Gliteree skinny-heeled platform pump was darling; I just wondered how Tony would feel about the shoes. They were a tad high for a fourteen-year-old. Just to be on the safe side, I e-mailed Izzy, agreeing that the shoes were cute, but suggested we not limit our choices until we had scoured the mall to see all the options. I'd make a point of taking her to the Betsey Johnson shop last. Hopefully she'd fall in love with another, more appropriate pair. I was already on Tony's crap list. I didn't relish the idea of throwing gas on that fire.

I lingered over a cup of coffee while I scanned eBay for any new listings. I hit pay dirt. A seller was offering four band links with no reserve. My kind of auction. I immediately placed a bid and was almost giddy when I was the high bidder. Now if it only stayed that way for the next six hours.

♦

Riviera Beach was a small town just north of West Palm. I had to MapQuest and GPS the directions since the sheriff's office wasn't on my radar. Suspenders and a belt—sometimes my GPS takes the long way around. Luckily I was going against the traffic, so I arrived at the station and didn't see Tony's BMW or the small compact I'd rented for Liam. I stayed in my car. I'd already had one interaction with detectives and I wasn't relishing a second round of questioning. Instead I tried Jane's number. It frustratingly went directly to voice mail. I pleaded with her to call me ASAP, then placed my phone on vibrate only.

I checked my lipstick in the mirror just as Tony and Liam pulled into the lot. They were together, so I wondered briefly what had happened to the rental. After all, it was being billed to my already-stressed VISA.

Liam looked pissed more than anxious and Tony was all business. We met up at the flagpole near the entrance to the single-story stucco building. The emblem of the PBSO was on the double glass doors leading into the station. As we entered, I smelled cleaning supplies mingling with coffee. There was a lone uniformed officer standing behind the counter.

He looked up and I saw recognition immediately register in his washed-out brown eyes.

Tony passed him a business card while I stood just behind the two of them with a death grip on my briefcase. "I'm Mr. McGarrity's counsel and he's come in voluntarily to speak to whoever is in charge of the Lopez shooting."

The officer seemed at a loss for a second before he grabbed a phone and called for Detective Wells.

I stepped forward. "He was at my house this morning," I whispered to Tony.

"Anything I should know?"

I shook my head. I hadn't technically lied, more like a version of truth avoidance.

A buzz sounded, then the door opened and Wells, with Metcalf on his heels, came out into the lobby.

Metcalf's eyes narrowed on Liam. "McGarrity," he said, almost as if it was a vile curse.

"How ya been, Harry?" Liam asked, as if they were the best of friends.

But I knew that wasn't possible. Metcalf looked like the top of his bald head was about to blow off.

The detective looked past Liam, right at me. "Miss Tanner."

"I'm Tony Caprelli," Tony said as he extended his hand. "I represent Mr. McGarrity, and Miss Tanner is my paralegal. We're here to answer any questions you may have about the death of Mr. Lopez."

"Deputy Sheriff Lopez," Metcalf corrected curtly. "Let's go into interrogation two."

The three of us followed through the door, down a small hallway to an even smaller interrogation room. There was a table in the center of the room, a two-way mirror on one wall, and only four metal chairs. Wells excused himself to get another chair and I tried not to notice the metal loops used to handcuff people to the table. I had some bad handcuff memories that I didn't care to revisit.

Wells returned and offered me the seat he placed at the end of the table. Liam and Tony sat opposite the two-way glass while Wells and Metcalf sat across from them. I retrieved my pad and paper as well as a small voice recorder.

"We'll be taping this interview," Tony explained after giving me a "good job" nod.

"So will we," Metcalf said. He loosened his tie and depressed a button on the antiquated machine in the center of the table. He said the date, the time, and named everyone in the room. Then from rote he said, "You have the right to remain silent and refuse to answer questions. Do you understand?"

"Yes."

"Anything you do say may be used against you in a court of law. Do you understand?"

"Yes."

"You have the right to consult an attorney before speaking to the police and to have an attorney present during questioning now or in the future. Do you understand?"

"I think I've got that one covered."

"If you cannot afford an attorney, one will be appointed for you before any questioning if you wish. Do you understand?"

"Ditto," Liam answered as he absently rubbed his side. I guessed the wound was not healing as fast as he pretended.

"If you decide to answer questions now without an attorney present you will still have the right to stop answering at any time until you talk to an attorney. Do you understand?"

"That's a dumb-ass question."

"Knowing and understanding your rights as I have explained them to you, are you willing to answer my questions?"

"I'm here, right?"

Wells reached into a drawer in the table and passed Liam a card, telling him, "Initial each and every right as they were just read to you and sign at the bottom."

Liam did as requested and shoved the five-by-seven card back at the detective.

"I'd like it noted that my client came in of his own volition."

"So noted," Metcalf said.

"Where were you Sunday evening between five and eleven P.M.?" Wells asked.

"I was home until about nine thirty."

Metcalf leaned back in his chair. "Can anyone verify that?"

"My dog, but he doesn't usually talk to strangers."

"Cut the bullshit, McGarrity," Metcalf warned.

"No," Tony responded. "My client was home alone until approximately nine thirty."

"Then you went to Deputy Lopez's home?"

"He called me and asked me to come over," Liam's voice dropped slightly and he seemed more somber.

"Was that a common occurrence?" Wells asked.

Liam shook his head. "I hadn't spoken to José for nearly five years. He called from out of the blue and told me he had something important he wanted to tell me."

"And what was that?" Metcalf asked.

"I have no idea. I got to his house around ten thirty and when I arrived I found José in a chair with a bullet in his head."

"Are you saying he was already deceased when you entered his house?"

"Yes."

"How did you get in?" Wells asked.

"The door was ajar. I went in, found him, checked for a pulse, and then someone took a shot at me."

Metcalf tilted his head, conveying his skepticism.

Liam lifted his shirt. "Wanna look for yourself?"

Wells frowned. "We need to stop for a moment. Mr. Mc-Garrity, do you require medical attention?"

"No."

"Yes," Tony said, overruling him. "I want his injury fully documented."

"Wells," Liam began angrily. "I want this over so they can move on and find out who killed José, 'cause it sure as hell wasn't me."

"Which will happen as soon as a doctor checks you out," Tony said forcefully. "Call the paramedics. Now."

Wells and Metcalf turned off the recorder and left the room and Tony immediately turned to Liam. "You have to stop antagonizing these guys."

"I will if they stop treating me like a perp."

Tony stood and rapped on the glass. "Privacy please. I want to talk to my client."

"Does that really work?" I asked.

"They won't risk violating attorney-client privilege. What's the deal with you and Metcalf?"

Liam shrugged. "He used to be Internal Affairs."

"Are you sure you can't think of any reason for Lopez calling you last Sunday?"

"Not a one," Liam said, then raked his fingers through his hair. "I told you this was a bad idea. Metcalf will do his best to link me to José's murder."

"That's a leap, Liam."

"Not for Metcalf. And I'm not stupid, look at the circumstances. I was there. I'm sure my fingerprints are on the doorknob and I could have left any number of footprints or fibers or other forensics at José's. Once the shooting started I was more concerned with getting out of there."

"And you didn't see the gunman?"

Liam shook his head. "I can only say for sure that he was in the house. I booked out the back door and hopped the fence."

"Did he chase you?"

"I don't think so. But it wasn't like I was standing around waiting for him."

Tony rubbed his face with both hands. "And you didn't return fire?"

"My gun was in the glove compartment of my car."

"So you didn't handle a gun at all that night?"

"It wouldn't matter anyway," I piped up. "Bleach and cleaning solutions and time make a gunshot residue test pointless."

Tony and Liam turned their heads and stared at me. Tony spoke. "Bleach and cleaning fluids?"

I felt my face grow warm. Apparently Ashley gave me up to the cops, but Liam had kept my involvement quiet. God, how stupid! I'd outed myself as complicit. "I helped Liam a little bit," I admitted.

"Dammit, Finley!"

"Hey!" Liam barked back. "Don't blame her. It was my idea. She didn't know about what went down at José's place. She helped me clean myself up after the shooting. That's all."

"You should have called me," Tony admonished.

"I did," I reminded him. "I put Liam on the phone under the impression that he would talk to you."

"Right," Liam said. "If you're going to be pissed at anyone, be pissed at me."

"I think I'll be pissed at both of you right now."

This was definitely not one of my better days.

Thankfully a team of paramedics came into the interrogation room. Liam stood and lifted his shirt. Aside from the bloody bandage, he was pure perfection. I was going to hell. Here the poor man was having a gunshot wound tended to and all I could think about were rippling abs and the way his jeans hung low on his hips.

And my selfish thoughts didn't end there. Oh no, I started doing a mental comparison between Liam and his gorgeously bared torso and Tony in his custom-tailored suit. I was smack in the middle of any girl's fantasy. Well, except for the fact that Liam was shot and we were in a police interrogation room. Minor details.

After some arguing it was decided that Liam would be taken by ambulance to Jupiter Medical Center. Tony offered me a ride, but I opted for my own car. Not only did I want the freedom of my own transportation, I still needed to talk to Jane to find out what the problem was that had her leaving me messages.

I could still hear the sirens of the ambulance as I dialed Jane's number. She answered on the first ring. "Finley, where have you been? I've been stalker-calling your office."

"Did you forget my cell number?" I asked.

"He told me not to tell you. I didn't know if your cell was safe or not."

"He who told you not to tell me what? And why wouldn't my cell be safe?"

"Liam told me and I was afraid he might be with you and I didn't want to get in the middle of anything until I talked to you."

I was confused. "You talked to Liam?"

"He said he needed someplace to park his car. I let him have my space at the apartment. Is he okay? He didn't look very good yesterday. I didn't let on that you told me he'd been shot. Was that the right thing to do?"

"You were fine. He's an ass for bringing you in on this."

"On what?"

"Long story," I replied as I turned down Military Trail, following closely behind Tony's BMW.

"Is there a short version?" she asked, kind of irritated.

I let out a breath. "Liam sorta witnessed a murder. We're all on the way to the hospital now. I'll call you as soon as I can and give you all the details. Promise."

"Are you in trouble?" she asked.

"With my boss, yes. With the cops, the jury is still out."

"Is there anything I can do?"

"Save the employment section of the newspaper for me."

We said our good-byes as I pulled into visitor parking. Tony was already at the door, waiting to hold it open for me. He still looked annoyed, but I no longer had the feeling he wanted to beat me about the head and neck. We entered an atrium and went to the volunteer's desk for visitors' badges. I cringed when they scanned my driver's license photo, stuck it on an adhesive-backed piece of paper, and told me to wear it at all times. It wasn't my most flattering photo. Especially not in blurred shades of black and white.

Wells and Metcalf were already in the waiting area. Neither of them had to wear nametags.

"He's with the doctor now," Wells said.

I thanked him. Unlike his partner, Wells seemed to be the more reasonable one. Metcalf had a terminal case of the nasties and I got the feeling I wasn't on his good side. Actually I wasn't sure he even had a good side. But I had to admit I was curious. He and Liam had a history and I could only surmise that it had to do with the shooting five years ago. The four of us sat in chairs, not speaking, sipping bad hospital coffee. When Tony excused himself to make a call, I was left alone with the two men. It was like a stereo version of a bad date with someone's loser brothers. The silence was deafening.

"Finley?" Tony called quietly.

I stood and joined him at the end of the short hallway. "I've got to get back to the office. Can you stay here and let me know when the doctor is finished with him?"

"Sure." Like I had any intention of leaving.

"I don't want either one of you talking to the cops without me present. Is that clear?"

"I'm good, but I don't know if I can keep Liam quiet."

"If he opens his mouth, shove gauze in it if you have to. No one talks without me in the room. Got it?"

"Yes."

I waited alone with officers nice and nasty for nearly an hour before a woman in scrubs carrying a clipboard came out and said, "Finley Tanner?"

"Yes," I said, standing up with Wells and Metcalf hot on my heels. "I'm Finley Tanner," I said, tilting my shoulder so she could see my badge of dishonor.

"The doctor is going to admit Mr. McGarrity, but he'd like to see you."

I felt a surge of panic lodge in my throat. Admit him? Had Ashley and I done something that caused gangrene or some other life-threatening complication? What the hell did I expect? Super Glue and some Steri-Strips. Seriously?

"We'll join you," Wells said.

"No you won't," I said firmly. "Mr. McGarrity has nothing to say without his attorney present."

"We'll have to hear that from him, not a secretary," Metcalf grumbled as a red flush ran up his neck.

I had my phone out and was dialing the office. "Then it's a good thing I'm not a secretary." Wendy/Cindy answered the phone. "This is Finley, I need to be put through to Tony immediately." I was following the woman in scrubs as we neared the curtain-partitioned portion of the ER. I quickly explained the situation to Tony, then handed Wells my phone.

Whatever Tony said to him worked. He handed me back my phone and grabbed hold of Metcalf's sleeve. "We'll have to wait."

Metcalf's red stain grew darker. "For how long?"

"Attorney said McGarrity won't be available to continue the interview until he's been released by the doctor."

"That's bullshit," Metcalf snapped.

I turned and met his angry stare. "Well, it's legal bullshit, so you can be on your way now." Metcalf turned away. "Maybe now you'll know not to screw with a secretary, Detective. Have a nice day."

The only difference between a
hospital room and a motel room is the
motel room is cheaper.

seven

"Hi," Liam said, greeting me with a lopsided grin.

"Yes you are," I said, unable to keep from chuckling. He had on one of those hideous gowns with the hospital's logo stamped on it—like anyone would want to steal one—and an IV running into his hand. Even morphined to the gills, he looked good. His color was better than it had been in two days. Whatever they were pumping into him was working.

"They cut through the Super Glue and put in stitches. I hate stitches."

"And I hate having medical procedures explained to me," I told him. "I know you're loopy, but under no circumstances are you to talk to anyone except me or Tony."

"I like talking to you more than Tony," he said with a sensual grin He patted the bed next to him. "Wanna join me?"

"Wanna heal first?"

"Ah," he said. "That wasn't a no, was it? How long do I have to wait?"

Luckily I was saved from having to respond by the appearance of a guy with arms the size of my thighs. His nametag was clipped to a crisp white polo shirt, as if Liam was about to be whisked off to some tennis match. "Do I follow you?" I asked.

He glanced at the pagerlike thing clipped to his belt. "No. You can meet us in room 347."

I had to go back out to the atrium, past the gift shop with cheap but cute bangles in the window. I considered flowers, but that just seemed too sick friendish. Not appropriate for a guy who'd just propositioned me while in an altered mental state.

I stopped long enough to call the office and Tony told me to return once Liam was settled in his room. I waited for the floor nurse to take his vitals, left strict instructions that Liam was not to have visitors who weren't from Dane-Lieberman, then I reluctantly left.

The bright late-afternoon sun was harsh as I stepped out into the daylight. I was so tired it felt as if it should be midnight, not a quarter to four. When I got to the office, an elderly couple was seated in the lobby and Margaret was back at her desk.

"You're late," she said in a hushed tone, her face all pinched and disapproving.

"Late for what?" I asked.

She nodded toward the couple and said, "That's Mrs. Lawson, she's been here for almost forty-five minutes." As she spoke, she passed a nearly empty folder to me.

Crap. Vain Dane's new estate client. When did this happen? And why did the widow have her boyfriend along?

"Give me five minutes, then send them up."

"You can take them up now," Margaret argued.

"Five minutes," I said, this time with force behind it.

I raced to my office and turned on my computer. I quickly upped my bid on the links with only forty-three seconds left on the eBay auction. While I watched the countdown, I tidied up my desk. As I shoved a legal pad in my drawer, I remembered the notes Tony had given me on the Travis Johnson murder case. I was running on caffeine and residual adrenaline and it looked like it wouldn't be an early night for me. I was also starving. As if in agreement, my stomach growled just as Mrs. Lawson and her paramour were shown into my office.

We got the preliminaries out of the way, including my apology for being tardy for our appointment. An appointment I thought I was supposed to make myself, but that Vain Dane had obviously taken upon himself without notifying me.

Gwendolyn Lawson introduced me to Joseph Lawson and I was confused. "He's my son," she explained. "He's been wonderful since my Harrison died."

Either she was well preserved or he'd spent too much time in the sun. Or maybe, I concluded after I started asking the usual questions, they were both just old. Gwendolyn was in her midnineties and Joseph was in his midseventies. Still, he looked at least a decade older. I kept looking at Mrs. Lawson's hairline, trying to find the telltale signs of a face-lift. Too tight. She'd definitely had some work done.

Joseph handed me a file. "This is my father's will and copies of financial statements I got from the family accountant."

"Thank you," I said. If I hadn't already guessed by the size of the diamonds dripping off her fingers and an equally impressive diamond-and-emerald broach on her shoulder, the "family accountant" was a dead giveaway. No wonder Vain Dane had rushed this process. We were probably talking major money here, which meant major administrative fees for the firm. So what if I was starving and sleep deprived? Vain Dane was all about the money.

Mrs. Lawson had perfectly coiffed white hair and watery blue eyes. She kept clutching her son's arm, and in return he patted her hand sympathetically. She was wearing Elie Saab Le Parfum and it hung like a cloud in my office. She was dressed from head to toe in Chanel, right down to her vintage handbag. What I would have given for that purse.

"Miss Tanner?"

"I'm sorry." I jerked back into the present. "You were saying?"

She repeated her late husband's date of birth. I was tired, not stupid, so I did the math. Harrison was just shy of 105. "Are there any other children?" I asked.

"Three others, but they're specifically excluded in the will."

Meaning I could expect at least three pissed-off phone calls in my future. "I find in these situations," I began delicately, "it is still better to keep all the heirs apprised of the terms and conditions of the will. It tends to keep any challenges to a minimum."

"I'll provide you with names and addresses," Joseph said. "Or do you prefer electronic information? It's so hard for me to tell what to do now that technology has taken over the world."

I discreetly wiggled my mouse only to see the hateful screen telling me I'd been outbid on the links. I didn't blame the grieving Lawsons, I blamed Vain Dane.

"I have to prepare a couple of documents for you to sign," I explained. "If you don't mind waiting in the lobby, it shouldn't take me long."

The two of them exchanged glances, then nodded.

"Let me show you to the elevator."

My stomach continued to growl as I used templates on my computer to print out the retainer agreement and the request for Letters of Administration as well as several blank letters of request for information I might need for life insurance or any other claims the estate might have as the process moved forward. I had the Lawsons signed, sealed, delivered, and out in less than fifteen minutes.

Now all I needed was Vain Dane's signature. It was well after five but I knew he'd still be in his office. I buzzed his direct line and asked for a few minutes of his time. I was granted an audience with the pope of the law firm.

Before going up to the much more posh fourth floor, I called the hospital and checked on Liam. To my utter frustration the nurse informed me that he was resting comfortably, his wife at his side.

"Put me through to his room," I instructed.

The line rang once before Ashley picked up. "Hello?" she said in a whisper.

"You shouldn't be there," I told her flat out. "Until things get straightened out with the police, Liam shouldn't be talking to anyone but his counsel."

"I was just worried when Tony called me and told me Liam was in the hospital."

"Well, get *un*-worried and," on a whim I added, "come by my office in about a half hour. Okay?"

"Sure, but what for?"

"We need to talk." And then I'd like to kick you in the shins. "Do you know where the office is?" She didn't, so I gave her directions, then hung up.

With the now indexed and tabbed Lawson file tucked under my arm, I took the elevator up and went down the hall to Dane's office. Hands down he had the best office in the place. The wall behind his glass-topped desk was floor-to-ceiling windows with panoramic views of the Intracoastal and the Palm Beach skyline. If you squinted hard enough, you could almost make out the Atlantic Ocean.

Dane had turned the place into a shrine to himself. The walls were littered with plaques, awards, and news clippings touting his various accomplishments, both legally and personally. The man himself was a tribute to self-indulgence. He sat in a cushy leather chair, his jacket hooked on the back. His monogrammed shirt was so crisp it looked as if he'd just put it on even though it was past the end of the official workday.

He waved me in with his manicured hand. I swear the man had his nails buffed more often than a trust fund debutante. His salt-and-pepper hair was gelled and lacquered into place and it took a second for him to glance up in my direction.

I took an equally posh seat opposite his desk and, as usual, waited to be spoken to before I opened my own mouth. Vain Dane liked deference in his employees. Especially me.

"I understand you were late meeting Gwendolyn," he began.

Leave it to Maudlin Margaret Ford to tattle. "I was in the hospital at Tony's request." Apparently today was my day for tossing people under the bus.

He shook his head and nary a hair so much as wiggled. "With your increased responsibilities you have to get better at time management. This firm has invested time and money in you, so we expect you to perform accordingly."

Big deal, so they dropped a few thousand dollars on me for some continuing-education courses as a refresher on criminal litigation. It wasn't like they'd paid my mortgage. And, it wasn't altruistic either. The firm billed for my hours, so they were doing just fine, thank you very much. "My apologies," I said, not meaning a single syllable.

I placed the folder on his desk. "If you could just sign these I'll take them to the courthouse first thing in the morning."

He made a production of reading them, probably hoping to find fault, then grabbed up his pretentious fountain pen and fluidly wrote his name. Little did he know that the early morning run meant I could get a late start and just claim I had to wait in surrogate's court. What Vain Dane didn't know couldn't hurt me.

"I would expect nothing else," he said as he returned the folder, saying nothing about my excellent organization. Was it so hard to voice a compliment?

"Where are you in reference to the McGarrity problem?"

"Tony hasn't asked me to do anything else," I answered.

"Well, keep time sheets just in case. I know Tony believes McGarrity deserves pro bono representation, but that may change."

"Okay." *Heartless bastard.*

"You can go," he said abruptly.

So could he, but I didn't think we were talking about the same place.

I dialed Mr. Chow's and ordered a delivery of moo shu, then waited for tardy Ashley. I was down in the lobby, hoping the food came before the ex-wife.

They arrived at the same time. I tipped the delivery guy generously. Mainly because they don't technically deliver, but Mr. Chow made an exception in my case because I was a good and loyal customer.

After he left, I locked the door behind Ashley and pointed to the elevator. "This way."

The moo shu smelled divine. Ashley smelled like Clinique Aromatics Elixir. She was an inch or two taller than I was, wearing a simple white sheath dress and strappy sandals. Her skin was tanned but I could tell by the slightly orange cast that it was sprayed on. I wanted to tell her the eighties were calling and they wanted their big hair back, but that seemed petty. Well, I was feeling petty. I didn't understand this woman's presence in Liam's life and, worse yet, how it affected me. Selfish, I know, but what kind of couple divorces, then hangs out all the time?

Ashley settled in on one of the chairs across from my desk. "So what did you need to talk to me about?" she asked.

I had to admit that even with the orange tinge, she did have perfectly flawless skin. "I need to know about the shooting."

"You know as much as I do. José Lopez was dead when Liam—"

"Not that shooting. The one five years ago."

Her expression sobered and she started rubbing her long, red nails together, making an annoying clicking sound. "Liam was accused of shooting an unarmed boy. It ruined his career. In a lot of ways it ruined him. He changed."

"How?"

"He completely shut me out, for one thing," she said. "That's what ended our marriage. It got to the point where he was barely talking to me. It took years for us to get back on an equal footing."

What did that mean? I couldn't let it drop. "So you're working out your relationship?"

"More like we've started a different one."

Well, that was no help. I had to stay focused. "How did Liam's gun get to the scene?"

"He never could figure that out. I always thought that maybe he forgot it was with him. He kept the thing locked up at work and no one but Liam checked it out. The property clerk testified to that at the grand jury hearing."

"How do you know that? Grand jury testimony is secret."

"Liam got hold of a transcript. I think Garza gave it to him. It was a long time ago."

"Garza the prosecutor?"

She nodded. "He was always nice to Liam. I don't think he wanted him to go to jail for an accident."

"So you believe Liam shot that kid?"

She shrugged. "I believe a lot can happen in a tense situation."

"But Liam was trained for tense situations. All cops are."

"And stuff happens in the middle of all hell breaking loose."

"So you don't think there was any conspiracy to frame him?"

She uncrossed and recrossed her legs. "Liam wasn't with the gang unit long enough to make enemies. At the time of the incident, he'd only been in that job for two months. Other than José, he didn't really know the other guys and vice versa. Only Deputy Cain testified that Liam was in the house at the time the fatal shot was fired."

Now we were getting somewhere. I wrote on my pad. "What was Cain's full name?" I asked.

"Stanley. Stan Cain. Nice guy. Tragedy what happened to him."

"What tragedy?" I asked her.

"He was killed in a fluke hunting accident in South Carolina. A stray bullet, I think. He'd taken some personal leave and I guess he went hunting. He left behind a wife and two little girls. Like I said, a real tragedy."

Or a real strange coincidence.

"What were the names of the other officers involved?"

Ashley blew out a breath. "Well, there was José Lopez. Armando Calderone. Diego Ferrer. Carlos Santiago. Stan Cain." She stopped and scratched her head, careful to use only one finger to keep from cracking the blond war-helmet hair. "Vasquez. Michael, maybe? Like I said, he wasn't with that unit very long. I didn't get to know everyone on the team."

"What about the property clerk? Do you know his name?"

She shook her head. "No. Hey, you aren't going to dredge all this up with Liam, are you? It was bad enough the first time, I'd hate to see him fall back into all that anger."

"We may have to. Someone went to a lot of trouble to place

Liam at José's house. Unless you have another idea, what else do the two things have in common?"

"Maybe some old case they worked? Liam and José were having some success with the Latin Bandits. They'd made a lot of arrests and were working their way up the food chain. From what I get on TV, gangs are into retribution."

But five years later? I didn't think so, but I made a note anyway.

"Do I really need to stay away from Liam?" she asked. "Tony said it was okay and that I didn't have to talk to the police unless they formally charged me with something. He said if they did, he would represent me."

Of course I didn't want her talking to Liam, but not because I gave a damn if she got in trouble with the police. But I had to keep that self-centered thought to myself. "If Tony says it's okay, then it is."

"Good, I want to go back to the hospital now. I don't want him to be alone."

I didn't want him to be alone either, I thought as I warmed up my moo shu in the firm's kitchen microwave after showing Beer Barbie the door, I just would have preferred to be the one standing sentry at his bedside. Knowing that made me acknowledge that my lust for Liam had entered a new and ugly phase. I was jealous. Jealousy meant I had feelings beyond just wanting to sleep with him. I knew he felt the same about the sleeping part, but everything else was up in the air. He could be mending fences with Ashley, and the last thing I wanted to be was a thorn in that mess.

After I wolfed down my dinner, I went to the law library and started doing the research for the Travis Johnson case. Reading case law is a lot like watching grass grow. Judges like to drone on and often give a twenty-page explanation when two pages would suffice, thank you very much. I copied the two cases Tony had asked for specifically and found seven others related to a battered-child defense. From what I read, it didn't sound promising.

Now for the real fun. I had to go back to my office and write abstracts of the cases. I worked my way through three of them, then I don't know what happened.

The next thing I knew I was being smacked in the head. I finally came awake and started to move, feeling every muscle in my neck ache from the attempt. "What?" I groused as Becky's smiling face came into view.

"You slept here," she said, holding up her iPhone. "I took a picture to post on Facebook."

"You did not," I insisted as I raked my hair off my face.

Becky smiled. "You have the imprint of the open book on your cheek."

I rubbed my face. "Great."

"And your mascara is all screwed up. You, my friend, are a hot mess."

"And you are a pain in the ass."

She walked around me to turn on the coffeepot. "Stay here all night looking for a way to get Liam out of trouble?"

I shook my head and told her about the abstracts. "I must have zoned out."

"Well, you'd better zone back in. It's almost eight."

Crap. "I'm going home to shower and change."

"Ah, the walk of shame."

"No, the walk of the overworked." I grabbed the first mug of coffee before the pot had even finished brewing. "I think I liked just doing estates."

"But now you make more money."

True. "But I never slept here."

"I'll mention your devotion to Ellen when I see her. She loves you now, by the way."

"Good, because Tony doesn't."

"Trouble in paradise?"

"A little. I need the support of two partners. It's job security. But right now I need a shower. I feel disgusting."

"You look disgusting."

"Aren't you supposed to be my friend?"

"I am being your friend. I'm telling you the truth. It's good for the soul."

"Yeah? Well, it sucks for the self-esteem."

You never know when it will strike,
but there comes a moment at work when
you know that you just aren't going to do anything
productive for the rest of the day.

eight

I felt much better in my Lilly Pulitzer Jai dress. It was one of my most impressive finds. The poor thing had a tiny tear at the seam, so I'd scored it at a wonderful 40 percent discount. It was sleeveless with a faux wrap bodice in a pattern called Hotty Pink Scorpion Bowl. Very flattering and very functional, since the November temperatures promised to hit a near record mideighties. Still, knowing that Florida is not the Sunshine State but rather the over-air-conditioned state, I grabbed a white cardigan with tiny pearl accents to keep from freezing. I wore a pair of sand-colored patent wedges—also Lilly—with a cute peep toe that allowed my OPI pedicure to shine.

I'd already gotten the Letters of Administration for the Lawson estate, which was pretty much all I could do for at least weeks until the accounts were transferred, so I headed to the office just before eleven.

Sour-faced Margaret gave me her usual surly look as I asked for messages, then went to my office. It was a disaster area. I had law books piled up like paperbergs, mocking me because I still had four abstracts to write.

Apparently Margaret had sounded the alarm because within five minutes, Tony was standing in my doorway. Unlike Ellen and Vain Dane, he was just as comfortable coming to me as he was asking me to venture to the fourth floor. What I didn't know was whether he was there to ream me again. I didn't like the tension strung between us.

"Still mad at me, I see?" I said with a smile, hoping to clear the air.

"I'm still mad," he assured me with a grin. "But I'll get over it."

"I'm sorry, but I haven't quite finished the Travis Johnson research. Give me about an hour and a half and I'll send everything up."

"That's fine. I just need you to be available after lunch. Liam's being released from the hospital, so we're going back to the station to finish the interview."

I was relieved that Liam was being discharged, but I didn't relish the notion of going back to see Wells and Metcalf. "Okay."

"Heard you slept here last night. Do we need to get you a sofa for your office?"

"Hopefully it won't be a regular thing."

"One thirty at the station."

"Okay."

"And bring your little tape recorder. That was a nice touch."

"Thanks."

I felt better after he left. His anger seemed to have dissipated for the most part, and thanks probably to Becky, he'd heard of my devoted night at my desk. I was reveling in the glow of a compliment when my intercom buzzed.

"Line two for you," Margaret said. She could have at least told me who was calling, but no, she had to be a snot.

"Finley Tanner."

"So you're finally reachable."

Reveling officially over. My mother's tone dripped disapproval. "Good morning, Mom."

"What if the story about your seedy date goes national?" she asked without preamble.

"Liam isn't seedy and he was a victim in the case, not the perpetrator."

"But they called him a person of interest on the news. What if your sister's new family gets wind of this?"

"It's not a problem, Mom."

"Everything with you is a problem, Finley."

"Sorry to be such a disappointment."

"Did I say that?" she asked in a huff. "I'm simply pointing out that unlike your sister, you seem intent on bringing attention to yourself. Negative attention."

"Then we have a lot in common."

"That was uncalled for. I'm only thinking of your best interests."

Yeah, right. Sometimes it is better to surrender than to fight on. I tried to muster some submission. "I'm sorry. I've just got a ton of work to do. Maybe you could call and berate me later." Okay, so I was only partially successful.

"Obviously you don't care about my opinion or my standing in this community. How am I supposed to explain you cavorting with criminals?"

"Liam isn't a criminal and we aren't cavorting."

"I have eyes, Finley, and I've seen the two of you together. Why couldn't you just stay with Patrick? He was such a gentleman."

And a bastard. "Mom, I've got another call," I lied in tribute to my crappy ex-boyfriend.

"I'm afraid we won't be able to have brunch on Sunday."

If this was my punishment, I was all in. "That's a shame."

"Don't you want to know why?"

"I just told you I have another call."

"Fine. Don't care what's happening in my life." Click.

I stared at the receiver for a few seconds, then placed it on the cradle. It took me only an hour to finish the abstracts, so I decided to make my life easy and do some housekeeping on the Lawson estate. In no time my printer was spitting out letters to various financial institutions so Mrs. Lawson could have complete control over the seven million little friends she was about to inherit. I also drafted letters for the disinherited, leaving spaces for the names and addresses once they were provided by Joseph. That left me with a half hour before I had to leave for the Riviera Beach Sheriff's Office.

I started a search on the late Stan Cain, which, thanks to all the database subscriptions at my fingertips, was a pretty easy thing to accomplish. Cain had married his college girlfriend and settled back in Palm Beach County. He had been a decorated deputy who'd achieved the rank of sergeant. The Cains had two children, just as Ashley had said.

I stopped reading for a minute and glanced at my phone. I wanted to call Liam, but I was afraid. Afraid that Ashley was with him. It would be like her to spend the night at his side, and it was in keeping with Liam's MO to let her. For months I'd been torn between my curiosity over Tony and my lust for Liam. Only now I was fairly sure what I was feeling was more than just lust. I used to believe that if we just slept together, it would scratch that itch and I could move on to someone less complicated. But I couldn't ignore the jealousy factor. Or the idiot factor. As always, I was attracted to the wrong man.

"And what do you really know about him?" I asked the air. Easy answer. Not much. Not enough and *really* not enough to be angsting over his relationship with his not-so-ex-wife.

Back to Stan Cain. Getting copies of his birth certificate, marriage certificate, and work history was easy. Now I'd moved on to news articles. I found a few column inches in the *Palm Beach Post* regarding the accident. It wasn't detailed, so all I could garner was that he'd had some sort of accident. I glanced at the byline. Luckily, I knew the reporter. We'd gone out a few times several years ago. He wasn't my type, but he was very persistent. It had taken me a month to shake his incessant calls. I weighed my options. There was a chance that by making contact I'd renew his interest. But if I didn't contact him, I'd have to go see the widow and that seemed like the worse option. Especially since I had no authority and she'd have no reason to share her pain with me.

Justin Haller picked up the phone on the third ring.

"Um, hi, Justin, this is Finley Tanner."

"Finley, it's been awhile." I could almost hear him grin.

For good reason. "Yes it has. I called because, well, because I need some information on a piece you wrote about a week ago."

"You follow my work?"

His "work" was mostly grunt assignments, but he thought of himself as South Florida's version of Woodward and Bernstein. I dodged the question. "I'm working on something that is tangential to a story you did. The Stan Cain hunting accident? The deputy sheriff killed in South Carolina?"

"Yeah. What do you need to know? And what's in it for me?"

"Something has to be in it for you?"

"Sure. Like getting Tony Caprelli to return my calls. I want an interview with Liam McGarrity. Your firm does represent him, right?"

I sighed heavily. "You know I can't comment on clients."

"I know you can't comment on privileged information, but your client list isn't confidential. Besides, my source at the sheriff's office already confirmed that McGarrity showed up with you and Caprelli in tow. I also know McGarrity was shot. Care to comment?"

"No."

"Then I don't think I can help you."

My stomach knotted. "C'mon, Justin."

"Sorry, Finney."

My teeth clenched. He was the only one who ever called me that and I hated it. I wasn't big on pet names, especially from a guy I thought was a total jerk. "I'll ask Mr. Caprelli. Good enough?"

"For now. What do you need to know?"

"What kind of accident did Stan Cain have?"

"Accidentally shot himself while he was hunting in South Carolina."

"I read that," I said, trying not to let my frustration bleed into my voice. "I mean, how did it happen?"

"According to the cops in South Carolina, he was climbing into a blind when his rifle discharged. Died instantly."

"So it was definitely an accident?"

"Now you sound like the widow."

"Because . . . ?"

I heard papers shuffling before he said, "She was adamant that something was wrong. Said her husband always hunted with a crossbow. She didn't even know he had a gun with him."

I was jotting down notes on a pad. "Was there any kind of investigation?"

"Just cursory. Cain was hunting alone, so there were no witnesses, and rifles, unlike handguns, don't have to be registered. The best they could do was confirm that the rifle was shipped by the manufacturer and sold at a store in Palm Beach County. Cash transaction. The receipt was made out to Cain. Like I told the widow, I couldn't find anything hinky about the accident."

"Okay. Thanks, Justin. Take care."

"Wait!" he called into the phone. "What are you doing Saturday night?"

"I, um, have a date." Partially true, I had a date to meet Izzy and then we'd grab some dinner after shoe shopping.

"Sunday?"

"I have a standing obligation with my mother." Again, mostly true. I usually was commanded to Sunday brunch, only not this week—but Justin the Jerk didn't need to know that.

"Okay," he said, a tad defeated and totally clueless. "When will you talk to Caprelli?"

"This afternoon," I promised. And that was true. I'd ask Tony, but I already knew his answer. Tony never tried cases in the press and he was always discreet when it came to his clients.

"I'll wait to hear from you."

"Works for me." *Hope you don't mind waiting a long, long time.*

I wrote Stan Cain's name down, then circled it. I also wrote "accident" with a question mark. Coincidences didn't sit well with me, so my mind began to wade into possibilities. Were José's murder and Cain's accident somehow connected or was I making some sort of giant leap? That was exactly the kind of question I'd discuss with Liam, only his plate was already full with the investigation into José's death. Maybe we could discuss it after his interview with the police. Which I was going to be late for if I didn't get moving.

I made a travel mug of coffee to stave off hunger as I drove to Riviera Beach. I wasn't looking forward to another round of questioning. I didn't like seeing Liam in the hot seat. I knew all too well what that was like.

Tony and Liam were already in the lobby when I arrived, briefcase and coffee in hand. I was glad I'd brought my own roadie; cop coffee was sludge. No wonder so many cops ate antacids. I was astonished that any of them even had stomach linings left.

There were three other people in the lobby. One large woman sat wringing her hands and a middle-aged couple sat calm and collected. All three of them looked at me as I entered and stood next to Tony at the desk. Liam looked better, but tired. Either it was a residual drug thing still in his system or he and Ashley had spent the night chatting. It had to be chatting, I told myself. The idea of the two of them getting frisky made me a little crazy.

A buzz sounded and the door marked NO UNAUTHORIZED ENTRY swung open. Wells came out and said, "This way."

We followed, me sandwiched between Liam and Tony. I could feel Liam's eyes on me, but I didn't dare return the gesture since I was afraid my eyes would give away my conflicted feelings about him. Better to be silent than stupid.

We were shown into the same interrogation room, which was already set up with the appropriate number of chairs. Again, Liam and Tony sat across from the two-way mirror while I sat at the end of the table, taking out my recorder and a pad of paper. I'd just settled in, thinking how much more at ease everyone was without Metcalf in the room when the man himself came striding in. He had a folder in his hands that he slapped on the table before sitting in his seat.

Metcalf's no-name cologne was enough to make me choke. What did he do, bathe in the stuff? Like Wells, he was wearing a different suit, this one gray with a yellow shirt and matching tie. The color gave him a jaundiced cast. Conversely, Wells was wearing khaki slacks, a blue blazer, and a striped tie. He looked more like he was going to a poor man's polo match than conducting an interview. Wells also had a softer expression. Businesslike, but without the condemnation that dripped off Metcalf's face.

I started my tape recorder at the same time Metcalf started the official recording. He gave the date, time, names of the people in the room, and reminded the forces that be that Liam had been read his rights and that this was a continuation of his statement in the presence of counsel. As a little dig, he added, "Also present is Mr. Caprelli's secretary, Finley Tanner."

Not that there's anything wrong with being a secretary. I actually felt sorry for them, especially the ones who worked at Dane-Lieberman. They often put in long hours, kept complex calendars, and were forced to work late at the whim of their bosses. And they had no backup.

As much as I longed to correct him, I knew it wasn't worth it.

Metcalf began. "Mr. McGarrity, is it your position that when you arrived at the home of Deputy Lopez he was already deceased?"

"Yeah."

"Walk me through it."

"We've already covered this."

Metcalf offered a humorless smile. "Humor me."

"I went inside, José was seated in an armchair in the family room. He'd been shot through the head. I was about to check for a pulse when I was shot by someone I can only assume was the killer."

"Then what?"

Liam cursed. "I was unarmed, so I went out the back door."

"You were unarmed?" Metcalf challenged.

Liam nodded.

Metcalf got sort of a Cheshire grin on his face. "Did you touch the weapon?"

"Yes, I picked it up off the floor for a few seconds. It fell out of my hand when the shooting started."

"Why not use it to protect yourself?"

"A—the room was pretty dark, and B—I didn't know where it fell. Plus, I didn't see the perp. And I wasn't about to crawl around on the floor while someone was taking potshots at me. Besides, it's hard to exchange fire with a ghost. Leaving seemed to be the most prudent thing to do under the circumstances."

Metcalf opened his folder and took out a single sheet of paper. "This came in this morning. Can you explain it?"

Liam glanced at the paper, then handed it to Tony.

Tony then said, "He just told you he handled the gun in question. Finding his fingerprints on the weapon doesn't mean anything."

"But we found only two sets of prints on the gun. McGarrity's and Lopez's," Metcalf countered. "If there was a mystery shooter, why weren't there three sets of prints on the gun?"

"Maybe the shooter wore gloves?" Liam suggested.

"Then we'd probably find smudges," Metcalf claimed. "In this case, we have partials matching Deputy Lopez and a pristine set from McGarrity."

"Again," Tony interjected, "Mr. McGarrity admitted he touched the gun."

"Then explain this," Metcalf said as he took another sheet of paper from his file. "Deputy Lopez was killed with your gun. How do you explain that?"

"I haven't seen that gun in five years. I have no idea how or why it ended up at José's place."

"According to this," Metcalf said, pausing and taking yet another sheet of paper from the file, "Deputy Lopez returned the gun to you a week ago."

"Impossible," Liam said. "Like I said, José and I hadn't spoken or seen each other in years."

"So you're claiming to know nothing about how the gun got from the property room to Deputy Lopez's house with your prints still on it?"

"I handled the barrel," Liam said, agitation in his voice. "Other than that I never touched the gun."

"Is this going somewhere?" Tony asked.

"As you can see, McGarrity's prints are on the butt and we lifted a ten-point partial match off the trigger. That sort of positioning shows he handled the gun with his left index finger on the trigger. So, is your client going to stick to his story that he never touched the trigger?"

Tony shoved the ballistics report back at Metcalf. "We both know you can't time-stamp fingerprints. They very easily could have been left there years ago when the gun was in my client's possession."

"Not possible," Metcalf said. "The gun was tested for prints five years ago and it was clean. The officers on-site that night said McGarrity was wearing gloves."

"That was bullshit then and it's bullshit now. I believe Sergeant Cain testified to that fact at the grand jury."

I wondered if Liam knew that Cain was now deceased.

"Are you saying you never wore gloves?"

"No, I often wore gloves. Department issue. They have special grips on them to make holding a weapon more stable."

"And the added bonus of leaving behind no prints."

"What's your point?" Tony asked.

"My point is, the gun was registered to your client. According to official reports, the gun was returned to your client by Lopez a week ago. Now suddenly that same gun is used to kill the deputy. Your client had the means, the motive, and the opportunity."

"You're forgetting about the gunshot," Tony argued. "Are you claiming that Liam shot Lopez, then turned the gun on himself?"

Metcalf shrugged. "It's a nothing wound. As a former officer he would know exactly where to shoot to avoid a major injury. Or he was shot by Lopez. Maybe there was a struggle for the gun."

"Does the autopsy report indicate Deputy Lopez was involved in a struggle before the shooting?" Tony asked.

"Report's not complete yet," the previously silent Wells conceded. "That's why it's better for your client to come clean now before any more evidence piles up against him. Assistant State's Attorney Garza is on his way down to take his statement. Maybe some sort of plea is appropriate. Maybe there was a struggle and the shots were fired by accident. Maybe your client got shot by accident. Maybe the bullet from Lopez's head nicked McGarrity in the side."

"So what are you saying?" Liam asked. "I shot him in the head, then ran around the chair in enough time to let the bullet go through me? That's an idiot theory."

Metcalf's neck began to turn red. I knew from experience that this was not a good sign. "Then Lopez shot you, you struggled for the gun after you got shot, then returned the favor."

"The bullet that hit me was a through-and-through. It has to be lodged somewhere at the scene."

"We only recovered one slug," Wells said. "The shot that killed Lopez was a through-and-through, too."

Liam raked his hands through his hair. I now recognized that as his tell. I don't think it was nerves, more like his pissed-off-o-meter. "So we're back to me moving faster than a bullet?"

"Possibly. Excuse us for a minute," Wells said, turning off the tape, then scraping the chair legs against the floor as he stood.

Wells and Metcalf left the room.

Liam instantly got to his feet. "I'm done with this crap," he told Tony. "Let's go."

I'd started to put my pad and tape recorder in my briefcase when the door opened. This time the detectives had a third person with them. I recognized him from television and the papers. ASA Alberto Garza was a career prosecutor with an impressive conviction rate. He was tall, maybe an inch or so shorter than Liam, with a shock of black hair and eyes so dark you couldn't tell where the iris ended and the pupils began. I put him somewhere in his early fifties. I could tell by the way his suit fit that he worked out regularly, and his dark complexion was even darker due to sun exposure. This guy was definitely fit. And I sensed an inkling of something—maybe skepticism—etched in the deep lines on either side of his eyes. He smiled and it seemed genuine.

He looked past me to Liam. "McGarrity," he said. Then he moved around me and extended his hand to Tony. "Counselor."

"Been listening in?" Tony asked.

"Yes."

"And?"

Garza took a deep breath, pushing his chest out, then releasing the air slowly. "Detective Wells?"

"Put your hands behind your back," Wells said to Liam.

"What the f—?"

"Liam McGarrity, you're being charged with suspicion of murder in the death of José Lopez."

"This is crazy," Liam said as he reluctantly followed the order. "I didn't kill José."

Panic flooded every cell in my body as I watched Wells snap on the cuffs. I wanted to leap up and scream at them that they were making a horrible mistake. But shock had me glued to my seat.

"What's the probable cause for the arrest?" Tony asked.

Metcalf smiled broadly. "He probably did it."

*Eventually one of two things will happen—either he'll
realize you're worth it or you'll realize he isn't.*

nine

"So what happens now?" I asked Tony as we left the PBSO station. I was trying not to think about Liam behind bars.

"They'll keep him in the infirmary because of his wound and his
law enforcement background," Tony explained. "They have forty-
eight hours to arraign him, then the judge, hopefully, will set bond."

Somehow that didn't make me feel better. Forty-eight hours
locked up is an eternity. "So what do we do for now?"

We were standing next to my leased Mercedes convertible.
"Nothing."

"We're just going to leave him here?" I practically whined.

Tony touched my arm. "He's tough, Finley. We just have to
hope he keeps his mouth shut."

"He will," I assured Tony. Liam was a lot of things, but stupid wasn't one of them.

"If it will make you feel any better, you can visit him on
your own time."

"Don't I have to be with you?" I asked.

Tony looked down at me, his dark eyes registering regret. "No. But I can tell you want to be with him."

I felt a blush. "You're making that sound—"

"True," he interrupted. "Izzy was right. I should never have pushed you away."

Well, what the hell was I supposed to say to that? It made me feel a little panicked. Liam and I weren't a *thing*, so I was a tad sorry to hear Tony throw in the towel so easily.

Was I really one of those women who needed a man in the wings just in case? A second-stringer if things didn't work out with man number one? Apparently so. Worse yet, it was something my mother would do. She never left a marriage without an exit strategy. I guess there comes a time in every woman's life when she has to admit that part of her is her mother. Only I wasn't going to do it willingly. No, they'd have to carry me kicking and screaming into Cassidyville.

"You didn't push me away," I said, suddenly aware of how he was keeping his distance. "You made a rational decision based on what you thought was best for your daughter." And screwed me in the process.

Tony let out a deep breath. "I think you just scare me."

I scoffed. "Scare you? What does that mean?"

"It means," he said as his hand rubbed my bare arm, "you were the first intriguing woman I'd met since my wife died. I didn't know how to handle it."

"Dinner and a movie?" I suggested.

He slowly shook his head. "I see what's going on with you and Liam."

My mother saw it, Becky saw it, now Tony? How come everyone but me was seeing it? All I saw was a man I was physically and slightly emotionally attracted to spending more time with his ex-wife than me. Hardly a rousing endorsement of my ability to pick men. "Liam and I are just friends," I insisted. Only I insisted a little too forcefully.

Tony laughed. "I've known Liam for more than a decade. I've never seen him look at a woman the way he looks at you."

"But there's Ashley."

Tony moved his hand off my arm and waved it dismissively. "They'll never get back together. That's old news."

For old news she certainly had staying power. "Liam's too complicated."

"He really isn't," Tony said. "He has his reasons for helping Ashley."

"Which are?"

"His to tell, not mine." He shrugged out of his suit coat.

Tony turned to go to his car. "Wait a sec," I said.

He turned back around and looked at me with those knee-weakening chocolate eyes.

I set my briefcase on the hood of my car and pulled out my pad of paper with the notes from my earlier phone call. "I've been doing a little digging."

Tony's expression registered instant disapproval. "This is a murder investigation, Finley. You shouldn't be digging around anything."

I pretended not to hear him. Instead I told him all about the facts surrounding Stan Cain's sudden demise just a week earlier.

"Good work," he said grudgingly. "Get the autopsy report

from the South Carolina medical examiner, and while you're at it, get the one for Lopez, too. It should be ready by now. The detectives were stalling. There has to be something in that report they don't want us to see."

"On it."

"And, Finley?"

"Yes?"

"We don't know what or who we're up against here so your investigating ends now. Understood?"

"Sure," I lied. There was no way I was going to sit on my hands while Liam was in custody.

"See you back at the office."

As soon as I hit my desk, I was in touch with the powers that be in South Carolina. In accordance with their rules, I had to send a formal, written request for the autopsy report. Thankfully South Carolina wasn't one of the few states that kept those records confidential. I quickly typed up my request on the firm's letterhead and had one of the interns fax it to the number provided by the clerk.

I repeated the process for Florida, only this time I grabbed my purse and went directly to the morgue. It was located in the basement of the largest trauma hospital in Palm Beach County.

It had a medicinal smell—kind of like the science labs at college. And it had a seriously creepy factor. There was a desk with a long hallway beyond it. Tile covered the floors and extended up the walls about three feet. I assumed this was for easy cleaning but I didn't want to think about *what* was being scrubbed away. The assistant behind the desk didn't look happy to see me at all, probably because it was fifteen minutes before closing time. I had no sympathy. After all, I'd slept the previous night at my desk. He'd just have to put on his big-boy pants and get the job done.

Every time someone came through the double metal doors at the end of the hallway, I jumped. I had this irrational fear that they were going to bring me José's body in person. Stupid, I know, but morgues don't bring out the smarts in me.

As time dragged on, I got bored and sent texts to Liv, Becky, and Jane to see if they were interested in an early dinner. It had been an exhausting day and I could use some girl time. Actually, I could use anything to divert my attention from the fact that Liam had been arrested.

As expected, I got three instant affirmatives, so we opted to meet at the Food Shack in Jupiter. It was probably my favorite funky eatery in all of South Florida. It was in a strip mall, nestled between a dentist's office and a surf shop. The food was Floribbean and never disappointed. I was almost salivating at the mere thought of a tuna-basil roll when the young man came back from the part where they keep the dead people with a file in his hand.

"Thank you," I said pleasantly.

He grunted something unintelligible in return. As I was leaving, my cell rang. It was Ellen Lieberman.

"We've hit another snag in the Egghardt estate," she said.

I rolled my eyes. "What is it now?"

"The Bollans have hired Frank Mertzberger as their attorney. He wants a meeting first thing in the morning."

Great. "What time do I need to come in?"

"You're going to them. Listen to what Mertzberger has to say, then call me and maybe we can wrap this up."

"I hope so. This is like the estate that won't die. What time?"

"Be at the Bollan place at eight thirty."

Seriously? Since when did I keep long hours and go above and beyond? I was salaried, so it wasn't like I'd be earning overtime. "I'll be there."

"Do you want me to send the file over to you by courier tonight to save you a trip here?" she asked.

"No, I'll come by now and get it." Liar, liar, pants on fire. I'd have Becky bring it to me. Only I didn't say anything to Ellen because Becky didn't want people at the firm knowing we were very close friends. She thought it might be a problem if and when she was being considered for a partnership. Like West Palm Beach and Palm Beach proper, Dane-Lieberman had its own hierarchy, and Becky wanted to give the appearance of knowing that line between the powerful and the powerless. I was in the second category.

I sent Becky a text telling her what I needed and where to find it. I had almost forty-five minutes to waste before dinner. I really wanted to go see Liam, but I knew I didn't have the time. It would take them twenty or more minutes just to process him into the visitors' section. So I drove to the Food Shack's parking lot, retouched my lipstick, then spotted a sign calling out to me. The high-end surf shop was having a fifty-percent-off sale on all swimwear.

As I walked to the store, I checked my eBay status on my iPhone. So far, so good, I was still winning the bid on the diamond bezel. The store was nearly deserted, meaning I had the full attention of the salesclerk. She looked like a surfer. Her ripped arms and muscled thighs were a tribute to days spent paddling out beyond the breakers. She also had shoulders like a swimmer, broad and tanned. It was easy for me to deduce all these things since she was wearing a tiny sleeveless T-shirt, surf shorts, and a weathered pair of Sperrys. Her hair was streaked with natural highlights from the sun, and when she smiled, it was in stark contrast to her deeply tanned skin.

"May I help you?"

I smelled board wax and what I guessed was leftover pizza. "Just looking," I replied casually. I don't like salespeople following me around like lap dogs. I skimmed the racks, finding three possibilities. Even at half price, the suits would still set me back at least seventy dollars, but I really needed—*correction*—wanted a new suit. I decided on a pink bikini with little white floral accents and paid for my purchase.

Then, like a guilty child, I took the package to my car and hid it in the trunk. I didn't want Jane to know I was out spending again. No sooner had I ferreted away my find than Jane pulled up with Liv in the passenger's seat. I smiled, happy to see friendly faces after my hellish day. I felt a pang of guilt knowing I was about to eat great food while Liam was probably dining on mush and beans.

Liv was dressed impeccably in a tailored tan shift with a patterned scarf around her neck. Not that I had a girl crush or anything, but the honest truth was that Liv Garrett was quite possibly the most attractive person on the planet. She had shoulder-length dark hair and the most exotic aquamarine eyes. They were so stunning people often thought they were contact lenses. I knew better.

If Liv was overdressed for the very casual, not far from the beach Food Shack, Jane was a little closer to the vibe of the place.

Today she was sporting a green pleather miniskirt paired with a corset. On anyone else it would have looked like she was on her way to the closest S and M club. But somehow Jane managed to carry off the look. She had her long brown hair pinned up and the heels of her stilettos clicked as she walked across the macadam.

Becky pulled in just then, getting out of her Volvo, then shedding her jacket and rolling up the sleeves of her blouse. She had a pencil skirt on in a shade of coral that matched the chunky necklace around her neck. She leaned in the car one last time and pulled out what I recognized as my Bollan file.

Liv bent down and gave me a hug. "I'm so sorry about Liam."

"It'll all work out," I said, though I wasn't quite sure how.

I also received shows of support from Becky and Jane. Then we went inside. The Food Shack is a narrow restaurant with a bar and about two dozen tables. It also has a surfboard at one end of the bar that seats four. As usual the place was packed, so we were shown to a small table where we sat elbow to elbow with the patrons on either side. The food was worth being squished in like sardines.

The server left us the regular menus as well as the daily specials. I didn't even bother to read the offerings, I knew exactly what I was going to order. One tuna-basil roll and a panko oyster salad with spiced melon and greens. I also asked for a glass of wine. A big one.

"So what happened?" Becky said as I tucked my file down by my feet.

I gave them a blow by blow of the past forty-eight hours. I knew I was breaking privilege, but my friends would keep my confidences. I finished with, "So he's sitting in jail awaiting arraignment."

"Maybe something will break before it gets to that," Becky suggested.

"I think it's part of a bigger thing," I said.

"Bigger how?" Jane asked.

I was quiet for a minute until the waitress delivered our drinks. I took a long sip of wine, loving the way it warmed me as it went down my throat. "I think the Lopez shooting and Stan Cain's supposed suicide are somehow related."

"A week apart and two states away?" Becky argued.

"So maybe I don't have all the pieces of the puzzle."

"And," Liv injected, "maybe you should leave this to Tony."

"Right," Becky agreed. "The firm can hire a different investigator. Tony was right, you have no business investigating murders."

"I've done okay in the past," I said, defending myself.

"With Liam's help," Jane reminded me. "This time you'd be on your own."

"But I owe it to him. He's saved my fanny from the fire more than once. The very least I can do is return the favor."

"You're being crazy," Becky said emphatically. "Besides, if Tony finds out you're doing this behind his back he may just decide to fire you."

"Dane-Lieberman has fired me before," I said with a shrug.

"But this is different," Liv said. "From what you've said you may be talking about some sort of corruption or something on the police force. If that's the case, you could be putting your life in danger!"

The idea sent a shiver down my spine. "What else can I do?"

"Let this play out," Jane answered. "Let it run its course."

I was feeling a complete lack of support.

Liv smiled. "Finley has nothing but bad news. Whereas I have terrific news."

"Which is?" Becky asked before putting a forkful of sweet-potato-crusted mahimahi in her mouth.

"Concierge Plus got a new client. Six events in six weeks and hefty budgets to work with."

"Congrats," I said as I clinked my wineglass with hers. "What kind of events are they?"

Liv shrugged. "Something about having your life changed forever in twenty-nine minutes. It's all about Kabbalah."

Jane's fork stalled in midair. "Isn't that like Scientology for Jews?"

"I don't think so," I said. "Maybe I should attend one of the seminars. I'm due for a life change. And twenty-nine minutes seems about right."

We spent the rest of dinner on myriad topics. The mood lightened enough so that we even ribbed Liv about her loser boy toy. By the time we finished, I had to admit I was in a slightly better mood.

We walked out to the now dark parking lot and said our good-byes. "Be careful, please," Becky whispered in my ear.

"I'll try."

"Try harder," she insisted.

Once I was home, I toted the hated Bollan file inside. I wanted to make sure I had everything I would need. As much as I despised the thought of going down lawn jockey lane again, the meeting was probably the Bollans crying uncle. "About damn time," I muttered. While I didn't know Attorney Mertzberger, I knew a lot about him thanks to at least fifty billboards lining I-95 and his hideous television ads that provided a phone number and claimed it would be answered by a lawyer, not a paralegal. Needless to say, I resented the implication.

Dumping the file on the coffee table and gingerly putting my briefcase with my laptop on the sofa, I went back into my bedroom and undressed, then put on a soft, cotton pair of boxers and a cami. After pulling my hair up, I washed my face. Mistake. Without concealer I looked like a blond raccoon. I swore I'd make it an early night.

Of course thinking of night only steered me toward the image of Liam locked in a five-by-seven cell. "The dog!" I thought aloud. His poor dog couldn't go two days without food and water. Only problem? I'm afraid of dogs, even the little lap kind that are forced to wear silly bows in their fur.

Against every intuitive bone in my body, I picked up my phone and called Ashley. She grabbed it on the third ring. "Is there news?" she asked.

"No. How did you know it was me?"

"I programmed your information into my smartphone. Oh, when you have a minute I need a picture of you to add to the contact number so your face will show whenever you call."

Was she serious? Well, I didn't want to be on her friends and family list. "I'll get on that. Listen, Liam's dog—"

"Already taken care of. I went over and brought Perry Mason to my house. He can stay here until you get Liam out of jail."

"It's not an imposition?"

"Of course not. I'll do anything for Liam."

I had to ask that question, I thought as I made a gun out of my fingers and shot myself in the brain. "Okay, then."

"Honey, what can I do to help?"

I swallowed the desire to tell her to stop calling me honey. "Do you happen to know Stan Cain's widow?"

"Yes, why?"

"Think you could get her to talk to me?"

"Sure. I mean, I think so."

"Ashley, see if you can arrange things for after five P.M. tomorrow. Okay?"

"Yeah, but what does Stan have to do with José's murder?"

"Probably nothing. I just need some more details."

"I'll call you first thing in the morning."

Oh joy. "Thanks. And, Ashley?"

"Yeah."

"Do me a favor. Keep this between us. Don't mention it to Liam or Tony."

"Why?"

Because I'll get fired. "Because I don't want to get anyone's hopes up."

"I see. I'll talk to you soon. Oh, Finley?"

"Yes?"

"Isn't there some way to get Liam out of jail? Bond or something? He can be released to me."

Not comforting. "We can't do anything until he's arraigned. If he gets bail, it will probably be high."

"I'll find some way to raise the money."

"Great. Talk to you later."

Finally some peace and quiet. And eBay.

After several minutes of surfing, I found a few more links for sale. I had a good shot at all five of them since most people went for connected links. Since I was building my watch from the ground up, I'd take whatever I could get. I placed my bids, then went to the "my auctions" page. I was still the high bidder with twenty-seven hours to go. However, the auto-bid feature had already jumped to eighteen hundred. Someone had joined the bid. *Damn.*

I got a glass of wine, then settled in on the sofa. I turned on and muted the television. I wanted to catch the evening news, just so I'd know how bad the spin would get. My mother would no doubt be watching, so I needed to be well armed for our next battle. I next focused on the Bollan file. I had all the information—plats, surveys, etc. In addition, I had the agreement Ellen had already drafted granting Sleepy and Wanda Jean five acres of land at the southwest portion of the property. Hopefully I'd just waltz in, meet Mertzberger, get some signatures, and be on my way. Only I was running low on hope when it came to the Bollans.

Going back to my laptop, I thought I might start making a list of potential suspects in the Lopez shooting. All I knew right then was that several sheriffs' deputies might be involved. I typed out my theory. But it would require a larger cast of characters. A property clerk. The fingerprint analyst. It would literally take a village to arrange a crime of this magnitude.

I was discouraged. Maybe I was looking at it the wrong way. Maybe the crime didn't start with the PBSO. Maybe it started with the Latin Bandits. I looked up a few articles. They were really bad guys, and a few girls. Into drug trafficking, the sale of illegal assault weapons, and suspects in at least a dozen shootings. Not exactly the kind of people I wanted to meet in a dark alley—or a brightly lit one, for that matter.

So, I decided, I had option a: corrupt cops, or option b: violent gang members.

An option c would be nice.

I yawned, then checked my e-mail since the news didn't start for another twenty minutes and I was struggling to stay awake. It was a bunch of nothing, really. Mostly e-mails from online stores advertising sales or containing links to coupons. I did have some Facebook messages but I just wasn't feeling the social media thing right now.

There was a message from Izzy with the subject "urgent." I clicked it open.

Sorry, Finley, but can we go shopping Friday night instead of Saturday? One of my friends offered to take me out on her boat on Saturday. If you can't, I totally understand. Izzy

I wrote her back letting her know that the switch was fine. Especially since I didn't know if Liam would still be in jail in two days. If he was still incarcerated, I'd probably have to work out some sort of visitation plan with Ashley.

I opened the last e-mail and it contained a photograph and three words. The picture was of me leaving the surf shop earlier in the evening. The text read: WANNA DIE, BITCH?

The wrong relationship will make you feel
more alone than you did when you were single.

ten

"Did you tell Tony?" Liam practically yelled as his hands yanked on the shackles holding him to the desk.

I glanced toward the glass partition separating the counsel room from the guard positioned just outside. "Keep your voice down."

"Someone threatened you, for Chrissake."

"I got that from the note. I'm going to leave my laptop with the IT guys at work. Hopefully they can backtrack the IP address all the way to the Stone Age."

Liam leaned forward so that his fingertips just grazed mine. Even that small touch was enough to scare away some of the fear pooled in my stomach. "Listen, Finley. I'm not in a position to have your back on this one. You stay away from the Latin Bandits. They're no joke."

"It may not be the Latin Bandits."

His brows drew together. He had a five o'clock shadow at eight in the morning. His black hair was mussed but his blue eyes were clear. Apparently he could get a good night's sleep in jail. "What did you do?" he asked.

"What do you know about Stan Cain?"

"Good guy. Stood up for me at the grand jury. Died recently. A hunting accident. I went to the funeral."

"Were your other unit members there?"

He nodded. "Some of them. Carlos Santiago, Miguel Vasquez, and Diego Ferrer. Garza paid his respects, too. Stan wasn't killed in the line of duty, so the funeral was more low-key. Sad, too. He left behind a couple of kids. Why are you asking?"

"I'm working on a theory."

"Well don't," he said forcefully. "You don't have the skills."

My spine straightened indignantly. "I've done pretty well these last few years."

"By accident."

"By deductive reasoning."

"Finley, really. You expect me to sit in here knowing you're out there doing dangerous stuff that could very well get you killed?"

"Only if you can die from a paper cut. I'm focusing on what I can garner in cyberspace."

"What do you hope to find?"

"I don't know yet."

"No interviews? No breaking and entering?"

"I promise not to talk to any of your unit buddies unless I'm in a public place, no contact with any Latin Bandits, and no breaking and entering." *Well, technically it wasn't a lie.* I was going to see Cain's widow. She wasn't a member of his unit. "Oh, and don't say anything to Tony about this. Please?"

"I should call him right now."

I reached forward to maintain the contact with his hands. Contact strictly forbidden by jail policy. "You've helped me and my friends. Now it's time for me to help you."

"Well, I have a conceal-and-carry permit and fifteen years on the job. A little different from your background and training."

"Insult me all you want," I said as I stood. "I'm still going to do whatever it takes to get you out of here."

"Ashley said the same thing last night."

"Then maybe the two of us can join forces."

Liam sent me an icy glare. "Ashley is even less equipped than you are. I don't want anything to happen to her. She's already been through enough on my account."

"Like?"

"It's all in the past." He adjusted himself in the chair, the movement setting off a symphony of leg irons rattling.

"It doesn't seem that way to me." God, did I really say that out loud?

The irritation on his handsome face morphed into a lascivious smile. "Jealous, Finley?"

"Afraid."

He tilted his head slightly and a lock of his hair fell against his forehead. Forgetting the rules for the moment, I quickly pushed it back into place. Then I glanced behind me to make sure the deputy wasn't paying attention. He wasn't.

As I started to pull my hand away, Liam quickly grabbed it in his and leaned forward enough to kiss each of my knuckles in turn. Heat surged through me, washing over rationality like a tsunami. I slipped my hand out of his grasp. "I am afraid. I'm afraid you'll say something to Ashley that could incriminate you."

"Won't happen," he assured me as his eyes scanned my face like a lingering touch. "Ash would never do anything to hurt me. At least not anymore."

In for a penny, in for a pound. "Just what is your *thing* with Ashley?"

"It's evolving," he answered. Or rather nonanswered.

"I've got to go." Regret and frustration made up the majority of my tone.

Liam chuckled at my back. "I'll be here."

◆

True to her word, Ashley had arranged a meeting between me and Marjorie Cain for two that afternoon. It gave me plenty of time to finish my business in Indiantown. The western portions of Martin and Palm Beach counties might as well have been a mountain range apart. Except that Florida sat below sea level in most places. The only way out there were the two lanes that followed the spillway from Lake Okeechobee. Grand golf and tennis estate homes melded into manicured equestrian estates, and those melded into abject poverty. The population of Indiantown was heavily Hispanic, most of whom toiled tirelessly in the fields and groves that dominated the inland areas.

I took the road to Sleepy and Wanda Jean's, just beyond the strip of feed stores and the iconic Seminole Inn, where the Duke and Duchess of Windsor once partied with their gentile crowd. Fearing a food-borne illness, I stopped at a gas station and bought a Diet Coke. Normally I would have gone for coffee but the sun was barely up and already the temperature was hovering around eighty. The weather folks said the high temps had something to do with El Niño or La Niña. I didn't really care; I was just missing my winter when temps hovered around the seventy-two mark. I had a closet full of really cute sweaters longing to see the light of day.

I turned right at the sombrero-wearing yard ornament and was about fifty feet down the potholed dirt driveway when the assault of the Baskervilles began. No less than a half dozen dogs of questionable lineage barked and leapt as I slowly cruised toward the dilapidated trailer. I immediately spotted an older-model, cherry red Corvette parked in front. Had to be Mertzberger's.

I heard a sharp whistle and the hounds retreated. Sleepy was on the porch, wearing his signature wife-beater T-shirt and a pair of tattered jeans. Cautiously, I got out of my car and made my approach, holding tight to my briefcase just in case of a rabid attack.

Once inside, I greeted Wanda Jean, who then introduced Mertzberger. Not that he needed an intro. I'd seen his face and heard his ads for so long that I almost felt like I knew him. And not in a good way. He was a legal generalist who promised to charge no fees if he didn't win a case. I was slightly intrigued though; he was a slip and fall/auto accident guy. So what was he doing on an estate matter?

He reached his pudgy fingers out and shook my hand. I smiled in return and told him to call me Finley.

Mertzberger was about five-five, which explained the penis-envy Corvette. He was nearly as large around as he was tall. He wore an ill-fitting suit with a dress shirt that was too tight to button at the throat. And he was a sweater. His forehead was sweaty. His hands were sweaty, and no matter how many times he wiped the moisture away with his handkerchief, it just kept on coming.

Me? I was all good in my Boy. by Band of Outsiders rabbit-print sleeveless top and matching skirt. The tie neck and stand collar were nice accents to the otherwise simple outfit.

Wanda Jean had cleaned the coffee table. Mertzberger and I sat opposite each other, while Sleepy stayed in his Barca-lounger and Wanda Jean carried over one of the torn Nauga-hyde seats from the dinette. The place smelled of bacon and cat food.

"Thank you for meeting us out here to discuss terms," Mertzberger said as he carefully wiped the sweat around his face without disturbing the odd and unflattering comb-over. Hey, if you're going to be bald, I say go all the way.

"The terms are quite clear," I said as I pulled out the agreements for Sleepy and Wanda Jean to sign. I handed them to Mertzberger. "The estate is still willing to allow the Bollans the acreage and location as set forth in the—" I stopped and pulled out the plat. "In here," I said, pointing. "That's twice the amount of land they currently have and Ms. Egghardt is generously willing to deed the land to them for ninety-nine years or life, depending on circumstances."

"What's that mean in English?" Sleepy asked.

"It means that once you and Wanda Jean are gone, the property reverts back to Leona Egghardt.

"Or her heirs," I added.

"So we'd be renters?" Sleepy asked, his tone a bit louder and more irritated.

"In a sense," I said before ambulance-chasing Mertzberger could chime in. "For the yearly sum of one dollar, you get to stay here."

Wanda looked sad. "Just not *here,* here."

"Correct," Mertzberger answered as he took a stack of forms out of his tattered briefcase.

I could read the caption upside down. "Voluntary Relocation Agreement." "We have a counteroffer," he said, passing me the document.

It was only two pages but I had to give the guy props for trying. "I can run this by Ms. Lieberman," I said reluctantly as I scanned the paperwork. "But your demands are excessive and unrealistic."

"I'd rather hear that from Lieberman," Mertzberger stated.

"Let me make a phone call." Leaving my briefcase in the house I stepped out onto the porch with the document and my phone in hand. Before I could dial the number, a big dog that looked part German shepherd and part wolf came around the scuff-worn porch.

Reflexively I backed up. The dog kept coming. He growled, then suddenly was in front of me. Not, to my surprise, to pounce and kill, but he was a crotch sniffer. I wanted to smack him away but I was afraid of losing a hand. I did the next best thing. I turned my back on him and walked briskly to my car.

It was hot inside the car so I dialed quickly.

"Dane, Lieberman, and Caprelli."

"This is Finley, Margaret. I need to be put through to Ellen immediately."

"I'm afraid she's on another call. Would you like me to transfer you to her voice mail?"

"No. I want you to put me through. Now." Wolf dog was keeping watch over me with his beady little blue eyes.

"What do you need?" Ellen asked rather sharply when she came on the line.

"Sleepy and Wanda Jean will relocate on one condition."

Ellen cursed. "What's the condition?"

"They want Lenora Egghardt to buy them a new double-wide trailer."

"Oh for shit's sake! Don't they get that they aren't in a position to bargain?"

"Mertzberger has them thinking otherwise."

"Mertzberger is an ass."

"Well, right now he's the ass pulling the strings. Want me to walk away?"

Ellen went silent for a minute. "A double-wide costs less than it will to litigate this case. Get their signatures on an addendum to our contract and I'll work it out with Lenora. But put a cap on the cost." She then gave me a figure and we hung up.

Dodging the dog and the two new ones who'd joined him, I made my way back into the trailer. "The estate will provide a double-wide trailer," I explained. "You'll be capped at thirty thousand dollars and you have thirty days to be out. Okay?"

Mertzberger was grinning as if he'd just won the Casey Anthony trial. "Then sign right here, Miss Tanner. You can be a witness."

"No." I wrote the amended terms on the back sheet of our agreement and told Mertzberger where he and his clients could sign. I explained that I would take the papers back to the office so Lenora could countersign and that the documents would be overnighted to them.

"I'll miss this old place," Wanda Jean said wistfully. For a minute I thought she was going to sob.

I might even have joined in. No more trips to the land of dogs and dirt was almost enough to bring tears of joy to my eyes.

◆

She drove a pink Jeep. Ashley, not the widow. It was parked in front of the window of the Cains' residence. Didn't Beer Barbie know it was a cliché to tool around town in a Barbiemobile?

The sun was still bright and warm as I walked up the crushed-shell walkway and knocked on the front door of the small but well-kept stucco house. The door opened and I looked down into an inquisitive pair of big brown eyes.

"Ellie!" I heard a woman call. "You know only Mommy answers the door."

A pretty but harried-looking woman in her thirties came up behind the child and shuffled her out of the doorway. "You must be Finley," she said as she tucked a few strands of brown hair behind one ear. I noted she was still wearing her wedding rings.

She offered her hand. "Marjorie Cain. Most people call me Ree."

The door swung wide and I saw Ashley seated on a couch in the midst of a sea of toys. The house smelled fresh and fruity.

Someone was burning a Yankee candle. Cherry-mango chutney if I had to guess.

A second, younger child was playing on the floor, putting her doll in a small wagon, then taking it for rides. The older child sat warily watching Ashley and me as we settled in with some iced tea.

"Time to play outside before dinner," Ree announced, opening the back door to a nice-size fenced-in yard.

Both kids grabbed toys and happily went out the door. Ree sat down, or rather fell into the chair. "Sorry, but with a three-year-old and a four-year-old, I'm outnumbered."

"I can imagine," I said, having no real clue what it was like to chase preschoolers. I tended to avoid children. I didn't think they liked me very much. "I just have a few questions about your husband's accident," I began.

Her demeanor changed dramatically. The smile slipped and tears began to pool in her eyes. I felt like a dirt bag. "If it's too much, we can do this at a later time," I suggested.

She waved her hands, then dabbed tears from her eyes. "It's just so new, ya know?"

I nodded. "And I really hate to ask you to relive your pain."

"Are you opening an investigation into Stan's death?" she asked, her expression hopeful.

"I'm a paralegal with a law firm and we're looking into the death of José Lopez. Your husband's name came up."

"That mess Liam is in?" she asked.

Ashley nodded. "And we wouldn't be here, Ree, if Liam did it. We're trying to clear him."

Ree sat on the edge of her seat. "Even when I saw it on the

news I was stunned. Liam isn't the murdering type. Stan used to talk about him. Said he was a great cop who got royally shafted."

"What can you tell me about your husband's accident?" I asked.

She shrugged. "It's a crock. Stan was super careful when it came to guns. And by guns I mean firearms, not rifles. He owned one rifle, it belonged to his father. It's still locked in the gun case."

"But records show he bought a new one just before his trip."

She smoothed her hair as she let out a breath. "Like I told the investigator and the reporter, Stan did not buy that gun."

"But the receipt . . ." I let the comment linger in the air.

"Didn't have his signature, just his name. And I would have known if he'd bought a rifle."

"Because you were close?" I asked, wondering if you could ever really know another person.

"Hang on," she said as she disappeared down a hallway then returned a second later with a large file box. She placed it in the center of the coffee table. "These are all our financial records for the last five years. Pay stubs, bank statements, phone bills, electric bills, credit card receipts, cash withdrawals, everything. Stan and I weren't poor, but with two kids we lived on a tight budget. And I always took care of the finances. Stan didn't have four hundred and fifty dollars to spend on a rifle. The money just wasn't there."

I sucked in a deep breath and gingerly asked, "Any chance he was getting money on the side? Working a second job or something?"

Her eyes narrowed. "Don't you mean was he taking bribes? No. If he had been, then he wouldn't have left me with a twenty-five-thousand-dollar life insurance policy that doesn't pay out in cases of suicide. If it wasn't for the department's widows' and children's fund, I'd have lost my house."

"I didn't mean to disparage your husband's memory," I promised her. "Was your husband friendly with José Lopez or any of the other men from the gang unit?"

"He transferred to major case after the shooting. He was something of a pariah after the grand jury." She blew out a breath. "Cops. They like to stick together. But the day before he left, José called here looking for him. I gave him Stan's cell number, but I don't know if they ever connected."

"Is it possible that—" My cell phone rang and I excused myself to take the call. It was from my security company. I gave them the code word and then a voice on the other end said something about an attempted break-in.

"I'm sorry," I said. "Something's come up. You've been most helpful, Ree. If we find anything important, we'll be sure to share it with you."

I think I said good-bye to Ashley but I wasn't sure and didn't care. The whole idea that someone would try to break in to my house gave me the jitters. What if it was the same person who'd sent me the threatening e-mail?

I made it back to my place and surveyed the damage. Someone had thrown a brick through my back door, smashing my sliders into tiny shards. "What happened?" I asked the deputy in charge.

"Kids, probably. Two other houses in this neighborhood had smash and grabs this week."

"What should I do?"

"Check to see if anything is missing."

My laptop was with the IT guys. My television was still on the wall with no signs of pry marks near the brackets. My jewelry was all accounted for. Nothing was taken.

The deputy spoke over the crackle of the radio clipped to his shoulder. "Do you know anyone who can fix that back door for you?"

I nodded. Harold the ex-con would help me in an instant.

"What was the response time?" I asked.

"We were on scene six minutes after we got the call from your alarm company."

"So it was definitely a smash and run?" I said, relieved.

"Looks that way." He reached into his pocket and handed me his card. "If you do find anything missing, give us a call."

"Was anything taken in the other break-ins?"

"Nope. This is why we think it's just bored kids. In five minutes a pro can clean out a house. Take all the stuff that's worth a quick buck to a pawnshop or a fence. So far these punks haven't graduated to that yet."

"Let's hope they don't."

Great, so now I have Ashley as my wingman; Liam is in jail; I get a creepy e-mail; and now my house gets broken into? Immediately my mind started to travel down a suspicious path.

*In order to get a loan, you must first prove
that you don't need it.*

eleven

I started my day with coffee and dead people. I sat in my darkened kitchen poring over the autopsy reports. Harold had come
in the middle of the night and put plywood over the broken
sliders, so I was cheated out of what was probably a beautiful
sunrise. He'd promised to reinstall new sliders today and I knew
his word was good in spite of the vulgar prison tats that decorated his hands, arms, and chest.

I began with Stan Cain. Unlike as seen on TV, autopsy reports are complicated, with lots of unfamiliar medical terms.
About the only things I understood were the *Xs* placed on the
body-outline diagrams. After reading Stan's twice, I finally gave
up and decided I needed to do the reading back at my office
where I had access to a medical dictionary.

It was still warmer than usual, so I looked longingly at my
sweater collection before choosing a sleeveless Vince Camuto
colorblock dress. It was black, white, and poppy, and fell just

above my knee. I added a simple pair of black patent Franco Sarto sandals with a stacked heel and a slight platform.

Once I got to the office, I grabbed the medical dictionary from the library and barricaded myself in my office. Before I could get started, Margaret buzzed my line.

"Yes?"

"You have a collect call from an inmate at the Palm Beach County jail. If you accept the charges, you'll have to reimburse the firm."

"Not if it's a client," I informed her. *Bitch.* "Accept the charges and put it through."

My line buzzed again and I picked it up. "Liam?"

"Know any other inmates?" he asked, his tone jovial.

How could he sound so cheery when his arraignment was just hours away? "Just one. But he's in juvie. What do you need? Oh, clothes for the arraignment?"

"Nope, I'll be the guy in the navy jumpsuit with PBJ stamped on the back. If I need clothes, Ashley can get them. She has a key to my place."

A key *and* a drawer? "Okay, so we're back to what you need."

"I just wanted to hear your voice."

Talk about mixed signals. Ashley has unfettered access to his life but it's my voice he wants to hear? Has he been playing me all this time? Could it be that Liam McGarrity is one of those guys who likes the chase but once the prey is in his sights he loses interest? Could I stop obsessing?

"You'll hear my voice at the arraignment."

"Yes," he agreed, his tone dropping lower and sexier if I did say so myself. "What happened last night?"

"What makes you think anything happened?"

"Heard there was a *thing* at your place."

How did he find this stuff out from behind bars? "It was nothing. Just some kids in my neighborhood entertaining themselves by breaking glass."

"Are you sure that's all it was?"

I twirled a lock of my hair. "There have been other similar glass-smashing incidents, so yes, I'm certain it was just an unfortunate and expensive bit of bad luck."

"I thought we had an agreement."

"We did?"

"Yeah. I wouldn't rat you out to Tony if you limited your investigating to computer searches."

"I have." *Mostly.*

"Then what do you call your little visit to Ree Cain's house last night? A recipe swap?" His tone was a tad sarcastic.

"How did you . . . Ashley?"

"I called her last night."

You didn't call me. "I wasn't doing anything dangerous. I just wanted to hear about her husband's accident."

"So what did you find out?"

"What? Ashley didn't give you all the juicy details?" I couldn't keep the derision out of the question.

"No. It wasn't that kind of phone call."

Now I was curious. And pathetic. "Don't they monitor your calls?"

"Not when I'm calling my attorney."

"I'm not an attorney."

"Paralegals count, too."

"I found out that Stan owned a perfectly good hunting rifle, but he left that behind when he went hunting. There is a receipt with his name on it for the purchase of a new rifle but Ree says they had no money in their accounts and no record of Stan spending that much cash. Swears it isn't possible."

The line was silent for a few seconds. "I gotta get out of here. And you've got to stop playing detective."

"First off, I am not playing. Second, it is part of my job to do pertinent research on cases." *And third, I want you out of jail, too.*

"One word to Tony and I bet he'll tie you to your desk."

"Promise me you won't," I pleaded. "I'm not going to do anything stupid. Consider it legwork for you once you get out of jail."

"Assuming I get out. Garza is a good guy, but judges often remand on murder charges."

My heart ached. I knew it could take a year or more for a criminal case to wind its way through the legal system. I couldn't imagine a whole year without Liam.

"Think positively," I insisted. "Tony is a great lawyer, and all the police have is circumstantial evidence and a theory."

"And people get life on circumstantial evidence."

"We'll be at the courthouse at twelve thirty. And promise me you won't tell Tony. I'm only trying to help. Can't you accept that?"

"I appreciate it, Finley. I just don't want you to get yourself in too deep. Not until we know what or who is behind this."

"Promise me, please?"

"Okay. For now."

"Thanks. I'll see you soon."

"Finley?"

"Yes?"

"Thanks."

I went back to the autopsy face sheet on Stan Cain. It was like a table of contents—historical summary; examination type; date, place, assistants, and attendees. All that told me was the name of the examiner and the people present at the autopsy. Then it moved on to the presentation of clothing and personal effects—Stan had only his ID and fifty-two dollars in his pockets. Under evidence of medical intervention, all that was listed was NONE since he was a DOA. Then as I continued into the document, I learned what postmortem changes had taken place—lividity in the back and lower extremities, meaning Stan had fallen backward from the shot. Imaging studies showed the gunshot went up through his chin and exited through the top of his head. There was some yucky stuff about brain matter that I skimmed. They noted the evidence of injury, internal and external exams, then moved on to toxicology samples—negative for any kind of medication, legal or illegal. Then I finally reached the summary, comments, and cause of death statement. Bottom line, the medical examiner determined that Stan's weapon had fired from below, consistent with the gun being lifted into position and discharged but also consistent with suicide. The medical examiner did not rule out suicide because of the stippling at the entrance wound. The presence of gunpowder meant the barrel was almost directly under his chin when the weapon discharged. No wonder Ree was so upset. Without a clear showing of an accident, she couldn't collect on his life insurance. How would she care for her family if that happened? That was a lot of worry resting on her shoulders.

Tony came to my door and knocked once on the jamb. He had on a gray suit that did wonders for him. He looked lean and fit and very handsome. No wonder he had such luck with jurors. But today wouldn't be about jurors. It would be only the judge, the ASA, Liam, Tony, and me. "Did you get the report?"

"Reading it now," I answered, hoping he wouldn't want it right then since I hadn't finished.

"How are your photography skills?" he asked.

"I'm not Ansel Adams but I can point and shoot. Why?"

"The cops have released José's house. I got an order this morning allowing us to go in. I want every inch of the place photographed before the arraignment." He stepped forward and handed me a slip of paper with an address on it. "Don't forget the backyard. I want to be able to see the path Liam took when he fled the scene."

I nodded. "Anything else?"

"Yeah. Here's the key to get in." He turned to leave, then turned back. "Nice job on the Travis Johnson abstracts. You'll be meeting him next week."

"Okay."

"See you at the courthouse."

I spent the next forty minutes trying to decipher the Lopez autopsy. It wasn't as complete as Stan's because it was a preliminary report. The toxicology wasn't back yet and some of the trace evidence was still being examined. All I really learned was that he was shot just below the right ear and the bullet went through his brain and exited through his jaw. My stomach was doing flip-flops. I envisioned the scenario in my head, with a downward wound pattern, and realized that one of two things was possible. Either José was seated when the bullet hit or he was shot by a much taller person. Then he either fell into the chair or was put there by someone.

Like Stan, there was stippling around the wound, meaning it was a close-contact injury. I flipped back a couple of pages and looked up José's height. He was five-eleven. If he died standing up, Liam could have made the shot. Not a bonus for our side.

I gave the autopsy reports to one of the interns to take up to Tony's office on my way out. After stopping at the store to buy disposable cameras, I went to the former crime scene. José's house was on a cul-de-sac. The fenced yard abutted a house one street over. It was a modest blue home with white trim and lots of hedges in dire need of trimming. I started my photo shoot on the outside, clicking away at every possible angle.

With more than a touch of trepidation, I went to the front door. A piece of yellow crime scene tape fluttered in the breeze where it was still taped to one side of the door. I let myself in and again snapped photo upon photo. The kitchen was a tad untidy but nothing major. Well, nothing except for the finger-print residue on every surface. The kitchen had two entrances, so I went past the range and entered the living room. There were two sofas, a recliner, an entertainment center with a television and a stereo, as well as a coffee table and matching end tables. The living room led out to a small cement patio and the fence, which was overgrown with wisteria vines. There was a grill and a plastic patio set that was dirty but undisturbed. I concentrated on the living room, my stomach lurching when I photographed the recliner with the dark brown bloodstain that had dripped along the chair, then pooled on the floor. There were flecks of what looked like sweetbreads. Just seeing them pushed bile into my throat. Moving closer, I captured the disgusting scene from several perspectives. I was about to go in search of bedrooms and bathrooms when something caught my eye.

The sunlight was shining through the glass doors and there was a reflection on the top of the coffee table. Two circles. Outlines really. I captured those on film as well. Maybe the killer had a beer with José before blowing his brains out. Not likely. And I had no way of knowing when those marks were left on the table.

The bedrooms and bathroom were devoid of any new clues. The windows were locked and I didn't see any disturbances in the fingerprint dust, indicating that nobody had found a lift on the sill. Trying to be thorough, I took pictures from the bedroom hallway, giving me long shots into the living room. Then I heard a noise and, startled, I hit the small table and sent a lamp crashing to the ground. As I started to collect the pieces, I was already dreading having to tell Tony that I'd broken something during my assignment. Then I saw it, right in the middle of all the ceramic shards. A small black button-size object with a tiny wire sticking out of one side. I placed it in my palm and stared at it. A fuse maybe? A timer for the light? I didn't know, but I decided to take it with me. I could always return it.

I'd managed to go through four cameras before I ran to Walgreens to have the films developed at their kiosk. There was a clerk stationed at the kiosk just in case anyone ran into trouble. I guessed he was late teens, early twenties. I knew he was staring at me. Or at least at my legs. I'd have smiled back if I thought it would get me a discount, but then I remembered Dane-Lieberman would reimburse me so I just ignored his misplaced adoration. Unlike Liv, I wasn't interested in having a plaything.

I arrived at the courthouse with fifteen minutes to spare. So had Tony, and we slipped into one of the counsel conference rooms and he looked at my photos. "Look at this," I said as he got to the ones with the coffee table circles. "What does that look like to you?"

"Condensation circles. Lopez had a visitor that night?" he wondered aloud.

"Or he had one a month ago and wasn't big on dusting and polishing."

Tony smiled. "I like my theory better."

"Me, too. Oh, and look at this one," I said, moving the photos around on the table until I found the one I wanted. "The wisteria shows signs of disturbance and I think that's a smear of dried blood on those flowers. Doesn't that prove Liam's story?"

"It goes a long way, except that the state's attorney can claim that Liam jumped the fence after he shot Lopez."

"What about this?" I said, taking the button with the wire out of my purse and handing it to him.

"Where did you get this?" he asked.

"I accidentally broke a lamp, which I will pay for, and it just came out. Do you know what it is?"

He nodded. "It's a listening device."

"José's house was bugged?"

"Looks like it."

My heart pounded with excitement. "Can we find out who was doing the bugging?"

"Maybe. These things have serial numbers. Maybe we can trace it."

Tony and I gathered everything together and packed up our respective briefcases. "Let's go down to lockup and see Liam before the arraignment."

Lockup smelled like sweat and desperation. It was a series of small rooms along a short corridor. There were at least a half dozen guards and an elaborate electronic board that controlled all access to those waiting in the small glass cells. Tony and I were buzzed into Liam's room, but not before I'd gotten a few catcalls.

"Sorry about that," Tony said. "I should have warned you."

"Not a problem." I said, then focused my full attention on Liam. His hair was damp and he was clean-shaven. The blue jumpsuit was hideous, yet it managed to show off his well-toned body. Leave it to me to be lusting after a guy in prison blues.

In spite of Liam's protests, Tony insisted on going over exactly what would happen at the arraignment. Then he produced the minute listening device and asked, "Recognize this?"

"It's a plant," he said. "You can get them at any spy shop in the country. Probably online, too."

"Well, this one came out of Lopez's house. Finley found it."

Liam looked up at me and smiled. "Finley went on a field trip?"

I braced myself. If he told Tony I was directly violating his instructions I'd be in deep shit.

"I asked her to photograph the scene for me."

Liam nodded. "Find anything interesting besides the bug?"

Tony had me take out the photos for Liam to examine. "Does this look like the house when you last saw it?" Tony asked.

"It was dark, but I'm pretty sure there were two cans of beer on the coffee table."

"The cops must have taken them for evidence," Tony said. "If they did, I'll ask to have access to them so we can do our own testing. At least we can infer that Lopez wasn't alone that night."

"Unless both cans were his. Lopez could down a six-pack, no problem."

There was a buzzing sound and then Liam's door slid open. The bailiff said, "They're about to call your case."

Liam stood, the action rattling the chains around his waist, hands, and ankles. Tony and I left first but I could hear the shuffle of Liam following behind us. It was enough to make my heart ache. I wanted this nightmare over. Maybe we'd get lucky and the judge would dismiss the charges.

And maybe it would snow in Miami.

I saw Jane, Liv, and Becky seated in the gallery. I mouthed "Thank you" to them. Ashley was ever present as usual. On the opposite side of the aisle, the place was packed with uniformed deputies showing their solidarity with the slain officer. I hoped that wouldn't have an effect on the judge. Assistant State's Attorney Garza was standing at his table. Tony and I were across from him facing the elevated bench. Once Liam was brought in, a guard stood behind him as if he'd make a mad dash for it. He was no longer in chains and restraints.

He sat between me and Tony and absently I reached over

and gave his hand a squeeze just as the bailiff told us to stand. The judge, whose nameplate identified him as the Honorable Sean Hastings, was a distinguished-looking man with salt-and-pepper hair and the symbolic black robe. Court was called to order, then Garza spoke.

"We're here in the matter of the State of Florida versus Liam Rory McGarrity. The charge is murder."

"Can I get a plea?" the judge asked.

"Your Honor," Tony began as he rose. "The defense respectfully requests that you drop these charges for lack of evidence."

The guy in the robe didn't even look up.

"I'm reading the charging documents, Mr. Caprelli, and everything seems in order. You'll have to take up the matter of suffiency with the trial judge. Now can I get a plea?"

"Not guilty," Tony said forcefully.

"Bail?" the judge asked.

Garza stood again. "The state requests remand. The facts in this case indicate that Mr. McGarrity committed a heinous act and then hid from the police."

Tony stayed on his feet. "The state is neglecting to tell the court that Mr. McGarrity willingly and of his own accord made himself available to the police and cooperated at all times during the interviews."

"Is that true, Mr. Garza?"

"Yes, Your Honor, but—"

"Then it appears the defendant was not hiding. Does he have ties to the community?"

"He's a lifelong resident of the county," Tony began. "He owns a home here and a business. He poses no risk of flight and looks forward to the opportunity to defend himself against these false charges."

The judge reached for his gavel. "Bail is set at one hundred fifty thousand. Cash or bond."

I was relieved and terrified at the same time. Did Liam have that kind of money?"

Tony said, "Can you get that much?"

Liam shook his head. "My house is mortgaged and I've got about fifteen grand in the bank."

Before I knew what I was doing I said, "I've got it. I can put my house up as collateral." I only hoped Jane didn't hear that pledge.

"You don't have to do that," Liam said.

"It's not a problem."

"Thanks," he said as the guard took him by the arm and started leading him to the exit that would take him back to the holding area.

"Finley," Tony warned. "We represent clients. We do not bail them out of jail."

"I'm not going to leave him here. Not when I know he didn't do it."

Tony shrugged just as ASA Garza made his way over to us. He had a folder in one hand that he passed to Tony. "Look, I like your client, but things are not looking good. Call me if you want to discuss a plea."

As he walked away, Tony opened the folder and held it so we could read it simultaneously. It was Lopez's toxicology report. A large amount of ketamine was found in his system and a puncture wound was noted as well. "What's ketamine?" I asked Tony.

"It's potent stuff. Called Special K on the streets. It's an animal tranquilizer but can be used on humans."

"So Lopez was drugged?"

Tony turned to the second page. "Yep. And according to this, the police have a confidential informant who says he sold ketamine to Liam the day before the shooting."

Happiness covers all things except poverty
and a bad haircut.

twelve

Deed in hand, I went to the nearest bail bondsman. It was a small, single-story building with glass partitions separating those who were arranging bail from those who were collecting the cash or collateral.

To say I was out of my element was an understatement. Very few people had all their teeth and at least three of the patrons looked as if they'd been in the same clothes for a week or more. Like some sort of deli counter, I pulled a ticket out of a machine and waited for my number to be called. Each minute felt like an hour and I was still ten people away from being picked.

I got a call from the IT guys at Dane-Lieberman and stepped out to take the call.

"Did you find the IP address?" I asked, hopeful that it would result in some sort of clue that would take us to a new place in the investigation.

"Yeah, but it isn't good news. Know that coffee shop on Australian, Wired?"

"Yes."

"The e-mail originated from one of their computers."

Shit. Shit. And double shit.

He promised to leave my laptop in my office, then I went back inside to discover my number was next in the rotation. Even though I knew Liam was not capable of shooting anyone for no good reason, I still felt panicked at the thought of gambling with my much-coveted house.

If I thought getting to my number was a triumph, I was sadly mistaken. I was handed a hefty stack of forms, told to go over to the chipped Formica counter on the adjacent wall and fill them out. Once that was done, I was to take the paperwork and my deed to window number 7.

The questionnaire was lengthy and covered everything from my date of birth to my relationship—if any—to the inmate. The options were in black and white. You were either a family member or a friend. No box to check if you were just in lust with the person you were bonding out.

Number 7 was a bleached blonde with some miles on her. She was as wrinkled as a slept-in linen skirt and never smiled or sent out any sort of positive vibe. What did I expect? "Welcome to Fred's Bonds, have a great day?" Instead she moistened her fingers, flipped through the pages, and stamped each one. She disappeared behind a door for a moment, then slipped some pages into the well between the glass and me.

On to step two. I went back to the courthouse and presented the bond to the clerk. He made a production out of making sure every *i* was dotted and every *t* was crossed. Then he told me I would have to wait an hour before the inmate would be released.

I wasn't going to sit around. I grabbed a chicken salad sandwich to go from the courthouse cafeteria and walked the two blocks back to my office. All the while my brain was spinning. I dropped my things off, reclaimed my laptop and secured it in my briefcase, then buzzed Becky.

"Are you free to come down here for a few minutes?"

"Is Liam with you?"

I explained the painfully slow turning of the wheels of justice. "I just need a sounding board."

"I'm due for a break," Becky said. "I'll be right there."

True to her word, within five minutes Becky was seated across from my desk. "You gonna finish that?" she asked as she spied the half sandwich on my desk.

"Go for it."

"So what's up?"

"First, thanks for coming to the arraignment."

She shrugged. "Liam was there for me when I needed help. Thought it was only right that I return the favor."

"I've been thinking."

Becky grinned. "With what part of your anatomy?"

"I'm serious. Liam was a cop for almost fifteen years. He had to have made enemies. Maybe one of those enemies lured Liam to José's house that night with the intention of killing them both?"

"Because?" she asked with her mouth full of half-masticated food.

"Because bad people do bad things."

"So why now?" she countered. "Liam's been off the force for five years. Long time to hold a grudge."

"Unless the person with the grudge has been incarcerated all this time."

"Possible," Becky acknowledged.

"How can I find out what cases Liam worked without going to the police?"

"Hit the criminal database and do a search for Liam's name. That will tell you every case he testified in or was the arresting officer on."

"It's that easy?"

Becky shook her head. "No. Then you'd have to get the transcripts and read what happened. If any threats were made. Why don't you just ask Liam?"

"I sorta want to do this on my own."

Becky's eyebrows arched. "Why, for God's sake?"

"I just want to show him that I am fully capable of figuring this out."

"You want him indebted to you?"

I took in a deep breath. "I don't know what I want. I just know that helping him is something I need to do."

"And how does Tony feel about you playing sleuth?"

"Hopefully he'll never know until I uncover something important."

"Or you'll get yourself killed trying. At least two people are dead already. Someone sent you a creepy e-mail and your window was smashed," Becky argued as she balled up the deli paper and tossed it in the trash.

"The window thing was a fluke. The cops told me so."

"Fin," Becky began earnestly. "You're great at tracking down heirs, but tracking down a killer is a whole different ball game."

"If I get in over my head, I promise I'll back off. Just don't say anything to Liam or Tony."

"I can't make that promise."

"You're my friend."

Becky nodded. "A friend who doesn't want to attend your funeral."

♦

I was battling a bit of a time crunch. I drove over to the courthouse, then started walking toward the door where inmates were released. I was not alone. There, standing in the shadows of the sun, was Ashley. She was all dolled up for the occasion—white skinny jeans and a top with a deep V that showed more cleavage than I even had.

She greeted me with a smile and then gave me an awkward hug. "Thanks so much for arranging Liam's bail. My salon is doing okay but I sure don't have a hundred and fifty grand in equity."

I shifted from foot to foot as I nervously waited for Liam to come through the fence with sharp razor wire looped on top. The temperatures were beginning to fall and I was sorry I'd left my sweater in the car.

"It's really good that Liam has a friend like you," Ashley said to break the silence. "Not everyone would do what you did for him today."

"It's not a big deal," I lied. I was already ducking calls from Jane. As my financial planner, she hated when I planned something without her.

A sirenlike noise sounded and Liam came out of the building flanked by a single guard. He smiled at me. He also smiled at Ashley.

It was Ashley who ran forward and jumped into his arms. Then she gave him a kiss. I wanted to go running and screaming out of there but I couldn't think of a way to extricate myself without being totally transparent.

When Liam reached me, Ashley still had her arm looped through his. "Ash, you want to give us a minute?"

"We don't need a minute," I said, trying my best to be all easy and breezy.

Liam gave me that sexy half smile and I was pretty sure he knew that I was not comfortable watching him lock lips with another woman.

"A minute," Ashley replied in an almost singsong way. "I went shopping and got all the stuff to make your favorite meal. Thai chicken with pasta." She walked toward the half-full parking lot.

"Come here," he said softly.

I stood my ground. A girl can take only so much humiliation in one sitting. "I just wanted to make sure you got out okay. No snafus with the bond."

"Then I'll come to you," he said, stepping forward so that mere inches separated us. He smelled of soap and I could almost feel the heat of his body.

As he slipped his arm around my waist, I turned my head to see if Ashley was bearing witness. She wasn't. She'd already turned the corner of the building.

"I need to thank you properly." His head lowered and hovered over my mouth.

My tongue slipped out to moisten my suddenly dry lips. That's when he made his move. And what a move it was. He pressed his mouth to mine and then gingerly took my lower lip between his and teased it with his tongue. My insides were melting along with my ability to reason. His hand moved up and laced through my hair, tilting my head ever so slightly before he slipped his tongue into my mouth. This time there was nothing gentle or tentative about it.

His other hand came to rest at my waist, but only for a second. Soon it was traveling up my rib cage until his fingers just grazed the side of my breast. A moan escaped from my lips and I carefully pressed closer to him, mindful of the stitches in his side.

His mouth broke from mine and he trailed tiny kisses down my jaw and then to my neck. He tugged at the top of my dress, giving himself access to the tender spot near my collarbone. My knees were mush. I was mush. I was also an idiot. I was reveling in sensations from a man who'd just kissed another woman.

That realization was like a bucket of ice water dousing my inflamed passions. With a jerk, I stepped out of his hold. "Ashley is waiting for you."

His eyes were hooded and he seemed to be mocking me. "She'll wait."

"Well, I can't. I have a *thing*."

His dark eyebrows pinched together. "What kind of thing?"

"Dinner with a friend," I told him, careful to keep my tone even. "You'd better get going. Don't want to keep that Thai chicken waiting."

He laughed softly. "You're going to run out of reasons to put me off one of these days."

Probably true, but I'd gnaw off my own tongue before I admitted that to him.

I tortured myself by adjusting my mirror and watching Ashley and Liam ride off, literally, into the sunset. Before putting my car in drive, I called Izzy to tell her I was on my way.

Her enthusiasm was catchy. After a few minutes of her being in my car, I found myself enjoying the trials and tribulations of a fourteen-year-old.

"If he's such a great guy, why aren't you letting your father in on it?"

Izzy frowned as she captured her long brown hair and twisted it up on her head. "Dad doesn't think I should date until I'm sixteen. That's so medieval. Cole is my age. It isn't like I'd be in a car with a boy. Dad's fears are like totally irrational."

"Maybe his fears are because he was once a fourteen-year-old boy," I suggested.

"That's a gross thought." She adjusted the seat belt so she could sit sideways in the seat. "Unless you're you? I mean, it would be okay if he had those thoughts about you."

I patted her leg. "Not gonna happen, kiddo. I work for your father."

"You could quit."

"Not according to my VISA bill."

We pulled into the Gardens Mall and I purposefully parked outside the Macy's entrance. I thought it was prudent to keep Izzy away from the outlandishly expensive shoes at Betsey Johnson. We started at Macy's, then moved on to Aldo and then Nordstrom. Luckily for me Izzy fell in love with a pair of cute sale pumps with a tiny bow accent that would complement the black lace dress she'd chosen for the fall formal. With the hard work done, we opted to hit Brio for dinner.

The restaurant's entrance was outside the mall. It was reminiscent of an Italian bistro and the food was excellent. The waitstaff was top-notch and the tables were perfectly dressed in white linens. Since I'd only had a half sandwich, I felt like splurging, so I went for the cheesy-goodness lasagna and a glass of red wine.

Izzy ordered a personal pizza. "So here's the plan for next Saturday.

"You come over to do my hair and makeup, then I'll tell my dad I want you to drive me to the dance because you have a cool car."

"Your father has two cool cars."

She frowned. "But he'll go for it. Then all you have to do is drop me off at Cole's house and I'll get a ride home with him and Dad will never know."

I sipped my wine. "Have you thought about what will happen if he finds out you broke his trust?" Something I was busy doing at the moment.

"If I tell him the truth, he won't let me go. I just know it."

"What if we tell him together?"

"Like a tag team?" Izzy asked.

"Look." I leaned closer so she could hear me over the din in the restaurant. "Your father isn't unreasonable, he's just concerned about you."

"Too concerned. I just want to go to a dance with a boy."

"Then let's make it happen," I said.

We practiced our pitch all the way back to Martin County. I could tell Izzy had gotten comfortable with the idea, so I had my fingers crossed.

Tony greeted us at the door. He'd shed his suit for more casual attire. I might be lusting after Liam, but I did have a pulse. He looked fabulous in slacks and a polo shirt. Very polished but in a relaxed way. Izzy handed him a box of her leftover pizza and said, "I bet you haven't eaten yet."

He patted her head, "You guessed right." Then he turned to me as I lingered in the U-shaped drive in front of his salmon-colored five-thousand-square-foot-plus estate home. "Thank you for bringing her home."

"Finley and I have to talk to you," Izzy said, waving me forward.

I followed father and daughter inside. Like his office, Tony's home was all decked out in midcentury modern. He had a lot of chrome and glass and molded plastic in bright colors. I recognized several Herman Miller pieces, only because Liv had taken me to an expo at an art gallery in Boca Raton.

I put my purse down on the floor, then sat in the surprisingly comfy lime green and chrome sofa. Tony sat opposite me in a chair that looked like it belonged on the starship *Enterprise,* while Izzy paced back and forth.

"What's up?" Tony asked.

"It's about the dance," Izzy began. "I, um, I . . . Finley, you start."

I clasped my hands and placed them in my lap as I met Tony's inquisitive stare. "Izzy has an invitation to the dance."

Tony's expression instantly changed and he turned on his daughter. "We've been over this. You're too young to date."

"Which is why," I interrupted. "She's come up with a compromise."

"I did?" She looked at me, then with self-assurance said, "I did."

"Instead of a date, Izzy is going to ride to and from the dance with parents as chaperones. The boy who asked her is only fourteen, so you don't need to worry."

"Who is this boy?" Tony asked, his tone flat.

"His name is Cole Gentry. He's in my bio class and all we want to do is hang out."

"See?" I said. "It's really not a big deal. All we're talking about is them riding to and from together. Other than that, they'll be chaperoned at school, just as they would be if they arrived separately."

"Please, Daddy?" Izzy went over and stood in front of him. "It's just hanging out. No sex or anything."

I cringed.

"Well, that's a rousing endorsement," Tony said. "You're too young to date."

"Which is why I'm just asking to take a baby step. Ya know, kinda ease you into it."

Tony rubbed his face. "I want to meet his parents before Saturday."

"Done," Izzy practically squealed.

"And don't think I won't be dusting you for fingerprints when you get home."

Izzy grabbed him around the neck and gave him a big squeeze. "You're the best dad ever."

I stood, figuring my job was done. "Not so fast," Tony said. "Izzy, take your shoes upstairs and play with them or something."

She took her bag, but stopped long enough to give me a hug. "You rock," she whispered.

As soon as she was out of earshot, Tony said, "Are you going to come clean now?"

"About what?"

He leaned forward, bracketing his hands on his knees. "Are you going to sit there and tell me you haven't been working on Liam's case?"

"Sounds like a plan," I joked, hoping to keep things on the light side.

"You really have a problem with authority, don't you?"

I shrugged. "I prefer to think of it as taking initiative."

"Murder cases aren't a game, Finley."

"No, they're a puzzle. I'm good at puzzles."

"You're also good at getting yourself in over your head."

I thought for a minute, then came clean. I told him everything I'd done as well as my theories on the case. "I haven't gone near any bad guys."

"Keep it that way," he said firmly. "But keep digging. Just don't let it consume you. Victor and Ellen won't like it if you shirk your other responsibilities."

"I won't." At least not any more than I normally shirk my responsibilities.

"I wanted to hire an investigator for this case."

"Who?"

"Liam shot me down. He's hell bent on doing this himself. The two of you are a lot alike. Work with him, but keep your distance at the first sign of trouble."

"I've already gotten the first sign of trouble," I said, explaining the threatening and untraceable e-mail.

He rubbed his hands together. "Then maybe you should hang back on this one."

"I can't," I confessed. "Please don't ask me to."

"For now, you stay behind the scenes. Let Liam do his thing."

I felt a little better as I drove home. At least I wasn't going behind Tony's back, but I still felt like he and Liam were tying my hands. As I pulled into my driveway, the floodlights didn't come on. Maybe the motion sensors were burned out or something. But in the illumination of my headlights, I saw Liam before I saw his Mustang parked at the far end of the drive.

He was sitting on the step, holding a longneck bottle of beer. He stood as I got out of my car. "How was your dinner date?" he asked.

"Great. Good company. Wonderful food."

"Really?" he asked. "What'd you talk about?"

"The pitfalls of dating. Current events. That sort of thing." It was true. Izzy caught me up on all her school gossip and we did discuss her dating dilemma.

"Doesn't sound very romantic."

"Well, it wasn't Thai chicken," I returned with a touch of attitude.

"I happen to love Thai chicken and Ashley makes a great Thai chicken."

"Good for you and Ashley."

"Of course," he began as I came within arm's reach. "I also like Italian."

"Good for you."

"No, good for you. I'm sure you and Izzy had a great evening."

How did he know these things?

I was pondering that question when he took me in his arms.

When one door closes, you usually
get your fingers stuck in it.

thirteen

"Ready to get to work?" he asked against my ear.

I had to defuse the situation, so I snaked my hand between us and checked my watch. "It's nearly ten. I'm off the clock."

"Tony told me about your theories."

I stepped around him and placed my key in the lock. "Well, if you're here to mock me, good night."

He stood pressed against me. I could feel the outline of his body and my mind was starting to turn into lust mush. He was so close. All I had to do was turn around and do the only thing I really wanted to do. Kiss him. With tongue. Followed by a quick call to the paramedics after we ripped open his wounds.

I practically raced into the house, chased by Liam's soft laughter. By habit, I turned on the coffeepot after I put my purse and my briefcase on the sofa. Liam was still standing in the doorway.

"Are you coming or going?" I asked.

"I'd like to go over a few things with you, if that's okay?"

"Sure. Like what?"

"Lemme get some stuff out of my car." He started to walk away, then reached in his pocket and pulled out a receipt and three twenty-dollar bills. "Ashley and I returned the rental at the kiosk. Here's the receipt and the money to cover it."

I would have told him to forget it, but since Ashley was his accomplice, I gladly accepted the cash. He returned a few seconds later with his arms loaded down by four big file boxes. Immediately I took the top one, stunned by how heavy it was. "You have stitches, you shouldn't be carrying stuff this heavy. Let's put them down here," I instructed as I placed them parallel to the coffee table.

"What is all this?"

"My case files from the gang unit. I always made a habit of making copies for myself."

"Maybe the real killer's identity is in one of those boxes," I said with renewed excitement. "Give me a second to change and we can start going through them."

"Want some help?" he asked softly.

"Nope. Been dressing myself since I was three."

What was the appropriate attire for hunting suspects? I needed casual. Nothing said casual louder than a pair of yoga pants and lord knew I didn't wear them for yoga. I opted for a simple white, short-sleeved blouse and left my feet bare.

When I returned, Liam looked up and gave me a once-over that felt a lot like being caressed. I was tingling from head to toe and wondering how I was going to keep my mind on the task at hand rather than the promise of great sex.

"There's another possible explanation for Stan and José dying seven days apart."

"Which is?" I asked.

"Someone is after the whole unit. Maybe all of us are targets."

The thought sent a chill through me. "The Latin Bandits?"

"We confiscated more than two million in drugs, cash, and weapons at that raid. That's a lot of reasons to want us all dead. I just can't figure out why now. Why wait five years for retribution?"

I took my laptop out of my briefcase and fired it up. "Do you have the names of the defendants?"

Liam listed names while I checked their status in the criminal justice system. One had been shanked the first week of his incarceration. Died in the infirmary. Two others were on work release, and the fourth, the ringleader, was still locked up.

"So we concentrate on the ones out on work release?" I asked.

"Maybe. But we can't take Jimmy Santos out of the running. It's pretty easy to order a hit from prison if you know what you're doing. He was the jefe and he got the most severe sentence."

"Should we alert the rest of your unit?"

"We shouldn't. You should. Can you do it on Dane-Leiberman stationery?"

I thought about it for a minute. "Why not? Tony won't mind." *I hope.* "I'll just tell him I thought he might call them as witnesses if it turns out the Latin Bandits are behind the killings. That I've served Liam up some reasonable doubt."

"I still think you're way off base about it being one of my

guys," Liam said with a certain sadness in his tone. "I never saw anything out of the ordinary. And besides, they all would have been conspirators, plus the gun cage guy, plus the property clerk. I just wasn't important enough for that to be an issue."

"Nothing about that night sticks out?"

He raked his hands through his hair. "It was OT for me."

"Overtime?"

"Yeah. Ashley and I were saving to rent salon space so she could start her own business. I was forever pulling OT just for the cash."

"So no one knew you'd be at the scene that night?"

"No, the duty roster goes up on Wednesdays. The bust was on a Friday."

My mind was racing as myriad thoughts tried to come together in some sort of cohesive fashion. "So anyone could have gone into the gun lockup between Wednesday and Friday and taken your gun."

Liam let out a heavy sigh. "In theory. But the cage guy knows just about everyone, so it would have been impossible for a civilian to remove the gun. And someone would have to have had access to the sign-in and -out sheet since they presented testimony to the grand jury that I was the one who did it. They had the records to back up what they were saying."

"Could someone have been in cahoots with the Latin Bandits?"

"Anything is possible," he said as he drained his coffee and then asked me for a beer. "Except we didn't know we were hitting the Bandits until Friday, just before the operation started. Only Armando Calderone knew. He was running point."

"Did he have anything against you? Something personal?"

"No."

"So if the cops are off the hook, for now, who did have it in for you?"

He shook his head vehemently. "I've asked myself that same question a million times. Nothing was out of order that night. Well, except for the kid getting shot."

I sat sideways and tucked my feet beneath me, then straddled my laptop against my knees. I couldn't resist, I went directly to eBay. Twenty-seven minutes and counting and I was still the high bidder. As a precaution, I upped my minimum another five hundred but didn't place the bid. No, I would hold it with less than thirty seconds to go just in case I was up against a seasoned player.

I happily noted that I'd won three of the five links, so I went through PayPal and dispatched payment rather quickly.

"How long does it take that thing to boot?" Liam asked, irritated.

"I just had to do some housekeeping. The IT guys had it for a day, remember?" And I could multitask, a skill I'd perfected at Dane-Leiberman.

"Where do you want to start? Cops or robbers?"

"What kind of information can you get?"

I twisted my hair and threw it over my shoulder. "From here? I can get the basics. Personal, criminal history—though not in detail—financials, and work history. I'll need to be at my desk to run full credit and background."

"Start with Jimmy Santos," Liam instructed. "He was pretty pissed when he lost cash, drugs, and dope in the raid."

"About how much did he lose?" I asked.

"The dope alone was worth about million on the street. The guns," he paused and stroked the sexy stubble on his chin. "Maybe a couple hundred grand. I think the final count on the cash was around fifty thousand."

"Who does the count?" I asked.

"The initial count is done at the scene, then it's bagged and tagged and turned over to CSI."

"So if some of the money went missing, no one but the thief would know, right?"

"There's always at least two guys doing the counting, so that's highly unlikely."

So much for that theory. Back to the Latin Bandits. I tapped my pen on the edge of my laptop until Liam placed his palm over it to silence it.

Liam removed my laptop and set it on the table as he moved close to me.

"No," I protested halfheartedly.

Liam's lips brushed against the sensitive skin just below my earlobe. The feel of his feather-light kisses drew my stomach into a tight ball of anticipation. Closing my eyes, I concentrated on the glorious sensations. His grip tightened as his tongue traced a path up to my ear. My breath caught when Liam teasingly nibbled the edge of my lobe.

His hands traveled up and rested against my rib cage. I swallowed the moan rumbling in my throat. I was aware of everything—his fingers; the feel of his solid body molded against mine; the magical kisses.

"You smell wonderful," he said against my superheated skin.

"Liam," I said, whispering his name. It was the best I could muster over the lump of desire clogging my throat. "I don't think this is such a good idea."

His mouth stilled and he gripped my waist. "Why?"

"You're wounded. Stitches, remember?"

His eyes were such a dazzling shade of blue and a devastating combination when rimmed with dark, soft lashes. Those same eyes were passionate and hooded. A lock of his jet-black hair had fallen forward and rested just above his eyebrows. His chiseled mouth was curved in an effortlessly sexy half smile.

"I've kept my hands off you since the wedding," he said. He applied pressure to the middle of my back, urging me closer to him.

"I know," I managed above my rapid heartbeat.

"We've tried to pretend this isn't happening," he continued, punctuating his remark with a kiss on my forehead. "I look at you and I can't think of anything but this."

His palms slid up my back until he cradled my face in his hands. Using his thumbs, Liam tilted my head back and hesitated only fractionally before his mouth found mine. Instinctively, my hands went to his waist. I could feel the tapered muscles stiffen in response to my touch.

The scent of soap and cologne filled my nostrils as the exquisite pressure of his mouth increased. His fingers began to slowly massage their way up my spine. Until the tips began an easy, sensual counting of each vertebra. My mind was no longer capable of rational thought. All my attention was homed in on the intense sensations filling me with fierce desire.

With my heart racing in my ears, I allowed myself to revel

in the feel of his strong body against mine. As Liam deepened the kiss into something more demanding, I succumbed to the potent dose of longing.

I began to explore the solid contours of his body beneath his soft cotton shirt. It was like feeling the smooth, sculpted surface of a granite statue. Everywhere I touched I felt the distinct outline of corded muscle. I could even feel the vibration from his erratic pulse.

All the nights of worrying if he too felt the strong tug of attraction were easily erased by the undeniable proof of his arousal. My heart soared with the knowledge that Liam obviously felt it, too.

When he lifted his head, I had to fight the urge to pull him back to me. His eyes met and held mine as he quietly searched my face. His breaths were coming in short, raspy gulps and I watched the tiny vein at his temple race in time with my own pulse.

"I've never done this," he said.

My eyes flew open wider and my expression must have registered obvious shock.

Liam's chuckle was deep and reached his eyes.

"I mean I've done *this*," he corrected. "I've just never been so attracted to a woman that I've put on the full-court press," he said as he claimed my mouth again. His kiss lasted for several heavenly moments. "I just wouldn't want you to think I make a habit of this sort of thing."

"I don't think I *am* thinking," I admitted as I rested my cheek against his chest.

"Maybe I don't want us to think, Finley."

"That isn't very responsible behavior," I said against the soft fabric covering his broad chest.

"Who says we have to be responsible?" he countered as his thumb hooked under my chin. "I can't tell you how responsibly I've been taking my cold showers lately."

I tried to ignore the sudden tightness in the pit of my stomach. But I decided to ignore the blatant invitation in his devastatingly blue eyes . . .

"We have to wait," I said as I inched back into the corner of the sofa.

"Wait for what?" he asked with regret but no signs of malice.

"You have stitches."

He rolled his eyes. "Other than the fact that they itch, I'm good to go."

"Well, once you are stitches free, we can talk about it."

Liam reached out and cradled my face in one hand. "Whatever you say."

"You give up too easily," I answered with a grin.

He smiled back at me. "No, I just know the stitches come out in two days. Then you won't have an excuse."

Oh yes I will. The ever-present Ashley.

"Can we get back to business?"

"You can waste your time investigating the members of my unit. I'll take care of the Latin Bandits."

"That's dangerous," I warned. "What do you think, they'll just calmly confess to killing two deputy sheriffs?"

"I was thinking Jimmy Santos might be lonely. He's been locked up since the raid. Maybe he's tired of shouldering the whole burden."

"Fine, then I'll start with Calderone. I'll ask Tony to get their IA files." I grabbed for my briefcase. "I almost forgot." Because I wanted to. "I got the final autopsy reports and photos on José."

"Let's see them," Liam said, his tone more resigned.

"They aren't pretty," I warned.

"They never are," he told me.

I passed the color photos to him one by one, careful not to linger on any single picture. I didn't have the stomach for dissected bodies even if it was in the name of science. On the other hand, Liam scanned each picture, stopping only to ask if I had a magnifying glass. I did. Kinda. I had one of those kits to fix eyeglasses and it came with a tiny magnifier.

"What is it?" I asked after he'd spent at least three minutes looking at José's upper arm.

"What does that look like to you?" he asked, handing me the mini-magnifier and the photo. It was a rectangular scar just below where the shoulder met the arm. The skin was discolored, but there was a faint outline in red visible just off to one side. It looked like a stylized letter *L*.

"Ever seen anything like that?"

I nodded. "One of the girls I went to college with got a tattoo and her parents went ballistic. Sent her to a plastic surgeon to have the thing removed."

"It's against policy to have visible tattoos in the department."

I still wasn't sure where he was going. "You think José had a tattoo removed?"

"Maybe. He once told me it was from a motorcycle accident. I never really paid attention."

"The *L* could be for Lopez. Maybe he had his own initials

tattooed on and then had them removed when he joined the sheriff's department. Only one way to tell," I said.

"Which is?"

"Tony gets an order preventing release of the body and brings in a specialist to examine the scar. Sometimes if they remove skin layer by layer the image becomes clear."

He kissed my forehead. "Excellent observation."

"Only if Tony goes along with it."

I grabbed my phone and handed it to Liam. After he explained the situation, Tony agreed to draft the emergency motion and get it signed over the weekend before Lopez's body could be cremated. Liam finished by saying, "Finley spotted the tattoo."

I felt almost giddy. I was an asset to this team, and hopefully now they'd both agree that I didn't need to be cloistered in my office working from afar.

"I've got to make another run to my car," Liam said.

While he was gone I poured myself another cup of coffee and got him another beer. It was kind of like a domestic scene right out of the fifties. I wasn't sure how I felt about that. I just knew I still felt the lingering effects of his kiss. Of course, that was tempered by the memory of Ashley getting a kiss as well.

When he returned, he had a small duffle bag over his shoulder.

"More files?" I asked.

"Clothes. I'm parking out here until we find out who sent you that e-mail."

I tilted my head to one side and sighed. "That could have just been a jerk I met being a bigger jerk."

"Meet a lot of threatening men, do you?

"Sometimes. I can think of three times in the last two weeks that I've been . . . well *less* than kind to half-drunk morons at bars."

"Maybe you should stay away from bars."

"Maybe you should not be telling me what to do."

"Just thinking of your well-being."

I was getting pissed. "You don't seem to mind that Ashley spends a lot of her free time in City Place."

"That's different." He started to walk toward the guest bedroom.

"Different?" I whispered. What the hell did that mean? Okay, I decided when he was settling into my sanctuary, it was time to confront the issue straight on.

Before he came back, I went to eBay only to find that my competition had outbid me already. With just under fifteen seconds to go, I pressed the button upping my bid. I won! I practically did a happy dance right there. I was the proud new owner of an aftermarket diamond bezel for my as-yet-to-be-built Rolex.

When Liam returned, he stopped for a second to admire Harold's work replacing the slider and cleaning the glass shards away. "I told you he was good," Liam said.

"Sit down, please," I said in my most professional voice.

While he did that I took a second and made myself a cosmopolitan. I hoped alcohol would give me the fortitude to press for the previously off-limits information. I was tired of brush-off answers and flippant replies. Especially when he was going out of his way to seduce me.

I handed him a fresh beer, then sat at the far end of the sofa. I knew if he touched me I'd get all hot and bothered, and I needed all my wits about me if I was going to get through this.

"Let's talk Ashley."

His initial response was a maddeningly sly grin. "She owns a salon in City Place. Hair, nail, facials, massages, pedicures. They serve finger sandwiches and wine to their clients and even have dog bowls and food for the clients who bring their furry friends."

"I know all about the salon. What I'm struggling with is the nature of your relationship with Ashley. As you know, I've already been burned once. I'm in no hurry to do it again."

"Are you suggesting you and I have a relationship?" He was amused and I longed to douse him with my cosmo.

"I'm suggesting that you're confusing me. One minute you act like I'm the only woman you want, and the next minute you're off on one of your infamous *things* with Ashley."

"Don't be confused. My *things* with Ashley are not a big deal. Put them out of your mind. Why don't you come here," he suggested as he patted the cushion next to him. "I'll be happy to demonstrate just how much I want you."

Tempting but stupid.

Tempting was winning.

"I'm going to take a bath and get some sleep," I announced.

"I'll walk you to your room," Liam offered.

His polite gesture inspired quite a response from my overloaded senses. As we headed toward the hallway, I was keenly aware of his fluid movements. My shoulder brushed against his solid chest, inciting a whole new array of thoughts and feelings.

When he placed his fingers at the small of my back, I couldn't ignore the warmth of his touch. I tried to convince myself that it was just some sort of reaction caused by recent events. The clean scent I had grown to associate with him caressed my senses.

"Why are you so interested in Ashley?" he asked when we reached the door to my bedroom.

I looked up into the full force of his eyes. He was so tall, his shoulders so broad, that I could feel my pulse beginning to quicken again. "I just want to understand if this is going anywhere."

One dark brow arched and his mouth curved into a lazy smile. "You wanted to know why I spend time with my ex. Are you really that insecure?"

"Maybe," I acknowledged softly. "I haven't exactly been batting a thousand lately."

He reached for me with one hand, allowing it to rest on my shoulder, near my collarbone. I could feel every inch of his squared fingers through the thin fabric of my blouse. The feel of his touch wasn't nearly as powerful as the simmering passion I read in those clear blue eyes.

I felt my breath catch in my throat as the space between us grew palpable. It was as if a current had engaged, filling the inches that separated us with a strong and powerful electricity. For several protracted seconds, we said nothing. I was too afraid of breaking the spell. I didn't know what might happen, but I didn't want to do anything that put the brakes on.

Liam's eyes traveled lower, until I could almost feel him staring hard at my slightly parted lips. I knew instinctively that his thoughts were taking the same path as mine. His hand moved slowly toward my face, until he cupped my cheek, his thumb resting just inches from where his eyes remained riveted.

His thumb burned a path toward my lower lip. I watched the intensity in his eyes deepen as his thumb brushed tentatively across my mouth. Gently at first, then with each successive movement he applied more pressure until I thought I might die from the anticipation knotting my stomach.

Raising my hand, I flattened it against his chest. I could feel Liam's heart beating against the solid muscle. A faint moan rumbled in his throat.

His head dipped fractionally closer and I held my breath, fully expecting and wanting his kiss. His thumb continued to work its magic. The friction had produced a heat that was carried to every cell in my body. I swallowed. Hard.

"That first time," he began in a husky, raspy voice.

"Yes?"

"When I said I was a patient man?"

"Yes?"

"I lied."

His breath washed over my face in warm, inviting waves but he made no move closer. Gathering a handful of his shirt, I urged him to me. His resistance was a surprise. His thumb stilled and rested just below my lip.

His eyes met and held mine. "I guess this is where we say good night."

"Guess it is," he said easily. Too easily.

"Or you could come into my room," I said.

"Not yet," he said.

Those two words inspired the first stirrings of embarrassment to creep into my consciousness. I felt my face grow warm with the realization that I had all but begged the man.

"Look," I said, stepping out of his arms with my head bowed. "I need a good night's sleep. Thanks for staying here tonight. I don't know how I'll ever be able to thank you enough."

"I can think of a way," Liam answered before he turned and walked down the hall.

Closing the door, I leaned against the cool wooden surface and fanned myself with my hand. "Close," I mumbled. "Dangerously close."

Some people learn from mistakes,
I run from mine.

fourteen

Liam left early, off in search of information on the listening device I'd accidentally discovered at José's house. Me? I had to go to the office to type the letters to Liam's former unit buddies. Well, I guess once someone rats you out to IA and a grand jury you don't consider them buddies anymore.

Even though it was eight thirty on a Saturday, I was already dressed and fully coiffed. I went without first-thing coffee so I could make myself presentable to Liam. I wasn't used to having a houseguest and I wanted to look my best.

"Who are you kidding?" I asked myself. I just didn't want him to see me all scraggly and messy. Which made no sense since he'd already seen me soaking wet and in a police station with nothing but my jammies on. Still, it mattered.

The temperature had dropped down into the upper seventies so I'd chosen a pair of fuchsia Piazza Sempione capri pants and a Michael Kors shirt with button cuffs and princess seams. Since it was the weekend, I decided to give my feet a rest by wearing a pair of gold metallic Kate Spade sandals with faceted jewels on the T-strap. They worked well with my metallic gold Coach bag, the bag with the offset stitching that allowed me to score it for less than half the price.

I arrived at the office only to find both Tony's and Vain Dane's cars parked in the lot. Good, maybe Vain Dane would give me some points for working on a Saturday. After settling into my office, I saw a manila folder in my in-box. I pinched the metal prongs and opened it. Joseph Lawson had sent me the addresses for the family members. Good, while I was there I could finish those letters and take them up to Vain Dane for his signature. Then he'd have to notice that I was in the building.

I took the list out of my bag and started searching the Internet for information on the other officers present the night of the shooting. DMV records gave me photographs and addresses to put with the names.

Diego Ferrer was thirty-seven, with a neck like a professional wrestler. Definitely not someone I'd want pissed at me. No huge surprise, he had no outstanding tickets or warrants. I switched over to the property records, and at first, I found nothing. Not even the address from his driver's license. I clicked my way to vital records and found a marriage license. Then went back and discovered the house in Wellington was in the wife's name alone. Odd, but not unheard of.

While I couldn't access Internal Affairs information, I could get a work history from the credit bureau. Nothing special there. Diego and his wife, Maria, lived within their means. Well, better than within their means. They were making double mortgage payments. Smart move in a bad real estate market. They paid their credit cards on time and had excellent credit ratings.

The next name on the list was Carlos Santiago. Thirty-nine and not exactly what I thought of when I thought sheriff's deputy. He was only five-five according to his driver's license, but like Diego, he had that "I work out every chance I get" look about him. Thick neck, bulging brow, the steroid look. He'd gone to Palm Beach College and joined the force right after graduation. He'd paid off his student loans ahead of schedule and had a mortgage and a boat loan outstanding. Hardly a lavish lifestyle; three-quarters of Florida owned boats. His house was in an area called the Acreage, a less-congested suburb of West Palm. His wife was named Cynthia and I couldn't find any dirt on her aside from the fact that she liked to shop at Nordstrom, but then again, so did I. They paid their bills every month on time. Nothing stood out there.

I moved on to Miguel Vasquez. He looked fierce in his license photo. Dark and brooding and given his vitals, 6'3" and 225 pounds, he was one scary-looking man. He was forty-one, divorced, and had five children. This explained why he had an apartment in North Palm Beach. He was probably paying out the ying in child support. The fact that he was divorce poor might give him a reason to . . . what? Shoot the Peña kid? Shoot José? Shoot Liam? That made no sense. Being cash poor just meant he had to budget like the rest of us.

Well, I don't budget so much as I pay attention to the limits on my credit cards.

That took me to Armando Calderone, the unit leader and

the one Liam said had been the point man on the operation. Though he was forty-four, I found no record of him ever being married. Between the real estate records and the personal property tax rolls, I learned the man liked his toys. Being single was a lot cheaper than having a family, and Armando seemed to be living a pretty high life. He had a condo on the ocean in Juno Beach. A BMW and a GTO muscle car. I stared at his picture for a minute, wondering why he wasn't married. He was attractive enough. Maybe he was gay. Or in sheriff's terms, in the closet.

I thought of my friend Sam. He's a decorator and gay and always has money. Maybe there's some correlation between being gay and being financially secure?

I stopped and stretched, rolling my head around to get out the kinks. I hadn't exactly rested peacefully last night. Not with Liam a mere wall away. Things were getting way complicated between us. Or at least they were too complicated in my brain, which was apparently being led around by my libido. My cell rang, ending my moment of not so pleasant introspection before it got out of hand.

"Hi," Izzy greeted me.

"Excited about tonight?" I asked as I leaned back in my chair.

"Totally. Will you still come over and do my hair and makeup?"

"Of course," I said even though I'd forgotten all about that promise. "What time again?"

"Five."

"I'll be there."

"Finley?"

"Yes?"

"Thanks again for running interference with my dad. He had coffee with Cole's dad this morning and then he called me and said everything was okay." She sounded relieved and eager all at once.

No sooner had I hung up the phone than Tony appeared at my door. "Bucking for employee of the month?"

I laughed. "Just doing what you said. I had some estate stuff for Vain . . . Mr. Dane and I thought it would be a good idea to contact the other officers from Liam's old unit."

"Why?" he asked as he sat down.

I told him Liam's theory about them all being targets. "Isn't it prudent for us to warn them?"

Tony stroked his chin. "I suppose so. Write the letters and I'll sign them."

As he got up and went to the door he turned and said, "Thank you for all your help with Izzy. I know she appreciates it and so do I."

"I'm happy to help."

"Happy enough to have dinner with me tonight?"

I froze. If he'd asked me that question a month ago, I would have said yes without any hesitation. I thought of Liam. Then I thought of Ashley. "I'd love to."

As soon as he left my office, I wanted to run after him and take it back. No matter how frustrated I was over the whole Liam/Ashley thing, having dinner with Tony felt wrong. Having it feel wrong felt even worse. It meant that yet again, I had fallen for the wrong guy. Hadn't Patrick's cheating taught me anything? And in some ways this was worse than Patrick. Patrick did everything behind my back. Liam was doing it to my face and telling me not to sweat it. What self-respecting woman doesn't sweat the other woman?

Time to turn over a new leaf. If Liam could have Ashley, I could have Tony. Only deep down, in a place I didn't want to go, I knew which one I really wanted.

Well. I could wallow in self-pity or do something constructive. I typed carefully worded letters to the guys from Liam's unit warning them of the potential danger they might be facing. After Tony signed them, I then went to Vain Dane's office and knocked on the doorjamb. He looked up and his hazel eyes registered shock.

"Finley?"

I handed him the three letters all neatly paper clipped to their corresponding envelopes. "I know this will cause a potential problem on the Lawson estate so I thought it would be best to get a jump on it."

He was wearing a dress shirt and a tie even though it was a weekend. I wondered if he slept in a tie. Tight ass. He signed the letters and returned them to me.

I returned to my office to collect my things. My cell was ringing when I arrived. "Hello?"

"You used your house as collateral?" Jane barked into the phone.

"Liam isn't going to jump bail," I said. "Where's your compassion?"

"Right now it's looking at your monthly bills. Finley, you're spending way too much money."

"Anyone ever tell you you're a buzz killer?"

"Several times, actually. But the house, Finley? Really?"

"It seems to me that Liam was there for you when you woke up with a dead guy next to you."

Jane grunted. "I know."

"Thanks for being at the arraignment yesterday."

"You're welcome. Finley, please, *please* stop shopping. And stop using your house like it's a bottomless pit of money. If you don't, you won't be able to swing the monthly payments."

"I got it." Now probably wasn't the best time to tell her I'd just spent fifteen hundred dollars on a watch part.

"I've got to go," Jane said. "I'm taking a run on the beach, want to join me?"

I smiled. "Like that's going to happen."

With the estate letters, I had seven pieces of outgoing mail. I put them in Margaret's in-box so she'd have to put postage on them Monday morning. Then I thought about it and retrieved the four letters to the deputies.

I keyed their addresses in my GPS and opted to go to Wellington first. It was south and west of Palm Beach. It took me about thirty-five minutes before I found myself at the gate of a lovely golf course community. I scrolled down until I found Diego's name, then pressed the button. I heard a childlike hello, then the gates swung open and I drove through. Following the rather stern voice of the GPS I found the Ferrer house.

It wasn't what I expected. It was pretty big, two stories, with archways and pillars. The front yard was littered with kids' toys and bikes. I parked on the street and walked on the path to the front door.

A small child—four or five maybe—opened the door and stared up at me. On her heels was Diego. I recognized him from his license picture. He placed an arm protectively over his daughter and asked, "May I help you?"

I put on my best smile and said, "I'm from Dane, Lieberman, and Caprelli."

His expression darkened. "I have nothing to say to you."

He reached for the door but I grabbed the edge. "I don't want to talk, I just need to drop this off to you."

"If it's a subpoena you can toss it on the floor."

"It's nothing like that," I said in a rush. "Mr. Caprelli is concerned about your well-being." I chose my words carefully because the child was still standing there. "He just wanted to make you aware of some developments in the Lopez case."

"Alicia, go find Mommy," he told the child. She turned and ran down the hall.

Diego stepped out onto the porch. He was a mass of coiled muscle and pretty damned scary. Maybe hand delivery wasn't such a good idea after all.

"Give it to me," he said as he grabbed it out of my hand. He tore into it, scanned it, then tossed it at me. "Tell your boss I've been sufficiently warned. Tell your client to rot in hell."

With that I got a door slammed in my face. I was actually shaking. People have gotten annoyed with me in the past but that guy was a big slice of angry.

Hopefully he was the worst of the lot. But no. I got a similar reception from everyone but Armando Calderone, and the only reason he didn't ream me out was because he wasn't home. I tucked the letter between the screen and the door and was secretly glad to be finished with the task. I walked back to my car slowly, enjoying the view of the ocean from the seventh floor.

It wasn't until I was behind the wheel that I noticed a curtain flutter in Armando's apartment. Either one of the others had called him or there was some other reason he didn't want to speak to me. I could go back up and pound like a lunatic, but time was getting away from me, thanks in no small part to the four stops I'd made for coffee as I zigzagged across the county. I was already halfway to Martin County, so I went up to Tony's community, arriving fifteen minutes early. Izzy was thrilled to see me. She was even more thrilled to give me the message that her father would be picking me up at seven for dinner.

"How cool is it that you're having dinner with my dad?" she asked as she sat at her vanity after plugging in her curling iron.

"It's just dinner, Izzy."

"Whatever."

"Hold still so I don't burn you," I told her.

Izzy had a lot of hair, so it took me a while to make the soft *S* waves she wanted. With her perfect olive skin, foundation wasn't necessary. I did her makeup, and as I was finishing, Tony came home.

"Don't come in!" Izzy yelled as we worked the zipper up her back. "I want you to be surprised."

She looked lovely in the beige and black lace dress and I could see on Tony's face that he thought so as well. They were in the hallway together and I felt every inch the third wheel. "I've got to run," I said.

"Don't you want to see Cole?" Izzy asked.

I shook my head. "That's a father-daughter moment."

"Don't worry," she said with a flick of her wrist. "He'll take like a gazillion pictures."

"I'll look forward to seeing them."

◆

I was torn between the Versus one-shoulder dress and the Versus ruched-front jersey dress. The one shoulder showed off my tan but the jersey dress clung in all the right places. The problem was, I didn't want to look all that sexy. At the end of the day, I was still having dinner with my boss, so I didn't want to send out the wrong vibe. I went with the ruched front and the much-coveted pair of Jimmy Choo shoes my sister had given me as a maid-of-honor gift. I was just putting my lipstick in a tiny silver shell clutch when I heard the door open.

I walked out into the living room; Liam stopped and his jaw literally dropped. "Wow."

I'd flat-ironed my hair, so I had swing factor going on. "What's that?" I asked, pointing to the brown paper bag in his hand.

"Dinner. I brought you moo shu."

"Sorry," I said in the most chipper tone possible. "I have a date tonight. And it isn't with Izzy."

"I figured that out from the dress. Who is it?"

As if on cue, the doorbell rang. I made a mental note to call the alarm company and let them know they had somehow killed the motion sensors when they responded to the window smashing.

I brushed by Liam and opened the door. Tony looked dreamy in his black suit, gray shirt, and monochromatic tie. He smiled broadly. "You look great." He looked past me. "Hey, Liam. How are you?"

"Fine," he answered in a clipped tone.

"Would you like something to drink, Tony?" I asked.

"No, we have seven-thirty reservations at the Breakers."

"Then let me get my wrap." I waltzed past a very pissy Liam and grabbed my pashmina off the back of the sofa.

"I'd invite you along," Tony said to Liam, "but the reservation is only for two."

"How nice."

Tony placed his hand at the small of my back. "Help yourself to anything you want," I called over my shoulder.

"I'll get right on that," he grumbled as I closed the door.

It wasn't until Tony pulled out of the driveway that he said, "I think that went well, don't you?"

"I thought Liam was going to hit you. Or maybe me."

Tony laughed. "That was the point."

"Excuse me?"

"I have a confession to make."

"We're going to Burger King?"

"No. When Liam told me he was staying at your place, I thought it would be a good time to give him a little shove."

I turned and looked at his profile, illuminated by the lights on the dash. "You've lost me."

"I didn't have an emergency the weekend of your sister's wedding."

"Then why didn't you go?"

"Because I knew Liam wanted to. I just didn't know he'd blow it."

"It was one dance," I said, just as I'd argued with my mother.

"We're not on the same page here. Look, Finley. Liam and Ashley had a nasty breakup."

"Coulda fooled me."

"They did. He's been a little gun shy since then. Well, until you."

"I think you're reading the signals wrong," I told him. "You're on the wrong page now."

"No," Tony insisted. "I'm on the right page. Liam will sit in your house all night wondering what we're doing."

"We're having dinner."

"I know that and you know that, but Liam doesn't."

"So you did this just to make Liam jealous? I'm playing the role of the pawn now?"

"Not a pawn. I thought seeing us together might get him off the fence."

"What makes you think he's on the fence?"

"I know Liam."

"Well, your daughter is going to be pissed. She thinks we're about to start something."

"I had a talk with Izzy. When I told her what I was doing, she thought I was terribly romantic. Apparently that appeals to her fourteen-year-old brain."

"You could have told me."

"It was more fun this way."

"Not for Liam," I told him.

"We'll eat. We'll walk along the seawall. You'll smudge your lipstick and we'll let Liam's imagination do the rest."

"He's going to be mad."

Tony smiled. "That's what I'm banking on."

When in doubt, lie.

fifteen

I came home to find Liam laid out on my sofa watching football. He barely glanced up when I walked in and tossed my pashmina on the chair. "Have a nice dinner?" he asked in a casual tone.

So much for Tony's grand plan. "Lovely, thanks for asking." I went to the countertop and checked my cell for messages. I hadn't taken it with me because the cute silver shell bag was only big enough to hold a lipstick and a credit card. It wasn't a problem. Tony was a wonderful conversationalist.

Liam got up and headed toward the hallway. "See you in the morning," he said.

"You're going to bed?" I asked. It was barely eleven.

"Long day. 'Night."

"Good night," I said as I slipped off my shoes.

I went back to my room and pulled on some soft cotton drawstring pants and double cami tops. I was more than a little annoyed by Liam's lack of reaction. His silence spoke volumes. Obviously I was in a one-sided lust-a-thon.

Barefoot, I went back into the living room where he'd rained paper and files all over the place. I wasn't the least bit tired, so I started reading the various pages. At the bottom of one box I found a copy of the grand jury transcript. Liam had dog-eared several pages.

Most of them were sections of testimony where each officer except Stan Cain testified that they'd seen Liam pull a gun from his ankle holster. Then each one detailed their duties and responsibilities after the shooting. Diego Ferrer had stayed with the cache of drugs. Miguel Vasquez stood sentry over the guns, and Armando Calderone secured the cash. Liam and José had followed the ambulance with Fernàndo Peña to the hospital. Carlos Santiago didn't seem to have a responsibility beyond hanging with ASA Alberto Garza, who'd shown up at the scene because of a police-involved shooting. Stan Cain was responsible for overseeing the arrests of the five Latin Bandits they had in custody.

Other than the fact that I believed Liam could not shoot an unarmed kid, the grand jury should have been a slam dunk. But it wasn't. No matter how hard he tried, Garza couldn't get his witnesses to testify clearly. The worst example was Armando Calderone when he was questioned by Garza:

Q: Garza: Approximately how much cash did you recover from the residence?

A: Calderone: Around three hundred thousand.

Q: Garza: Would you take a look at the evidence sheet, please?

A: Calderone: Oh, sorry, I got confused between the guns, the drugs, and the cash. We confiscated fifty thousand in cash.

Q: Garza: Did you participate in counting the cash?

A: Calderone: Yes, myself and Deputy Santiago did the on-site count. Then we drove the money, the drugs, and the weapons back to the station house. A second verification count was done by the crime scene unit as well as the property clerk, Deputy Kronck.

Q: Garza: What was the rest of your unit doing while you were handling the evidence?

A: Calderone: I'd have to review my notes.

I may not be Gloria Allred, but I knew assistant state's attorneys prepped their witnesses. Calderone had come off like a buffoon who couldn't keep his numbers straight, and the only one who didn't fumble the ball was Stan Cain. No wonder Liam didn't get indicted. The witnesses sucked.

Or maybe Garza just did him a favor and didn't prep the witnesses. Liam said he was a nice guy. Which was good to know because the officers I'd seen today weren't exactly there to serve and protect. At least not me.

I went surfing through the files on the Latin Bandits. Jimmy Santos had been a member since the ripe age of thirteen. According to his rap sheet he'd been arrested more times than he'd had birthdays, and by the time of the raid, he was the prime suspect in at least three murders. The other Latin Bandits arrested that night were all low-level gofers. They just had the bad luck of being in the wrong place at the wrong time. Not that they were angels, but none of them had violent crimes on their sheets.

My cell phone rang and I leapt off the sofa to get it before it disturbed Liam. Not that I would have been crushed if he was disturbed. I was disturbed that he wasn't disturbed. No, I was just being an ass. Why I thought that high school move would work is beyond me.

"Did you get my text?" It was Izzy.

"No." Which was weird since I'd checked my phone as soon as I'd walked in the door. "How was the dance?"

"Cole was great. He can dance, too."

"Good. I'm glad you had a good time."

"Well?" she squealed.

"Well what?"

"Did Liam go all nuts and stuff? Dad wouldn't tell me and you didn't answer my text."

"Hang on," I said, then I scrolled over to my text messages and there it was, big as life. *Did you fool Liam with the fake date?* That smarmy bastard. He knew it was a sham! "Izzy, I'm glad things went well. But it's almost one, you should be asleep."

"Hang on, Dad wants to talk to you."

"Finley?"

"Hi. Thanks again for dinner."

"Did it work?"

"It kinda backfired. Nothing I can't handle. What do you need?"

"My forensic pathologist is only available tomorrow. Can you meet him at the morgue at eight?"

I rolled my eyes and my shoulders slumped. "Sure. If you'll

call Justin Haller at the *Palm Beach Post*. I sorta told him you'd call."

"Why?"

"Long story. I'll let you know if the pathologist finds anything."

"Great. Call me when he's done."

Call him? Was he going to sleep in while I did dead person duty? "Are you sure you want me to go? I'm not great with all that pathology stuff."

"I need you. I've got to go see Travis Johnson at juvie in the morning."

"Okay then. I'll talk to you tomorrow."

" 'Night, Finley."

I wasn't sure what had me more pissed. Going to work at the morgue at the crack of dawn on a Sunday morning or knowing that Liam had read Izzy's text and that's why he'd been so nonchalant about the whole situation. It was my own fault. It may have been Tony's idea, but I should have known better than to try to trick Liam into bed.

I set down my phone and took a vow of celibacy.

One of the boxes contained all the reports and statements the officers had given to Internal Affairs. Again, with the exception of Stan Cain, they all told the same story. The raid was over and then the Peña kid was shot. No one actually witnessed the shooting, but the ballistics reports all confirmed that it had been Liam's gun that had fired the fatal shot.

I looked at Liam's signed statement, then at the sign-out sheet from the gun cage. It looked like Liam's signature. In fact it looked exactly like Liam's signature. I placed one sheet on top of the other and held them up to the light. They weren't close. They were exact. As in traced. Someone had gone out of their way to make Liam look guilty. Someone inside the department.

I found the name of the gun cage attendant, Deputy Young. I turned on my laptop and did a Google search. It was the best I had until I went by my office. The only reference I could find was a commendation ceremony for Deputy Young, held on his retirement day three years earlier. I checked the white pages and found seventeen Donald Youngs listed. Frustrating.

I made a note to myself to find out everything I could about the retired deputy. Then I moved on to the property clerk. Deputy Kronck had signed the evidence receipts. I tried Googling him but all I found was his obituary. Still, I added his name to my list.

◆

"You're up early," Liam remarked when I dragged myself into the kitchen and made a beeline for the coffeepot.

"I've got to go to an autopsy this morning."

"You have such an exciting job. Want company?"

I glanced up at him as I brushed the hair off my face. "You can stop being all nice and chipper. I know you read the text from Izzy. And just for the record, I knew nothing about Tony's plan."

"I know that."

I took a long sip of hot coffee. "How?"

"You're not into games. That's one of the things I like about you."

I smiled. "One of the things? There's more?"

"Yeah, but they're all X-rated."

"Thanks for making coffee. I've got to shower and dress."

"Want me to wash your back?"

"Sure," I said as I came around the counter. "Only not when I'm rushed for time."

"It's a date."

"Right," I joked as I returned to my room.

I did have to admit that the thought of Liam naked in my shower was a pleasant fantasy. An image I had to banish so I could focus on the task at hand—picking the right outfit for a weekend trip to the morgue. I decided on white jeans, a cropped top, and flat sandals. I dried my hair and put on a modest amount of makeup. Who did I need to impress? The dead people?

Liam insisted on coming along, which, as it turned out, was a good thing because sometime during the night two of my tires had gone flat.

"Don't sweat it," he told me as I climbed into his in-the-middle-of-being-restored '65 Mustang. "We'll buy two new tires and I can change them for you."

"Thank you," I said as I clipped the seat belt.

Half the car was painted with gray primer. The muffler coughed and spit out bluish smoke and smelled god-awful. I waved my hand in front of my face until the exhaust fumes cleared. "This thing is a death trap."

"Wait till she's all fixed up," he promised. "You'll be begging me to borrow it."

"Why drive a Mercedes when I can have a junk heap?"

"Anyone ever tell you you're a little cranky in the morning?"

"No. I tend not to speak to people before nine A.M."

"Who are we meeting?"

"Dr. Wilkes. He's some big-deal guy out of Miami." I shifted in my seat so I could look at Liam. "Did you have an attorney during the grand jury hearing?"

"A very expensive one," Liam confirmed.

"Did he have the gun cage log reviewed by a handwriting expert?"

Liam glanced at me for a second. "Not that I know of, why?"

"I think your signature on the gun log was counterfeit. I'm no expert, but it looks like a tracing."

Liam raked his hand through his hair. "Do you know what you're saying?"

"I'm saying someone with access to the gun cage set you up."

"No," he said with an edge in his tone. "You're saying it was another cop."

"Five guys said they saw you draw a weapon from an ankle holster. If that never happened, I'm saying five cops plus the gun cage guy were all in on it."

"Or five cops got confused in the middle of a gunfight and you're barking up the wrong tree."

"Then fine. I'll prove myself wrong by having the signatures analyzed. Okay?"

"Finley," he said as he patted my thigh. "I appreciate your concern, but the real issue here is José's shooting. If he was involved in framing me, why would he be killed five years after the fact?"

"I don't know. Guilty conscience? Something must have happened."

"Like?"

"Like Stan Cain dying in the woods in South Carolina. Someone was keeping tabs on José or I wouldn't have found that listening device."

"Which I tracked to a spy shop in Wellington."

"Diego Ferrer lives in Wellington."

"So you think Diego killed Stan and José and took a shot at me?"

"Stop raising your voice. I'm just throwing out ideas."

"Well, they're dumb ideas."

"Anyone ever tell you you're a jerk before nine A.M.?"

We rode the rest of the way in silence. I guess I saw his side of it. They were men he called his friends. What I didn't understand was why there was still a thin blue line after they'd been instrumental in forcing his retirement. Once a cop always a cop, I guess.

Dr. Wilkes was waiting at the morgue. He had a black bag with him but I didn't even want to guess at what was inside. All sorts of poking and probing things. The Palm Beach medical examiner was present too, at the request of ASA Garza. The legal system is very territorial.

I sat outside while Liam paced in front of me. His expression was hard, as if he was deep in thought. Me? I was just bored. Until an hour and a half later when Dr. Wilkes came out carrying a Polaroid.

He smiled as if he'd just come from a party rather than from dissecting a body. It gave me the creeps. "Give this to your boss," he said, handing me the photo.

I was almost afraid to look at it. "Thank you."

"Tell Tony I'll send him my bill," the doctor said as he quickly left the building.

"What is it?" Liam asked.

I flipped the picture over and felt my stomach lurch. It was José's upper arm, with the skin shaved back in layers. The final flap revealed a perfect image of a stylized L linked through a larger B. "Little brother?" I asked.

Liam's expression was grim. "Latin Bandits."

"I don't understand," I said.

"José was a member," Liam said. "Probably in the past, but it does explain one thing."

"What?"

"How come our unit was always a step behind them."

There's only one thing to do
in the face of danger . . . run!

sixteen

"He was my partner. If he was dirty, I want to know," Liam said as soon as we got back to my place.

"You said your unit was always one step behind the Latin Bandits. How so?"

He followed me into the house. "We knew from CIs that they were moving a lot of product and a lot of guns. But we never caught them with the kinds of money or drugs you'd expect. The night of the raid we all thought we'd be looking at dope, guns, and money in the millions."

"What's a CI?"

"Confidential informant. Usually a low-level guy with information he or she trades to keep from doing time."

"Didn't Garza tell Tony he had a CI who could prove you bought the ketamine that was injected into José the night he was killed?"

"Uh-huh."

"Can we talk to him? I mean, if all this is a setup, the CI would have to be told what to say by someone."

"Except we don't have a name."

I rubbed my temples. "Maybe Tony can get us one."

"Good luck with that," he said sarcastically.

"Have some faith," I suggested. I called Tony, gave him the information about José's connection to the Latin Bandits, then asked what he could do about the CI Garza had mentioned. Unfortunately, he said nothing could be done. While I was on the phone, Liam was frantically going through the files spread out all over my living room.

"Tell me what you're looking for," I said. "I'll help find it."

"Armando had a CI the night of the raid. He testified at the grand jury."

"Hand me the transcript." I moistened my fingertip and began flipping through the pages. "Here it is," I said. My heart sank. "They call him John Doe."

"Damn, I was hoping I might use that to convince Jimmy Santos to talk to me."

"You still can," I said. "Listen to this:

Q: Garza: How long have you been a police informant?

A: Doe: Three months. I started cooperating after I was busted for meth.

Q: Garza: And which officer did you contact in reference to the Latin Bandits?

A: Doe: Officer Vasquez.

"So see, it wasn't Calderone's CI. We just have to ask Vasquez."

"Who wouldn't spit on me if I was on fire," Liam said.

"Maybe he'll be nicer to me," I suggested.

"No way," Liam said emphatically. "I'll handle Vasquez."

"What makes you think he'll talk to you?"

"Because I happen to know he has a thing going with a stripper. I don't think he'd want that to become common knowledge."

"What am I supposed to do?"

"I changed your tires. Go shopping or whatever it is you do for fun."

I crossed my arms. "That was a shitty thing to say. In case you haven't noticed, I can be helpful."

Liam reached me in two long strides. "I didn't mean you weren't helpful. I just want to make sure you stay in public places and don't do anything dangerous. Remember the e-mail? And I'm not so sure your tires were a fluke. I want you locked up here tight."

"That e-mail was days ago and we both know there's road debris all over I-95. If someone was at the house last night, why not just come in and do whatever? I'm sure if someone really wanted to hurt me, I'd be hurt by now."

"Please," he said, then kissed my forehead. "Either stay here or stay out in public. That's the safest way to go."

"Fine," I said, though I had no intention of sitting back while he did all the heavy lifting. I'd go to a public place, just not the kind with shops and cafés.

Once Liam went off in search of Vasquez, I called information to get the number for South Bay prison. I called to make sure they had visiting hours today. Grabbing my briefcase I put my hair up in a clip, trying to look as unfeminine as possible. I switched to a blouse that was less formfitting, then went out to my car. Liam could try to track down a CI while I decided on a more direct approach.

It took me over an hour to get to South Bay prison. It was a foreboding place—cement walls, razor wire, and guard towers. I joined the line of people waiting to get inside.

There was a chance that Jimmy Santos wouldn't talk to me, but I had a suspicion that he didn't get a lot of visitors. If nothing else, curiosity might work in my favor. I had to go through an elaborate series of screenings to get to the visitors' room. My purse was checked for sharp items—they confiscated my pen and travel tweezers—then it was on to the metal detector and finally a pat down by a no-nonsense female correctional officer.

I entered a long, wide room with vending machines along one wall. The room had dozens of bright blue metal tables and chairs bolted to the floor. I couldn't get over how many people brought children, both young and old, to the prison. Nothing says family like a day behind bars with daddy.

I saw one of the corrections officers point at me. Then I saw who he was pointing for and I got an instant case of the jitters. A tall, thin but muscular man was walking my way. He had that kind of bend, bounce, and glide walk that was popular among lowlifes on the street. The worst part was seeing the six teardrops tattooed on his face. I knew enough about gangs to know each teardrop represented a kill. What the hell was I thinking?

I had to place my hands on my knees to keep them from visibly shaking. His hair was slicked back into a ponytail that fell about three inches below his shoulders. As he walked closer to me, he did that disgusting hand-grabbing-the-crotch thing. Classy.

"What's up, chica?" he asked as he lifted one leg over the bolted stool and sat right next to me. "Do we know each other? I think I'd remember a fine piece of—"

"I'm Finley Tanner," I interrupted before he could finish the sentence. "I work for a law firm."

"You're here about getting me out of this place." He smiled, revealing one gold-capped tooth. "I'm looking at another dime inside and I'm all set to use my get-out-of-jail card."

"Actually I'm here about the murder of Deputy José Lopez. My firm represents the man accused of the murder."

Santos leaned forward. His shirtsleeve pulled up and I could just make out the tattoo on his upper arm. It was one of many tattoos, mostly skulls and snakes and other creepy things. But the one that caught my attention was the Latin Bandits tattoo.

"It wasn't me," he said with amusement. "I've been in here for five years. Besides, you kill a cop, they kill you back. Know what I mean?"

"Could it have been an, um, associate of yours?" I asked.

He stroked the length of hair growing just at the center of his lower lip. "A place like this makes your memory bad. Maybe if you unbuttoned the top button of your blouse, it might come to me."

I felt my face flush. "Think harder."

"I'm getting harder, chica."

I sucked in a deep breath and unbuttoned the top button of my blouse. So what if he got an eyeful of collarbone? I didn't want Liam to go to trial for a murder I knew he didn't commit.

"Nice," Jimmy said. "Maybe I do know something."

"Which is?"

"The Latin Bandits had nothing to do with killing no deputy. Bad for business, ya know?"

"How did you get caught five years ago?"

Jimmy moved closer so I could smell the acrid scent of his breath. "It wasn't supposed to go down like it did. Someone tipped the cops off. Then they ripped us off. But hey, it isn't like I can sue. Judge Judy ain't interested in gangs getting double-crossed."

"How were you double-crossed?"

"How about you undo another button?"

Great, I was about to show the lace of my bra to a pig like Santos. I complied, though I pinched the edges closed and met his icy stare. "How?" I demanded.

He sat, silent, until I released my death grip on my blouse. His Cheshire grin was enough to make my stomach turn. "The money. We got ripped off. Not the first time either."

"Are you telling me the gang unit was shaking you down?"

He nodded. "Still are as far as I know. Cost of doing business, ya know?"

"Thank you, Mr. Santos," I said as I rebuttoned my blouse.

"You got more buttons, I got more answers."

"Thanks, but I got what I needed."

"Me, too," he answered back, grabbing his crotch. "I'll have me some sweet dreams tonight."

I drove home and immediately took a shower. I wanted to wash the prison and Jimmy Santos off me. I knew Liam would be crushed when I told him about my meeting, but I was pretty sure Santos was telling the truth. Not because I thought he was a trustworthy guy, but because of Armando's botched testimony in front of the grand jury. If they'd found three hundred thousand and only turned in fifty thousand of it, where was the rest? Were they all in on it? The only one I could prove had any link to the Latin Bandits was José, and he was dead.

"Maybe Stan figured it out and he was killed to keep him quiet," I mused as I towel-dried my hair before turning on the blow dryer. I pulled on a pair of boxers and button-down knit top before I tossed my Jimmy shirt in the rag pile. It wasn't like I could keep wearing it. It would forever be known as my prison shirt.

I was in the kitchen making myself a very potent cosmo when Liam came back. He looked irritated. "Well?" I asked.

"I hit the usual spots and found out who might be the CI in Garza's case."

"Did you talk to him?"

Liam shook his head. "Seems this kid named Rodney has gone into hiding. Word on the street was there was a thousand-dollar finder's fee for anyone who saw me buy Special K the week José was killed."

"Is that normal?"

Liam shrugged. "Usually we're talking a hundred bucks or so. A grand to a heroin addict is all the money in the world. All

I could get was a description that fits most of the residents of Forty-fifth Street. Tall, lanky, strung out, always looking to score."

I took a long sip of my drink. "I did a little investigating myself."

Liam's head tilted to one side and he gave me an icy glare. "What happened to stay home or go to a public place?"

"I did go to a public place and it was very secure."

"How can you know that?"

"It had razor wire, metal detectors, pat downs, and guards everywhere."

"You went to see Santos?"

I nodded. "He was very helpful."

"He's also a full-of-shit felon who only talked to you so he could get his rocks off."

"That, too," I admitted. "But don't you want to know what I found out?"

"I want to put you over my knee and spank you."

"Sorry, I'm not into that kind of stuff."

The corners of his mouth twitched. "Okay, talk."

I repeated the encounter, sans the parts about unbuttoning my shirt. "I honestly don't think he knows who all was involved. Just that someone was orchestrating raids with large cash deposits that never made it into evidence. Someone or some*ones* were skimming off the top."

Liam came around and got himself a beer. "Santos isn't reliable."

"What did Vasquez say when you saw him?"

"Lots of profanity. He was a dead end."

"So all we really know is that José had a history with the

Latin Bandits and my guess is neither you nor Stan Cain was in on it. That's why Stan was killed."

"Then why kill José if he was the inside man?"

"I haven't figured that out yet," I admitted. "Maybe José wasn't alone in skimming. Maybe he was in it with other officers and for some reason, they had to shut him up. Think maybe Garza might know if there was some sort of secret investigation going on?"

"If he did, he wouldn't have pressed charges against me. He'd never go along with a sham prosecution."

I nodded. "Good point."

Liam placed his barely touched beer on the countertop.

I took an involuntary step backward when he was close. The action didn't go unnoticed, not if his satisfied smirk was any indication.

"Liam," I cautioned as I held up one hand, palm out. "We aren't going to do this. You have stitches."

"We haven't done anything yet and I heal fast. The stitches come out in the morning."

I backed up farther, only to find myself against the cool wall. Liam kept coming, his intense eyes belying the small smile curving his chiseled mouth.

"Please?" I said, not sure what I was asking for.

Without a word, Liam took the glass from my hand and deposited it on the counter. Then he flattened his palms on the wall on either side of my head.

I could smell his musky cologne and hear his slightly uneven breath. There was a smoldering intensity in his eyes that sent a ripple of desire through me.

"Please what?" he asked.

His warm, mint-scented breath washed over my face. Tilting my head back, I searched his eyes beneath the thick outline of his dark lashes.

"I've been very, very patient," he said.

Bending at the waist, Liam leaned forward until his lips barely grazed mine. Wide-eyed, I experienced the first tentative seconds of the kiss through a haze of surprise. The pressure from his mouth increased almost instantly. It was no longer tentative. It was demanding and confident. Apparently fueled by the months of touches and meaningful looks that had punctuated our coexistence. His hands moved slowly, purposefully to my waist. His strong fingers slipped beneath the fabric of my top and came to rest just below the swell of my rib cage. My mouth burned where he incited fires with his expert exploration of my mouth. A sigh inspired by purely animal desire rose in my throat. I was being bombarded with so many sensations at once, one more pleasurable than the last. The callused pad of his thumb brushed the bared flesh at my midriff. His kiss was so thorough, so wonderful that my knees were actually beginning to tremble.

When he pulled away, I very nearly reached out to keep him close to me. It wasn't necessary, he didn't go far. Resting his forehead on mine, I listened to the harmony of our labored breathing.

"What am I going to do with you?" he asked.

"Kissing me is a good place to start."

"I kissed you. You responded. Why have we been pretending?"

"It's not pretending," I said, feeling sad and lonely all of a sudden. "Maybe deep down we both know this isn't such a great idea."

"That," he began as he lifted his head and met my eyes, "is the dumbest thing I've ever heard you say."

Liam wasn't subtle with his second kiss. There was nothing even remotely sweet about it. This kiss was meant to do one thing, convey desire. Even before he pressed his hardness into my belly, I knew he was aroused like he'd never been before. I also knew that I had to keep this from happening, no matter how much I wanted it myself. Sex changes people. The whole relationship becomes tainted. If Liam was my lover, chances were he'd no longer be my friend.

"Don't," I said as I placed my hands flat against his chest and gave a little shove. "This is wrong."

"How can you say that?" he countered. "How can anything this good be wrong?"

"Because it ends," I said on a long breath. "We go along fine for a while, then something happens and we walk away from each other. I want you in my life, and if that means no sex, so be it." I watched him from behind the safety of my lashes.

"Finley." He said my name on a rush of breath. "I don't want to make love to you just for the hell of it."

"Then why?" I asked, truly confused.

He looked at me with eyes so full of tenderness I almost sighed. "I've wanted to do this since the first time I laid eyes on you." He brushed his lips across my forehead. "Because of everything you've done for me."

"Gratitude isn't a good reason to have sex."

"Not gratitude," he insisted as his fingers moved to grip my upper arms. His lips touched mine. His voice deepened to a husky whisper as he continued. "Like it or not, there's more here than just lust." He kissed me lightly. "Do we really have to put a label on it? I love the way you laugh. I love the fire in your eyes when you're angry."

"Liam?" I whispered, feeling my defenses crumble.

"I know it will be incredible between us. Let's just go with that for now."

He kissed me with equal measures of passion and pleading.

"You're confusing me," I admitted.

"I'm trying not to," he said quietly. His hand came up and he captured a lock of my hair between his thumb and forefinger. He silently studied the pale strands, his expression dark and intense.

"I don't know what to do, Liam. I don't want to make a mistake."

"You won't," he promised, his voice low, and definitely seductive.

The sincerity in his voice worked like a vise on my throat. The lump of emotion threatened to strangle me as the moments of silence dragged on.

"We don't even know if we have anything in common."

"Well, I know a good place to start," he countered, his voice rising a notch. "We can deal with the other stuff later," he said as he scooped me up in his arms, cradling me against his solid chest.

Liam carried me down the hall to my bedroom. As if I was some fragile object, he placed me on the bed, gently arranging me against the pillows.

I was silent as I watched him shrug out of his shirt and jeans before joining me on the bed. Through passion-dilated eyes, I took in the impressive sight of him, absently checking to make sure his injury was little more than a faint red line. His body was a true thing of beauty. Rolling on his side, Liam pulled me closer, until I encountered the solid outline of him. His expression was fixed, his mouth little more than a taut line.

"This'll be good, Finley. You'll see," he said as he gently pulled me into the circle of his arms.

It felt so good, so right. I needed this. Closing my eyes, I reminded myself of how many times I'd dreamed of this moment.

I surrendered completely.

Cradling me in one arm, Liam used his free hand to stroke the hair away from my face. I greedily drank in the scent of his cologne as I cautiously allowed my fingers to rest against his thigh. His skin was warm and smooth, a startling contrast to the very defined muscle I could feel beneath my hand. I remained perfectly still, comforted by his scent, his touch, and his nearness. Strange that I could find such solace in his arms. Being here in this room with Liam was enough to erase the uncertainty that had plagued me for days. What could be the harm in just a few hours of the pleasure I knew I could find here? He was right. We could work the rest of the stuff out later.

He tilted my head back until his face was mere fractions of an inch from mine. I could feel the ragged expulsion of his breath. Instinctively, my palms flattened against his chest. The thick mat of dark hair served as a cushion for my touch. Still, beneath the softness, I could easily feel the hard outline of muscle.

"I want you so badly," he said in a near whisper.

My lashes fluttered as his words washed over my upturned face. I needed to hear those words, perhaps even wished for them. Liam's lips tentatively brushed mine. So feather light was the kiss that I wasn't even certain it could qualify as such. His movements were careful, measured. His thumbs stroked the hollows of my cheeks.

Slowly and deliberately he stripped off my shirt and shorts, trailing little kisses everywhere he exposed new skin. With skill and agility, he made quick work of my bra and thong. His dexterity continued as he removed the last barrier of his clothing until we were both gloriously naked.

I banished all thought from my mind. I wanted this, almost desperately. The feel of his hands and his lips made me feel alive. The ache in my chest was changing, evolving, being taken over by some new emotions. I became acutely aware of every aspect of him. The pressure of his thigh where it touched mine. The sound of his uneven breathing. The magical sensation of his mouth kissing me in places I didn't even know needed kissing.

When he lifted his head, I grabbed his broad shoulders. "Don't," I whispered, urging him back to me.

His resistance was both surprising and short-lived. It was almost totally forgotten when he dipped his head. His lips did more than brush against mine. His hands left my face and wound around my body. Liam crushed me against him. I could actually feel the pounding of his heart beneath my hands.

The encounter quickly turned into something intense and consuming. His tongue moistened my parted lips. The kiss became demanding, and I was a very willing participant. I managed to work my hands across his chest, until I felt the outline of his erect nipples beneath my palms. He responded to my action by running his hands all over my back and nibbling my lower lip. It was a purely erotic action, one that inspired great need and desire in me.

A small moan escaped my lips as I kneaded the muscles of his chest. He tasted vaguely of mint and he continued to work magic with his mouth. I felt the kiss in the pit of my stomach. What had started as a pleasant warmth had grown into a full-fledged heat emanating from my very core, fueled by the sensation of his fingers snaking up my back, entwining in my hair and guiding my head back at a severe angle. Passion flared as he hungrily devoured first my mouth, then the tender flesh at the base of my throat. His mouth was hot, the stubble of his beard slightly abrasive. I felt it all. I was aware of everything—the outline of his body, the almost arrogant expectation in his kiss. Liam was obviously a skilled and talented lover. I was a compliant and demanding partner.

This was a wondrous new place for me, special and beautiful. The controlled urgency of his need was a heady thing. It gave me the sense that I had a certain primal power over this man.

He kissed, touched, and tasted until I literally cried out for him. It was no longer a physical act, it was a need. I needed Liam inside me to feel complete.

Poised above me, his brow glistening with perspiration, Liam looked down at me with smoldering, heavy eyes. He waited for me to guide him, then filled me with one long, powerful thrust. Then he moved. Rhythmically, faster and faster, until I was nearly out of my mind.

The sights and sounds around me became a blur as the knot in my stomach wound tighter with each passing minute. Building fiercely until I felt the spasm of satisfaction begin to wrack my body. Liam groaned against my ear as he joined in my release. His hold didn't diminish and he kept placing tiny kisses against my damp brow.

"Told you it would be good," he said without conceit.

"You didn't tell me it would be fantastic," I responded before realizing I'd spoken the words aloud. I felt kind of foolish at the admission.

He fell silent and gently stroked my hair.

I'd never had sex like that. I wasn't even sure if sex was the right word. It was more like a fusion of man and woman, primordial, punctuated by the most mind-blowing orgasm I'd ever experienced. Only now came the hard part. After-sex silence or awkward chitchat? Should I discreetly slip into the bathroom and freshen up, or should I lie there, lingering in his arms? Someone needed to create a manual. *Postcoital etiquette for the woman who probably just blew a great friendship.*

Sometimes the truth hurts—literally.

seventeen

The awkwardness was still there in the morning when I was pouring two mugs of steamy coffee. I couldn't look him in the eyes. Not because we had had sex, but because we had done it twice. My shower had been officially christened.

I was like a tightly wound watch, while Liam was the very picture of relaxed. It's so much easier for guys. That's because they don't dissect every little nuance.

"Are you going to remain silent?" he asked, grinning.

"It's the best plan I've got right now."

"I've got to go to Ashley's place this morning."

I wanted to throw my coffee mug at him. "You're a busy guy."

He sighed. "I'm going over to let the dog out. You can come along if you want. You'd like Perry Mason."

"I'm afraid of dogs."

"Perry is harmless."

"He has teeth, doesn't he?"

"Well, you'll have to meet eventually. I can't leave him at Ashley's forever."

Pass, thanks, on the dog meet and greet. "I have a job," I reminded him. "Tony has something he needs me to do on a case, and I want to take a second look at the guys from your unit. If Santos was telling the truth, someone's sitting on some serious cash."

"And if he was full of crap?"

"Then I'll just have wasted some time." I set my mug in the sink. "Why are you so resistant to the idea that some people on the force could be corrupt?"

"I worked with these guys. Trusted them. Cops have a special bond. We put our lives in each other's hands. It's just hard for me to think they intentionally got me booted from the force. Even harder to imagine that they're responsible for the deaths of Stan and José."

"But they threw you under the bus the first chance they got."

"Now you sound like Ashley. Next thing I know you'll be telling me you think I shot that kid."

"Why would I do that?" I asked, puzzled.

"That was Ashley's theory. She never thought I meant for it to happen, she was just convinced by the evidence and my attorney's suggestion that I take a plea."

"I'm sorry," I said, thinking it was a lame response to what he'd just said.

"It got worse. I spent all the money we'd saved for her salon on my jackass lawyer. Cleaned us out. Ashley had to go back to work in one of those quickie nail salons."

"But things turned out okay. She has her place now."

"That didn't seem like it was in the cards five years ago. She was convinced we'd go bankrupt before I went to prison." He wasn't looking at me anymore. His stare was far off in the distance and his face was devoid of emotion. "She made a decision that ended our marriage."

"Ashley wanted the divorce?"

He scoffed. "I was not a very pleasant person back then. I was mad at the world and she was convenient. We were on shaky ground. She put up a united front for the media, but she had so many doubts. About me. About our future. I realize now I can't blame her for what she did. And I've worked hard to replace every penny we spent on the attorney's fees."

"You're partners?" I asked.

He shook his head. "No. The salon is all hers. I just made good on what I'd taken from her."

"If you don't mind me asking, why? It wasn't like you intentionally blew through your savings. Your career—your *life*—was on the line."

"That's exactly what she said when she told me she'd had an abortion. She said she didn't want to be a single parent raising a kid in poverty. We'd been trying for a baby for a year. It took me a long time to forgive her for that. She never even told me she was pregnant."

"That's a huge thing. But you're past it now."

"It took a while, but we learned to be friends again."

I took a steadying breath. "Friends with benefits?"

His gaze met and held mine. "No," he said with so much clarity something tense subsided in me. "Anything else you want to know?"

I felt my face warm. "Nope, I think I've embarrassed myself enough for one morning."

He laughed. "Why would you be embarrassed?"

"For asking a question I had no business asking."

Liam came around and drew me into a tender embrace. "You can ask me anything."

"Really?" A day ago I had like a zillion questions. Now I could barely remember my own name. I guess things had changed between us. But for how long?

"Sure."

"Could you save this hug for later? I've got to get to work."

He kissed the top of my head. "Consider it a date."

I smiled all the way to work. Who wouldn't? Liam made me happy and it felt like forever since I'd been happy. I was more than happy, I was ecstatic. I didn't even mind Margaret's scowl as I breezed through the lobby and went to my office. I had a message from Tony to meet him in his office in thirty minutes. That gave me plenty of time to send e-mails to Jane, Liv, and Becky to arrange for a lunch. I just had to share my good news.

We made plans to meet at Five Brothers at one.

I gathered up my Travis Johnson material and a pad and headed up to the fourth floor. The executive secretary announced my arrival and I was allowed to walk down the hall to Tony's office.

He looked a little tired. "You okay?" I asked.

"Only if you tell me I have a shrink for Travis."

"He'll be at the detention center at eleven."

"Thank God. I spoke to the prosecutor this morning and

he's out for blood. He really wants that kid tried for murder as an adult."

"Is there anything you need me to do?" I asked.

"How are things going on getting the records on Travis?" he asked.

I shrugged. "DCF will only provide information under subpoena. The school won't release the information without a waiver from the parent or legal guardian, which is DCF. Ditto with the medical records. I filled out the subpoenas and they'll be messengered over this morning. We should have the paperwork in a day or so, then I can get the information. Is there anything else I can do?"

Tony rubbed his hands over his face. "Yeah, I need a miracle."

"Then you're in luck," I said. "I think I have a lead on Liam's case."

Tony sat back in his chair. "Shoot."

"The Latin Bandits had an inside man."

"A cop?" he asked, his interest piqued. "José? He had the tattoo."

"I don't know yet. I was thinking of going to see José's ex-wife to see if she can shed any light on the accusation."

"Just who made this accusation?" Tony asked.

I squirmed a little in my seat. "Jimmy Santos."

He leaned forward. "Please tell me Liam went to see Santos and you didn't ignore my very specific instructions."

"I went to South Bay prison yesterday."

"Jesus, Finley."

"It's a secure facility. I wasn't in any danger. The worst part was getting through security," I lied. No need to tell him I needed to tease Santos with a lacy bra to get him to talk.

"Do I need to staple you to your chair?"

"Not in this skirt. I paid full price," I joked. It didn't seem to help.

"Just so we don't have any more misunderstandings, stay away from high-security prisons. Besides, Santos would lie about his own mother just for the fun of it."

"But," I argued, "why lie about being ripped off? According to Santos, every time there was a bust, cash went missing."

"According to Santos. And he's not very reliable."

"Then let me talk to the ex–Mrs. Lopez."

He was shaking his head. "I doubt she'll want to talk to a paralegal representing the man who is accused of killing José."

"They're divorced. Maybe she won't care. At least let me try."

"Fine. But no one else. Let me or Liam handle talking to the cops."

"Fair enough." Good thing he didn't know I had hand-delivered the letters. Although he might find it helpful to know Armando hid from me and the others all met me with hostility.

Once I was back at my office, I decided to dig a little deeper into the lives of the officers in the gang unit. I started with José Lopez only because I had a suspicion that whatever was going on had started with him. He was the only one I could tie directly to the Latin Bandits.

José was divorced, so I used LexisNexis to get information from the pleadings. It wasn't a typical divorce. Mrs. Lopez got it all. And I mean all. The house in Ibis, the car, the boat, and the kids. What she didn't get was alimony. And I think I knew why. Alimony is taxable, so instead José was paying a ton in child support. It didn't look good. I added up the figures and José's expenditures far exceeded his salary. I also checked the property records and discovered José and his wife had bought the house in Ibis at the height of the real estate boom. On first blush, the house was now valued in the low three hundreds. But when they purchased it, the price was a hefty six hundred and seventy-five. They'd put down a 70 percent deposit, and up until the time of his death, José was paying the mortgage plus the rent on his house in Riviera Beach.

Now that I knew something about the scam, I rechecked the other officers' assets. All had bought expensive properties using hefty down payments so their mortgages were in line with their income. The homes were well out of their price ranges. Well, everyone but Stan Cain. He and his wife had a nice ranch in the Acreage with a tax base of one hundred and ninety thousand. Whatever was going on, Stan wasn't involved. Which was probably what got him killed.

I dialed Liam's cell. "Hey," he answered.

"Are you in a tunnel?" I asked.

"You're on speakerphone. I'm heating up moo shu unless you've got a better offer."

"Sorry, lunch with the girls."

"Too bad. What's up?"

"I know how they were hiding the money."

"Who?"

"All of them. Well, except Stan Cain." I explained how they had all invested in homes, boats, and cars and put assets in their wives' names. It was really quite creative. Liam was quiet for a moment. "Liam?"

"I'm here," he said. "José was the leak. The other guys must have caught on and taken a cut."

"I know what they did with the money, I just don't know how it actually worked."

"Pretty well, obviously. I didn't even get a whiff of it when I was in the unit."

"I'm guessing they were afraid you'd catch on, so that's why they set you up for the Peña shooting."

"Sons of bitches."

"How did a raid work? Who would have had knowledge of it?"

"Depended on who got a tip or who had the intel."

"Then what?"

"We'd type out a probable-cause document to get the no-knock warrants from the judge."

"Was it always the same judge?" I asked, excited.

"No. It was whoever was up in rotation."

"So they had to coordinate things themselves. Maybe one of them shared that with a wife or a girlfriend."

"I wouldn't," he said. "Marriages go south."

"Well, they had to know *something*. They're all living like queens, even the divorced ones. I'm going to see if I can get Ina Lopez to talk to me."

"Good luck. If I remember correctly, she's shy and not comfortable with strangers."

"All I need is one person to tell the truth and the whole scheme falls apart."

"And you put a target on your back. Maybe now would be a good time for you to step back. Finley, I don't want anything to happen to you."

"That makes two of us. Why don't you come with me? But stay in the car. I doubt she'll speak freely with the man accused of killing the father of her children."

"What time?"

"Give me a few hours. Say, two thirty. Meet me here at the office."

◆

"Really?"

"You did?"

"Well, it's about freaking time," Becky said before taking a sip of her iced tea.

Jane looked positively giddy, while Liv wore an I-told-you-so smirk. The restaurant was hopping and we'd waited ten minutes for a table. Since I had no excuse for a prolonged absence from the office, and I was going out that afternoon, I had no choice but to stick to the one-hour rule overseen by Maudlin Margaret. She ate her lunch in the firm's lunchroom and proudly exclaimed to one and all that she took a mere fifteen minutes to eat.

You pay me for lunch, I'm taking lunch.

"Was it amazing?" Liv asked.

"No details," I answered with a straight face. Then added, "It was better than amazing."

"Your place or his?" Jane asked.

"Mine, why?"

"If you do it at his place, you can check his drawers and stuff while he's in the shower."

"Jane Spencer! When did you get so sneaky?"

"When I woke up next to a dead guy. Now I'm not taking any guy back to my place unless I've run a full background check on him."

Becky took a bite of her burger, then said, "I don't think I remember what sex is like."

I smiled. "That's because you work eighty hours a week."

"No," she countered. "It's because the only people more loathed than lawyers are tow truck drivers and I haven't met one of those yet."

"I'm telling you," Liv added. "Go for the young guys. They always want sex."

"Your young guy still lives at home," I said pointedly.

"He's an artist. He's trying to get established."

Becky scoffed. "He's sold one painting and that was to you."

As usual, Liv was drawing the attention of every man who entered the place. Her unusual beauty had that effect on the opposite sex. It also had a downside. Whenever the four of us went out, it was Liv who was never asked to dance. I guess men were afraid of being shot down by the prettiest girl in the room.

"I heard you went to prison," Becky said.

"For an interview," I clarified. Then I shared what I knew to date.

"Shouldn't Tony be doing this legwork?" Liv asked.

"He's got a client with immediate needs. A thirteen-year-old he's trying to keep out of adult court."

"The kid who stabbed his father to death?" Jane asked.

I nodded. "But it isn't that simple."

"It is for the dead guy," Becky said.

"I'm waiting for school records, medical records, and records from Child Protective Services. Tony and a shrink are with him now."

"This is depressing," Liv said. "Let's get back to Finley and Liam. Where is this going?"

I shrugged. "I wish I knew."

"The Ashley factor?" Jane asked.

I shook my head. "No. He explained all that to me."

"Do tell," Liv urged.

I shook my head again. "Not for public consumption. I don't think Liam would appreciate my broadcasting his past. He's kind of secretive that way."

"But he told you," Becky pointed out. "That implies trust."

"He wants me to meet his dog," I said with a definite lack of enthusiasm. "I guess that's a step in the right direction."

"So you can get bitten on the butt again?" Jane teased.

"My point exactly. It's the Liam version of meeting the folks. Swears I'll love the thing." That would be a miracle. Fear trumps everything.

"You might," Liv suggested. "At least give it a try."

"The dog could be a deal breaker," Jane said.

"We don't have a deal," I told them.

"What do you call a guy who's living at your house and who you're sleeping with?"

"I don't know. That's the problem." I checked my watch. "I've got to get back."

"A Margaret bed check?" Becky teased. As a firm attorney, the rules didn't apply to her.

"Yes. I wish she'd take a vacation. She's got to have about a year's worth saved up. I'll see you guys later." I stood and wadded my trash into its wrapper. "Oh, Jane, before I forget, I bought a couple of watch parts on eBay."

"Finley?" she warned.

"Gotta go," I said as I quickly left the restaurant.

Once I was back at work, I made a copy of Liam's signature from his DMV records and added the copy of the sign-out sheet I'd taken from the files then sent them by courier to the expert we used when we had to verify signatures on will or estate documents. He was good and he was quick. If Liam wasn't on his way I would have walked them over to Darrell's office myself; it was only four blocks away.

Instead I handed it to Margaret. "This needs to go right away," I told her.

She took out her trusty pad. "What's the name of the client?"

"Liam McGarrity," I told her.

She met my answer with a pointed stare. "He's one of Tony's clients," I said. "If you've got a problem, take it up with him."

She pursed her lips and wrote the name down as if she was signing her own death warrant.

I saw Liam standing by my car, which I'd carefully parked next to Vain Dane's Hummer. I still didn't understand why he needed an urban assault vehicle in the flattest state in the union. I guessed it made him feel powerful.

Briefcase and keys in hand, I left the building. Liam was smiling at me. "Hi," he greeted me. "How was lunch with the girls?"

"Interesting," I said, not wanting to tell him the sordid details.

"You have Ina's address?" he asked.

I nodded. "Let's take my car. Fewer toxic fumes." I went to hand him my keys but dropped them. In unison we bent to pick them up, knocking heads in the process. It must have been a hard knock because I heard a buzzing sound whoosh by my ear. Then my brain processed the sound of breaking glass.

Liam reacted, tackling me and shoving me between the two cars, shielding me with his body. The air rushed from my lungs. I heard something ping off the pavement and Liam half-rolled off me and cursed.

"I don't suppose you own a gun?" he asked.

"Why would I own a gun?"

"Because someone is shooting at us."

It's always good to know you're needed
but even better to know you're wanted.

eighteen

In what felt like an eternity but was probably only a matter of minutes, several squad cars arrived on the scene. It was only then that Liam and I stood up, still shielded for the most part by my car.

I'd started to brush my hair off my face when I felt a sharp pain in my palm. I looked down and saw a ragged piece of glass sticking out from where blood trickled from the wound. I looked at Liam, hardly able to hear over the pounding of my heart and the very real sensation of wanting to wet myself. I was shaking as he took my hand. "It's not deep," he assured me.

His dark hair glistened from the shower of glass and I could hear the siren of an ambulance coming closer. I glanced over at my office building and noticed several faces pressed up against the windows.

"Ma'am?"

I turned toward the sound of the voice. It was a deputy,

around my age, and he was securing his gun back in the holster on his hip. "What?"

"Are you hurt?"

I looked at my hand, then back at him. "Not really."

"Sir?" he asked Liam.

He shook his head. "But I think she might be going into shock."

He wrapped his arms around me. I was shaking like a leaf. "What just happened?" I asked.

"Someone shot at us."

"Which one of us?" I said, my voice trembling.

"Don't worry about that now," he said as a gloved paramedic appeared at my side.

"Let's go to the ambulance," he said.

First they wrapped me in a blanket and then they put an oxygen mask over my face. Only then did they inspect the cut on my palm. With relative ease and a very long pair of tweezers, they removed the thick piece of glass and assessed my wound. Someone else was taking my vitals. I only knew that because of the pinch on my arm as the blood pressure cuff inflated. My stomach was doing flip-flops when Becky appeared at the opened ambulance doors.

"Is she okay?" Becky asked the paramedic.

I was lightheaded and felt as if I couldn't gulp in enough air to sustain life.

"BP is 107 over 45," one paramedic said to the other.

"Ma'am. We're going to take you to the hospital as a precaution. Do you understand?"

I nodded.

"I'll follow you," Liam said

I spent an hour in the emergency room. Most of it with a CNA gently combing glass out of my hair. My clothes were smudged with dirt and I had road rash on one knee. Liam stayed at my side while a deputy stood watch at the edge of the curtain. The wound to my left hand was shallow and required nothing more than a butterfly bandage. I was finally able to breathe again but the shaking still hadn't abated.

"Your color is coming back," Liam said as soon as we were alone.

"Getting shot at isn't an everyday occurrence for me."

"That's a good thing," he said as he gently kissed my wounded palm. "The cops want to talk to us."

"I can't tell them anything."

The curtain yanked open and Tony entered the small cubicle. "Are you both okay?" he asked in a rush of breath.

I nodded while Liam answered, "She's shaken up pretty bad."

"I'm staying while you give your statements."

"I have nothing to state," I reiterated.

"Deputy?" Tony called. And a uniformed cop stepped inside.

Tony said, "Tell the detectives Miss Tanner and Mr. McGarrity are available."

The officer spoke into the radio clipped to his shoulder.

Much to my displeasure, Metcalf and Wells arrived a few minutes later. Wells looked sympathetic, while Metcalf was his usual churlish self.

"We'd like to interview them separately," Metcalf said.

"Then you'll have to do it one at a time," Tony said. "I represent Mr. McGarrity, and Miss Tanner is my employee, so I need to be sure you don't ask her for privileged information."

Metcalf sighed. "Fine. Miss Tanner, you go first. Can you describe what happened in the parking lot?"

"I dropped my keys. I went to pick them up and then I heard a whoosh and Liam pushed me to the ground. We were showered with glass. That kinda all happened at one time. Then I heard a ping. Then nothing."

"So you didn't see the shooter or where the shots came from?"

I shook my head. "I didn't even know they were shots. It all happened too fast."

"So you don't know whether the person was shooting at you or Mr. McGarrity?"

"No."

Metcalf turned his attention to Liam. "Are you going to tell me the same story?"

"Pretty much. I didn't hear the shots, so I'm thinking it was a sniper rifle."

"I'm not interested in your theories. Just the facts," Metcalf chastised.

"The facts are that someone was shooting at one of us. Or both."

Wells cleared his throat. "Any idea why?"

Liam took in a breath and let it out slowly. "It's the second time in a week someone's taken a shot at me."

"Miss Tanner?" Wells prompted. "Anyone angry at you? An ex-boyfriend? A client?"

I looked up at Tony. He gave me a nod. "Not that I know of. I did get a threatening e-mail about a week ago."

"From?"

"The best I could do was trace it back to an Internet café. I have no idea who sent it or why."

"What did it say?" Metcalf asked, actually sounding curious.

"'Wanna die, bitch?'" I quoted.

"Did you report this incident?"

"It didn't seem important. I assumed it was just some jerk I'd met at a bar with too much time on his hands."

"Do you often aggravate men in bars?" Metcalf asked.

I gave him a screw-you look. "No. But if I sense a guy is a jerk, I don't encourage him."

"Do you have any names for these men?"

"Of course not. That's the point in blowing someone off. And before you ask, no, I don't know how anyone would get my name, let alone my e-mail address."

"We'd like to take a look at your computer."

"Not gonna happen," Tony said. "Miss Tanner often works on her laptop. That makes it attorney work product and therefore privileged."

"Don't you want to get the guy who shot at you?"

"No," Tony said. "She wants you to get the guy."

"What about you, Mr. McGarrity? Piss anyone off lately?"

"Um, you."

Wells fought back a smile.

"Aside from me?"

"I had a little talking to with—"

"Privileged," Tony cut in. "Mr. McGarrity is under no obligation to tell you what he's been doing to aid in his defense of the bogus charges against him. Since he's been shot at a second time, perhaps you'll want to rethink the charges."

"That's Garza's call," Metcalf said. "But I'll pass along your request."

"If we have any more questions, where can we reach you?"

Liam and I both provided our cell phone numbers and the detectives went on their way. I don't know what I expected, but it wasn't to be left hanging, knowing someone wanted me dead.

"What do we do now?" I asked Tony.

"It would help if we knew which one of you was the target."

"My money's on me," Liam said. "It would be too coincidental for Finley and me both to attract a gunman in the space of one week."

"Then you have to go someplace," I insisted. "Someplace no one will know where to find you."

He shook his head. "Not my style."

"I know your style," Tony said. "Carrying a concealed weapon is a violation of the conditions of your bond. If you get caught, Finley could lose a big chunk of money."

"I don't care about the money," I said. "I want Liam to be safe."

"Finley, do you have an alarm system?"

"Yes."

"Then I think the two of you should stay there until we figure out someplace safe," Tony said.

"Can you take her home?" Liam asked. "I have an errand."

"Liam?" I practically whined.

"Nothing dangerous. Promise."

"Can I get my car?" I asked.

Tony nodded. "I'll follow you and stay until Liam gets there."

"Wait," I said. "That's asking too much. What if something happens? What about Izzy?"

"Then stay here," Liam said. "I'll be back in an hour."

"I have a job," I reminded him.

"Which is on hold," Tony said.

"But Ellen and Mr. Dane . . ."

"Ellen agrees and Victor is so pissed about his car that he doesn't really want to see you right now."

"Pissed about his car?"

"The glass that shattered came from the Hummer. The second bullet dinged his bumper."

I slouched forward. "Great. He'll probably take the repair costs out of my check."

Tony laughed. "You leave that to me. I'll stay here with you until Liam gets back."

♦

"I'm not sure I want to go back to the scene of the crime," I said as Liam drove me back to Dane-Lieberman.

"You have to get your car."

"Why? We have yours. Such as it is."

"Just trust me. Stay off the phone. Drive directly home." His tone was strident and his expression was tense.

"You're scaring me."

He reached over and gave my hand a gentle squeeze. "Don't be scared. I'll be with you."

But for how long? I wondered. Oh great, now I was *that* girl. The one who puts a stopwatch on a relationship. Only I was worse. I wasn't even sure if we had a relationship. Maybe for Liam it was just sex. But then again, he was so attentive and caring. Maybe because he wanted more sex. Inside my head was a lost and confused world.

The parking lot was devoid of glass as Liam swung into the place next to my Mercedes. "Here," he said as he reached under the driver's seat and produced a small but lethal-looking gun.

"I don't want that!"

"I don't care. Take it."

"The only time I ever fired a gun I missed by like ten yards."

"This," he said as he pulled out a portion of the grip. "This is the clip. I have extras. You just tap it in and pull back like this." He did something that made the gun click. "Now there's a bullet in the chamber. This," he said as he pointed to a small lever by the trigger. "Is the safety. This is on, this is off. Put it in your purse."

"I don't want a gun."

"Would you rather get shot?" he asked.

I couldn't argue with that logic. Of course I didn't want to get shot. "How am I supposed to shoot at someone I can't see? Didn't you say it was a sniper?"

"Yeah. It was a desperate move. One I don't think they'll repeat."

"Who are *they*?"

"Not sure yet."

"Great, so I could end up shooting the FedEx guy."

"Let's hope not. Now drive and don't say a word. Blast the music and stay off the phone."

"Why?"

"I have a theory, but we have to get to your place first."

"Why?"

"Just trust me."

"Okay."

The shaking started again once I was behind the wheel of my car. I kept checking the rearview, making sure Liam was right behind me. Still, every time a car passed me I had to fight the urge to duck. I was very happy when we finally reached my place. At least there I knew I had an alarm and Tony had called the Palm Beach police and asked them to make periodic drive-bys.

Before we went inside, Liam placed his finger to his mouth and shushed me. As soon as we were inside, he reset the alarm and pulled a black box out of the backpack he'd brought in. He turned on the stereo and blasted it so loudly I could feel the bass in my back teeth.

I stood by while he extended an antenna and started scanning my living room. It beeped like one of those metal detectors people used on the beach. When the beeps got closer together, he followed that direction. His first stop was my television. From behind the bracket, he pulled a small black button with a wire that looked exactly like the one I'd found at José's house. He repeated the same steps in every room and closet until he had a total of six of them in his hand. He motioned for me to kill the alarm, then he opened the back slider, walked to the water's edge, and threw all of them into the Atlantic.

He came back and we reset the alarm. "How did you know someone was listening to us?" I asked.

"Too much of a coincidence that we agreed to meet at a

certain time and a shooter was in place. Where's your electrical box?"

"Guest room closet. Why?"

He didn't answer so I followed him down the hall and into the bedroom. He opened the breaker box and there was an open slot. "Now we know why your motion sensors aren't working. You don't have a spare breaker, do you?"

I shook my head. "Harold did all the electrical."

"Did you call your alarm company?"

I nodded. "They're supposed to send someone out tomorrow to fix the problem."

"They'll have a breaker. Got a flashlight?" he asked.

"It's daylight," I said.

"Flashlight?"

He followed me back to the kitchen. "Here."

"I've got to go outside for a minute. Turn the alarm on while I'm out there."

"Don't go outside," I pleaded.

"It'll just take me a second," he said. Then he pulled up the leg of his jeans enough for me to see the gun he had strapped to his ankle.

He went outside and got next to his car, then turned on the flashlight and scooted beneath the Mustang. True to his word, he was back out from under the car quickly, then he went to the Dumpster and attached something to the side.

"What was that?"

"A GPS tracker. That's why they flattened your tires. You have a car alarm, I don't. By forcing us to use my car, they could follow us everywhere."

"And the window smashes?"

"My guess is they did a couple of houses before yours to throw the locals off the track. Do you all use the same alarm company?"

"I think so."

"Then they waited around and got the response time."

"So they knew how long they had to plant listening devices in my house."

"Right," he said as he bent down and gave me a kiss.

"Oh my God!"

"What?" he asked in a near panic.

"They heard us having sex." I know I must have turned eight shades of red.

Liam laughed. "I'm sure it wasn't as good for them as it was for me."

Never trust anyone who lies to you.
Never lie to anyone who trusts you.

nineteen

Tony called to check in just as the afternoon news was starting. Of course, the shooting at Dane-Lieberman was the lead story. I could only imagine what that was doing to Vain Dane. He was probably thinking of ways to kill me. Well, he'd have to get in line.

"Have you had a chance to talk to Garza yet?" I asked.

"I've got a call in," Tony said.

"Surely once he hears what Jimmy Santos had to say, plus the shooting, he'll have to see that Liam isn't responsible for José Lopez's death."

"We have a problem with Santos."

"If he won't talk, I can testify as to what he said to me. It's a statement against his interests and therefore admissible."

"In a case against Santos," Tony agreed.

"Well, Santos was running a criminal enterprise. Surely Garza can come up with some sort of charge to hold over his head."

"It isn't Garza who's the problem. It's Santos. He's dead."

"Dead?" I asked, stunned. "I thought he was some bigwig in the Latin Bandits. How could he get killed?"

"By an even bigger wig."

"Does the Department of Corrections have any suspects?"

"They're treating this like an NHI."

"NHI?"

"No humans involved. Santos was responsible for a lot of murders. He was a dirtbag, so we shouldn't expect there to be much of an investigation. Besides, hits inside prisons are, unfortunately, common. I'm surprised Santos made it this long. Usually when the youngbloods move in on the outside, the ones on the inside have a magical way of getting dead."

I needed a diversion. "What happened with Travis Johnson and the shrink?" I asked.

"He was severely abused. How long will it take to get those records?"

"They should come back this week. Just make sure Margaret knows to give them to you or else she'll bury them in my in-box."

"How are you and Liam holding up?"

I told him all about the listening devices. "I'm now creeped out in my own home."

"Maybe the two of you should get out of town."

"Liam can't leave the county."

"I can go see the judge about that. It definitely qualifies as a change in circumstances."

"Would you?" I asked. Not so much for myself, but I knew Liam. He wasn't the type to sit around and wait for something to happen. He was just too proactive.

"First thing in the morning," he promised, then hung up.

Liam came down the hallway, shirtless and drying his hair with a towel. My nerves might be shot, but my libido was just fine, thank you very much. I couldn't help but admire the ripple of muscle, broad shoulders, and thick mat of dark hair that veered downward like a big arrow pointing to the good stuff. I also noticed the scar was healing nicely.

I turned away before he caught me gawking. I'd already showered and changed into some drawstring pants and a T-shirt. Unlike my normal routine, I'd reapplied makeup. Liam and I weren't yet to the no-makeup stage in our relationship. I wasn't exactly sure where we were. Just that we definitely had the sex part covered.

"Who called?" he asked.

"Checking up on me?" I joked.

"Just making conversation. You don't have to answer."

"Lighten up, Liam. It was Tony. He was just making sure everything was okay and give me the news that Santos was killed in prison after speaking to me."

Liam's hand stilled. "Santos is dead?"

"Yep."

"Suspects?"

"No, and Tony isn't holding out much hope that there will be much more than a cursory investigation. He thinks we should get out of town for a while. I'm game."

"Good. Go pack a bag and we'll take you anywhere," he said as he pulled me into his arms. As wonderful as that was, I ducked away and went to the kitchen to take stock. It was a sad state of affairs. "I hope you like Lucky Charms," I said.

"Why?"

"It's that or mustard. I'm not terribly good at grocery shopping."

"We can get takeout," he suggested.

"Is that smart?"

"Only if you know a delivery guy on sight, which I'm guessing you do."

"Then chicken or Chinese?"

"Chicken."

I lifted the phone off its cradle and pressed the speed-dial number assigned to my favorite rotisserie place. I ordered a chicken and two sides. "Dinner will arrive in about a half hour."

"That's just about enough time to—"

"Think north of your waistband or I'll start to think you're only here for the sex."

"The sex is a plus."

We sat on the sofa and I muted the news. "Don't the police use listening devices?" I asked.

"Yeah. But you have to sign them in and out with the undercover unit. Besides, the one from José's was traced back to a store here. The police don't order devices one at a time. They buy the things by the gross."

"So the ones here and the one at José's weren't police issue." My mind was spinning with the sensation that I was missing something right in front of my nose.

Liam wrapped the towel around his shoulders. "Definitely not. Besides, if they were department issue, you'd need to expand your conspiracy theory to include about twenty more guys."

"There's no way to find out who bought them?"

He shrugged. "I guess I could go back to the store in Wellington with pictures."

"You're not going anywhere."

"I'm not going to be a sitting duck."

"So you'll leave me here alone?"

"No. I'll figure something out."

"What? A babysitter with an Uzi?"

"There's a thought," he teased as he took my hand in his. "I've got a guy I throw some work when I'm too busy. I trust him."

"Is he an ex-cop, too?"

He shook his head. "Nope. Ex-special forces. His name's Paul Booker. Good guy."

"That still doesn't solve the problem of you putting yourself out there in harm's way. I'd feel better if you stayed here with me."

"I will," he said as he kissed my hand. "Most of the time."

"So when do I meet this guy?"

"Soon. I've already called him. He's up to speed."

The doorbell rang and for some dumb reason I leapt over the sofa and cowered in a huddled ball. I heard Liam get off the sofa and walk to the front window. "You can come out now. There's a car here with a big chicken on the top."

Dragging my humiliation with me, I moved toward the door. Liam was standing there with a gun at his side. "I thought you said it was okay?" I whispered.

"Just being cautious," he said as he stood behind me when I opened the door a crack.

"Hi, Miss Finley."

"Hi, Frankie. How are you tonight?" I asked as I pressed the code on the alarm so I could leave the door open.

"Great. You?"

"Dandy. Hang on and let me get my wallet." I went to the kitchen counter and opened my purse. The gun stared back at me. Note to self, the next time you hide, take the gun with you.

I gave Frankie a generous tip and took the bag. Liam closed the door, locked the dead bolt, and reset the alarm. "Smells great," he said.

I took plates down and put out utensils before I unloaded the chicken, potatoes, and spinach. "Hope this is okay," I said. "I probably should have asked you if you liked spinach."

"It's fine. The only thing I don't eat is sushi."

"That's a problem. I love sushi."

"That's why you have Becky, Liv, and Jane."

"Point taken. I also have my mother."

"The shooting was on the news. Why hasn't she called to make sure you're okay?"

I blew out a breath. "It's complicated. You saw her at the wedding. Did it seem to you like we were close?"

"Not really. But I thought she was just . . . distracted."

I smiled. "She is now. She's set her sights on husband number six. Or is it five? Whatever. I'm sure she has other things on her mind right now."

"If you want to call her, I can give you privacy."

"If you want to stay my friend, you won't make suggestions like that."

We were quiet as we ate. Apparently, getting shot at works

up an appetite. "There's more chicken," I said, passing him the container.

"You sure?"

I pushed my plate away. "Yes. I'm full."

"I'm not," he said as he finished up the remaining food.

Just as I started to clear the dishes, my cell rang. While I was on the line, Liam placed a distracting series of kisses along my neck. I swatted him away but it did no good. He kept flustering me until I hung up the phone.

"Don't do that," I said halfheartedly.

"I like to watch you squirm."

"Well, you'll like this even better. That was Darrell."

His eyebrows pinched. "Darrell who?"

"He does handwriting analysis for us," I explained. "Your signature on the sign-out sheet is a forgery."

"Which sign-out sheet?" he asked.

"The week before José was killed he signed out your gun and the document has you signing as the registered owner. Only you didn't sign it."

"José did?" he asked.

I shrugged my shoulders. "Darrell can only tell if a signature is real. Without an exemplar of the forger's handwriting, he can't tell me anything more than that."

"Can we get exemplars from the other team members?"

"It won't help," I explained. "Not with a tracing. When someone traces a name, the way they tell is in the flow of the ink. People aren't fluid when they're copying something, so all the examiner can tell is that there were starts and stops in the questioned document."

"So our best bet is still the spy store in Wellington?"

"And talking to Ina Lopez. Which reminds me—didn't Cain's wife say Stan was transferred out of the gang unit after the Peña grand jury?"

Liam nodded. "José went to traffic division."

"So if Stan and José were both out of the unit, that would mean someone else was the inside man. Or men."

Liam stood and took a shirt out of his duffel bag and pulled it on, buttoning the buttons as I watched with unabashed interest. Here I was, center stage in a murder plot, and I was thinking about his biceps.

"If you were going to play both sides, what would you do?" I asked Liam.

"I wouldn't."

I rolled my eyes. "Pretend. We're tossing around ideas here. What would it have taken for you to betray your friends?"

"If someone had something on me. Something that would end my career or my marriage."

I stroked my chin. "Maybe that's how they got José to turn. Would the police force hire a former gang member for the gang unit?"

Liam shook his head. "Not if he had a record or some other thing that would have deemed him unfit for service."

"Like?"

"A bad psych eval. Any arrest. Juvie problems. You'd be amazed by the number of fruitcakes who want to join the force."

"But aren't most juvie records sealed?" I asked.

"Depending on the crime and the whim of the judge, but yes, usually."

I got up and grabbed my laptop. After logging in to Lexis-Nexis I tried searching for José's name. I came up empty. "This isn't going to work," I told Liam. "Is he from Palm Beach County?"

"Miami, I think. But I'm not sure."

"We've got to talk to his widow, or whatever you call the ex-wife of a dead guy."

Liam shook his head. "We are not leaving this house. Besides, Booker and a friend are coming over in a little while."

"So you can do what?"

"I thought I might go see my old buddy Deputy Young."

"The gun cage guy? Going out in the dark is just plain stupid."

"But necessary," Liam countered. "I can handle myself."

"But—" I was cut off by the sound of Liam's cell ringing.

He covered the receiver and mouthed "Garza." I sat quietly while he grunted "uh-hum" and "yeah" into the phone. "Thank you for calling," he said, then ended the call. "They got the shooter."

I felt relief wash over me. "Really? That fast?"

"Someone called in to Crime Stoppers. Led them right to the guy."

"Did he say why he was shooting at us?"

Liam's expression hardened. "He was shot at the scene after he got off a few rounds. DOA."

"Do they know who it was at least?"

"Low-level member of the Latin Bandits. He had ID on him and he had the tattoo."

"Well, that should convince Garza to drop the charges against you."

"The shooter had something else, Finley."

"What?"

"A picture of you. You were the target."

Liam held me until I stopped shaking. "Garza is going to talk to Tony about relocating you until this is over."

"Why just me?" I asked, terrified. "I only feel safe when you're around."

"I know but—" His phone rang again and he cursed before answering.

I heard him giving directions to my house. As soon as he hung up he said, "That was Booker, he's on his way. Can you get me a current address for Deputy Young?"

Reluctantly I went to my laptop and pulled up the information I'd e-mailed myself when I'd done the research at the office. According to the records, he didn't really have a home address. "It just says slip nineteen, Singer Island Marina," I said.

"That's good enough," Liam told me. "He won't be hard to find."

"I wish you wouldn't do this," I said quietly.

"I have to," he replied as the doorbell rang.

At least this time I didn't dive for cover, but I did cower behind Liam as he checked out the window, then hit the alarm pad.

He opened the door to a giant human being with a military brush cut and arms the size of cannons. He was well over six feet, with muscles on top of muscles. And he wasn't alone. Standing next to him was a very large dog with its tail wagging.

"Hey, boy," Liam said as he bent and scratched the dog behind the ears. "Booker," he said, acknowledging the man. "In," he told the dog, then Booker followed, dropping the leash and adjusting the large sack of dog food beneath his arm and a small black duffel looped over his shoulder.

The dog entered and started sniffing everything. I was praying he wouldn't pee on my expensive furniture. "Why is a dog here?" I asked as I automatically backed into a corner, hoping not to be noticed by the pony-size animal.

"Think of Perry as a backup alarm," Liam said. "If anyone comes near this house, he'll let you know it."

"If he doesn't eat me first," I grumbled.

"I'm Booker," the huge man said as he shook my hand, swallowing it completely with his beefy fingers.

"Finley," I said, though my eyes remained fixed on Cujo.

Liam noticed my discomfort and called the dog over. "Sit," he said. The dog did as instructed. "Shake," he said and the dog offered me his large paw. "Now it's your turn," he said to me.

"My turn to do what?"

"Give him a command."

"Like what?"

Liam was grinning at me. "Perry, be dead." The dog fell over in a heap. "Now you."

"Perry, sit," I said unsteadily. The dog complied.

"See, gentle as ever so long as he knows you're a friend."

"What if he gets confused?" I asked.

"He won't. Booker will be in the guest room and Perry will be right next to you on the floor when I'm not around. Between the two of them, you'll be perfectly safe."

Great, big man with gun and big dog with teeth. When did my life go to shit?

No matter how much I begged, I couldn't convince Liam to refrain from going to see retired Deputy Young. Knowing the sign-out sheet was a forgery was pressing him on. At least he took his gun and his cell phone. That made it seem a little less stupid.

Booker turned out to be the strong, silent type. No matter what I asked, he managed to answer with a single word. The dog was more animated than the man. Wanting to make sure Perry Mason was happy, I went into my room and filled a sock with an old pair of hose, then tied a knot. I returned to the living room and played with him. He was like a small child. My arm was tired of tossing it in the air for him to catch, but he wasn't even winded. We were warming up to each other. Mainly because he hadn't jumped up on any of my furniture. One stray hair and we'd have issues.

"Shouldn't Liam have called by now?" I asked Booker.

"Maybe."

He was so not helpful.

"How long does it take to talk to one guy?" I asked as I glanced at the clock on the end table. "He's been gone for two hours." Alarm sounded in my head. "What if he's hurt? Or what if he got caught with the gun?" I had a hundred and fifty thousand reasons to be worried about that. Though the money didn't matter much when I thought of Liam hurt or worse. "I'm calling him," I announced.

"Not a good idea."

"Too damned bad," I replied as I grabbed my cell and dialed.

Liam answered quickly but quietly. "What?"

"Where are you?"

"Young's boat."

"What did he say?"

"Nothing. He's not here."

"Then get out of there before he comes back."

"I don't think that'll be a problem."

"Why not?"

"This place is covered in blood."

The cure for boredom is curiosity,
but there is no cure for curiosity.

twenty

The dog whimpered and his ears straightened. I immediately sat up in bed. I didn't hear a sound, but Perry Mason got up and started toward the living room. Very quietly, I took the gun out of my bedside table and prayed my hands would be steady.

As soon as I reached the hallway, a large arm came out and shoved me back inside. Booker held one finger up to keep me silent. Like I could talk over the lump of terror in my throat.

Perry Mason barked once, then I heard the front door open. Booker had a gun out and he held his elbows locked, with the gun pointing in the direction of the living room.

"It's me!" Liam called.

My pulse stopped thudding in my ears.

I put the gun back and walked out to join Liam, Booker, and my new best friend Perry in the living room. Liam looked sexy and disheveled. Well, except for the blood smears on his hands. "What have you been doing all this time?" I asked as he went to the sink to wash up.

"I was going over Deputy Young's things," he said. "Discovered he had a habit of taping stuff under drawers."

"Is he dead?" I asked.

"Based on the amount of blood, I'd say yes."

Liam came over to my coffee table and took several blood-spattered pages from his back pocket. Carefully, he unfolded them and lined them up in a row.

"That guy looks familiar," I said as I pointed to the mug shot of a kid in his teens holding an informational card at chest height. The sign said GARCIA, JOSÉ.

"It's a younger version of José," Liam explained. "Taken in 1993 in New York."

I studied the picture. "How do you know that? Is the information on the back?"

"Look at the sign he's holding up. See the NYPD and then the number, 933682? The first two digits are the year. The last four are his ID numbers."

"So how does a criminal from New York named José Garcia become a sheriff's deputy in Florida as José Lopez?"

"That's something I was hoping you could work your magic on," he said to me. "Can you track him, or whatever it is you do on your computer?"

"Maybe. But I can do more on my machine at work."

Booker spoke up. "I've got a contact with the NYPD, maybe he can help."

"Great," Liam said. "Can you call him right now?"

"It's one thirty in the morning," I reminded Liam.

"Cops work shifts. He could be up."

Booker had me disengage the alarm so he could go out and speak privately to his contact.

"I also found this." Liam pointed to another sheet of paper. This one was older, the paper had begun to yellow and disintegrate. I scanned it: JL, DF, CS, MV, AC, SA. Beside each set of initials were amounts. "This is a payout sheet?" I asked Liam.

"I think so. I think that's probably why Deputy Young was killed. They had to suspect that Young had something on them. Maybe he figured it out and kept this for insurance."

"If we go to my office, I can run a work history," I said excitedly. "There has to be some correlation between the gun cage deputy and the gang unit." I yawned. "Sorry. Adrenaline crash."

"That's okay," he said as he rubbed my thigh. I got a tingling sensation from his touch.

Booker came in and I gave him the code to reset the alarm. "Birth date?" he asked.

I nodded. He just shook his head and gave me a knowing smile. "I know. I'll have the alarm company reset it when they come tomorrow."

"The initials fit my former team members except the last one," Liam said. "Does SA mean anything to you?" he asked me.

I searched my brain for any connection, going over all the names I'd come across during my investigation. "No. Could it be the initials of one of the Latin Bandits?" I asked.

Liam shrugged and raked his fingers through his hair. "What about one of the ex-wives? Could any of them be SA?"

I wiggled my finger across the touchpad on my computer,

bringing it out of hibernate. I quickly read the information I'd e-mailed to myself. "José's ex-wife's surname was Aldoña, but her first name is Ina." My hopes were dashed.

"If José changed his name, maybe she did, too," Liam suggested.

"Then we take a road trip," I said. "I need my office computer to do a complete search of the databases."

Liam looked perplexed. He glanced at Booker whose only response was a tilt of his head. Perry Mason was lying down at my feet as if he didn't have a care in the world. While I wasn't ready to join the American Kennel Club, I was growing used to having the dog in the house. Especially now that I knew he was in a perpetual state of readiness.

"I'll pull up in front of the door," Booker said. "We can limit her exposure."

"Thank you for talking *about* me instead of *to* me," I said. "Besides, the shooter was killed. Doesn't that mean I'm safe now?"

Liam reached out and tucked some hair behind my ear. "Probably, yes. But the photograph isn't a good sign."

"What is it a sign of?" I was pretty sure I didn't want to know the answer.

Liam met and held my gaze. "A hit for hire. The shooter obviously didn't know you on sight."

"Okay," I said, trying to keep my nerves in check. "But what sense does that make?" I asked. "You're the one who was on the gang unit. You're the one they tried to kill at José's house. So how did I become the target?"

"I'd rather it was me, too," Liam said.

I reached out and took his hand in both of mine. "I didn't mean that the way it sounded. Of course I don't want you being hunted like a dog." Perry Mason's ears went up. "Sorry," I said as I let go of Liam and scratched Perry's head. "But when I got the creepy e-mail I'd done nothing other than show up at the police station with you. If someone had a problem with that, why not go after Tony? He's your attorney. All I'd done till then was a few cursory database checks. We're missing something. I shouldn't be a target."

"But you got Santos to spill his guts," Liam countered.

"Why?" I asked, more for myself than the two men in the room.

"Because he hasn't seen a pretty woman in five years," Liam answered.

I shook my head. "He was completely cavalier about it. Tossed it all out on the table. Correct me if I'm wrong, but if an inmate has information about a serious crime, don't they usually trade that information for something they want?"

Both men nodded.

"Santos thought I was an attorney when he first met me. I didn't think anything of it at the time, but he made mention of getting out of prison early. Maybe he spilled his guts to me because he was about to go to the authorities with what he knew about the police skimming money off gang busts."

Liam rubbed his face. His brow was strained and I could almost hear his brain working. "So someone got wind of it and had him killed," Liam said. "But this someone doesn't know what Santos told you."

"Right," I agreed quickly. "Only why wait five years?"

"Because for Santos to talk about police corruption he'd also have to name the names of the Latin Bandits. That's a death sentence," Booker offered.

"But they could have put him in witness protection or something. He could have told his story and then been whisked off to Nebraska to work in a hardware store."

"Right. Jimmy Santos wouldn't stand out in the middle of a bunch of tumbleweeds," Liam said with a scoff.

"Tumbleweeds are mostly found in arid parts of the United States, like Texas and—" Liam shot me a glare. I held up both hands. "I'm just saying."

"Forget SA for a minute. The other initials are JL, José Lopez. DF, Diego Ferrer. AC, Armando Calderone. CS, Carlos Santiago. And MV, Miguel Vasquez. That's everyone in the unit except Stan and me."

Liam looked so dejected. All I wanted to do was pull him into my arms, but not with Booker and Perry Mason watching. I had to keep reminding myself that our relationship didn't have a definition. I didn't know the rules. Public affection or not? I went with the safe choice and decided not.

"Who did you replace?" I asked Liam.

"I don't remember his name."

"Then let's go to my office. Maybe something will pop up on LexisNexis."

"Let's do it," Booker agreed.

I felt a little like the First Lady. I remained with Liam in the house while Booker pulled up his Explorer. We set the alarm, locked the door, and made a mad dash for the car. I leapt inside, landing half sitting, half lying on the seat with the cup holder rammed into my ribs. I bet that never happened to Michelle Obama.

It was pitch black out, and thus far, we hadn't seen another car on the road. I didn't feel panicked at all. Being surrounded by strapping men with guns can have that effect on a girl.

When we reached the office, I used my key and we went inside, locking the door behind us. Booker decided to stand guard in the lobby while Liam accompanied me to my office. Through force of habit, I made a pot of coffee. I needed a caffeine fix to get my brain to focus.

I logged into the database and searched for a member of the sheriff's office with a last name that started with an A. The results were impossible. There had to be nearly fifty names on the list. I printed it out. "You go over these to see if you can find the elusive SA while I look through case files."

The plaintiff-defendant database seemed like a good place to start. I put in José's name and a long list of cases appeared. He had fifteen years on the force, so this wasn't going to be a quickie task. Thank God for coffee.

His most recent cases were all traffic-oriented—DUIs, speeding, resisting arrest, nothing major. "How long was José in the gang unit?"

"Eight or nine years," Liam answered. "I can't find any officers with SA as a first or a last name. Does this include retired officers?" he asked.

"No," I said as I narrowed my search to the dates Liam had given me and found another long list of arrests and court appearances. The way the database was configured, I could get the names of the major players involved, like the judge and the court reporter, as well as a two- or three-paragraph recap of the court proceedings, followed by the disposition—jail time, probation, and community service. I was scanning the fifth report when I noticed something odd. "Every trial José testified in was overseen by Assistant State's Attorney Garza."

"I know," Liam said as he looked up from the list that was alphabetical by last name. "Judges specialize. Some handle only capital cases, others do drug cases, others do traffic, others do misdemeanors, and the low guys on the totem pole get stuck with night court. It helps when a judge knows the players and their attorneys."

"If Garza only does drug cases, why is he on your case?"

"Probably because it involves the murder of a former gang unit cop." Liam let the paper fall into his lap. "Unless . . ."

"SA stands for state's attorney," I said, finishing the thought.

"It fits," Liam said. "But Garza has always struck me as a fair guy."

"Maybe that's because he wanted you to think that," I suggested. "We should call Tony."

"Hang on," Liam said. "It's a big leap from Stan to José to an attempt on our lives to Garza. We can't just make an accusation. Garza is a smart guy. I'm sure he's covered his ass."

"Then let's see if he's covered his assets."

I searched every possible database and Internet site out there but couldn't find anything out of the ordinary. No large investments, no sudden windfalls. In fact, he'd lost a decent amount when tech stocks tanked. A house with a mortgage that was in keeping with his government salary. I couldn't find a thing.

"So what do we do now?" I asked. "Call Tony in the morning and ask his advice?"

Liam shook his head. "The fewer people we involve in this the better. Especially Tony. He's got a kid to think about."

His comment reminded me about the breakup of his marriage. As much as I wanted to hate Ashley for making a rash decision, I kind of understood her position. It would be awfully hard to raise a child whose father was in prison when your one skill was doing nails. I tip my manicurist well, but not enough to buy diapers and formula. What I didn't get was why she would think for a minute that Liam had shot an unarmed kid. My heart ached for Liam. Then it ached for me. I had a sneaking suspicion that I wasn't in lust anymore. I had entered the scary zone. Not love, but definitely headed in that direction. A very bad thing when all I'd done was spend one night with him. Granted, it was a wonderful night, but really, I was thinking like a stalker. I all but had us married in my brain. Definite stalker behavior.

"So how do we connect the dots?" I asked.

"Carefully and discreetly," Liam answered.

◆

I woke up to the sound of Perry Mason whining. Liam was just getting out from under my comforter when I glanced at the clock. It was already after seven.

"Crap," I said as I quickly stood up, shielding my nakedness with the clothes on the floor next to the bed. "I'm gonna be late for work."

"Tony told you to take some time off," Liam said.

"That was before they caught the shooter," I replied, exasperated, as I made a dash for the shower. I stood under the spray freezing for a few seconds until the hot water kicked in. I moved at warp speed, dreaming of coffee as I rinsed the shampoo from my hair.

Wrapped in a towel, I went to my closet and did the hard thing—finding the right outfit for the day. After some searching I settled on a Kate Spade A-line skirt in bright pink and a simple Burberry white blouse. I'd gotten both items on eBay, and after a trip to the dry cleaner's, no one would ever know they were preworn. At least no one but me and PayPal. I slipped on a pair of Nine West taupe platform pumps. They were comfortable, probably because I'd gotten them on a 50 percent off red-dot sale.

It was nearly eight fifteen when I emerged with mostly dry hair and full makeup. Booker was sitting in the living room and Liam was in the kitchen. And bless him, he'd made coffee. I gulped down the first cup, then passed him the mug for a refill.

"I'll follow you to work," Liam said as he gave me the once-over. The perusal was almost as exciting as his touch.

"And then do what?" I asked.

"I'm a client. We can have a meeting."

"You're a pro bono client. Vain Dane will get an aneurysm."

"We'll figure it out."

Booker was left in charge of the dog and waiting for the information from New York regarding José. Assuming Garza was the mastermind of the cash-skimming scheme, I was a tad wary of being out in public. I was comforted by seeing Liam right on my tail the whole way to the parking lot.

There was a rental Hummer in the lot, so just as a precaution, I parked as far away from it as possible. Vain Dane was probably halfway to a heart attack already; no need to make it worse.

I had a rational fear of the parking lot, so I walked quickly inside the building. Margaret looked up, then made a note. It was 9:05.

"Messages?" I asked.

She passed me three pink slips. "May I help you, Mr. McGarrity?"

"I'm with her," he said.

"So you might want to put on some Kevlar," I joked as we walked to the elevator.

"She's chipper in the morning," Liam observed.

"That was actually a good morning," I told him. "Oh, crap," I groaned as I read the notes.

"What?" he asked.

"Three messages from three disinherited people. Not exactly how I wanted to start my morning."

"I guess they aren't calling to say thanks."

"No, it's more like being bitch-slapped over the phone. It's my fault their father chose to exclude them."

"Was it?"

I turned to glare at him as the elevator door opened. "I never even met the dead guy."

I noticed that the room went completely silent as the interns and administrative assistants all turned and looked my way. Obviously they didn't relish the idea of working alongside a moving target.

Ignoring their stares, I went to my office with Liam in tow. Becky was sitting at my desk.

"You just won me fifty bucks," she said with a smile as she got out of my chair. "Thanks."

"Fifty bucks for what?" I asked.

"Hi, Liam. Oh, we had a little office pool going on whether you'd show up for work or not."

"Thank you for assuming correctly that I would perform my duties as expected."

Becky's smile broadened and she absently played with the amber pendant hanging around her neck. "Actually, I won because I said you'd be here, but you'd be late."

"Gee, thanks."

"How's the hand?"

I glanced down at the curling edges of the bandage. "A nonevent. I've had worse paper cuts."

She had on a flowing coral skirt and patterned blouse along with her chunky bracelets and chandelier earrings. "Glad it wasn't worse."

"You and me both. Want some coffee?"

"I've got to get back upstairs. Just wanted to check in with you."

I gave her a hug. "Thanks, but I'm all good."

Liam parked himself in one of the chairs opposite my desk. I went out to the kitchenette and rinsed my coffeepot, then filled it with water. As I passed through the bullpen area, I was still garnering stares. Hopefully that would end soon. I didn't want to be treated like a star when, at best, I was an understudy.

I took the Lawson file out of my credenza and clipped the

three messages inside. I flipped to the bottom one and dialed the number. In less than ten seconds, I was sorry I had. I was being reamed by Virginia Lawson Reynolds, who was insisting her father had dementia and the will couldn't possibly be valid. She blamed the whole thing on her greedy brother and easily manipulated mother and she promised to fight it with everything in her power.

For part of the one-sided conversation, I'd held the phone away from my ear while she was screaming at me. Liam seemed a little stunned and said as much when I ended the call.

"Are they all like that?"

"With seven million up for grabs, yeah. Pretty much."

I got lucky with the second and third calls, reaching machines both times. I knew they'd call back, I just hoped they'd take their time doing it.

Tony appeared at my door. "Glad you're here," he said. "I've got good news."

"That will be a nice change."

"Garza wants Liam and me in his office in an hour. I think he's going to drop all charges."

You can be fearless or you can be smart.

twenty-one

"We have to tell Tony," I whispered as soon as I knew he was out of earshot.

"You think Garza's going to invite the two of us to his office and then open fire? It's the courthouse, Finley. Let's see where this goes. Maybe Garza isn't the SA from the list."

"But if Tony knew, he could help."

"We could also be putting him in danger. The best thing we can do for him is to keep him out of the loop. You don't want anyone going after him, do you?"

"Of course not," I answered. I rested my cheek against his chest and focused on the even rhythm of his heartbeat. "So what happens when we see Garza?"

"You're not going," he said. "You don't have to be there. Tell Tony you've got a migraine or something. Anything."

"You're going in alone?"

"No, I'm going with Tony. You're going home to Booker."

I grabbed fistfuls of his shirt. "Are you sure this is safe?"

He cradled my face in his hands. "I'm positive.

"Wait here until Tony and I leave. Then drive home. No stops."

My nerves were on edge. Even though Tony was with Liam, I still had a nagging suspicion that something was all wrong about the whole situation. Maybe Booker could do something.

I arrived home and heard the reassuring sound of Perry Mason barking. Maybe a dog wasn't the end of the world. I stuck my key in the lock and as soon as I opened the door, I saw Booker on the sofa with his gun pointed at me.

The dog stood at my feet looking up as if it was perfectly normal to be greeted by a large man with a large gun pointed at your head. I gave him a pet. "I'm taking a partial sick day," I explained. Then I told him about Liam.

"Smart move," Booker said.

"He could be walking right into a trap," I argued.

"Garza wouldn't dare do anything in public, and there are guards all over the building, so it may be the safest place for him."

I felt slightly mollified. "Has the alarm company shown up yet?"

He shook his head. "But I know how José Garcia became José Lopez."

"How?" I asked as I sat at the opposite end of the sofa.

"Ran his social. It wasn't issued until José was seventeen. My guy at the NYPD said Lopez, then Garcia, was busted and looking at some serious drug time so he rolled on the Latin Bandits. The feds set him up in Miami with a new ID and a clean slate."

"So he joined the sheriff's office?" I asked, incredulous.

Booker smiled. "Seems his brush with the law took him to Jesus. From everything I could find, José turned into an altar boy once he got to Miami."

"Then how did he end up being the point man ripping off drug dealers?"

"Turns out I wasn't the first person to check on José. His file with the feds shows an inquiry by the Palm Beach Sheriff's Office eight years ago."

"Not Garza?"

"I haven't been able to find anything that leads back to Garza. Either he isn't the right SA or he's one very clever dude."

"Anything that links José to Santos?" I asked.

He took a notepad out of his back pocket. "I can't find anything that puts them together before the drug busts here in Palm Beach County."

"Would Jimmy Santos have recognized him as a Latin Bandit?"

Booker shook his square-topped head. "They aren't like those White Pride assholes. Each gang in each city has its own hierarchy. They don't have annual conventions. Besides, Lopez/Garcia hasn't been active for more than twenty years. And, if the Latin Bandits here found out, they'd have killed the guy on sight years ago."

"I'm going to change," I said. "We can call for Chinese."

I put on a pair of skinny jeans and a flowy top I'd found on sale at Bealls Outlet. After slipping on some ballerina flats, I rejoined Booker. "There has to be something," I told him. "What if we went to see Ina Lopez? She might know something."

"Liam wants you here."

"Liam doesn't always get what he wants," I countered. "Fine. You stay here, I'll go alone."

He laughed. "No wonder Liam likes you."

I wanted to ask him to define "like" but I couldn't think of a way that didn't drip with desperation. "Let's go. No Chinese, we can hit a drive-through on the way. My treat."

We ate as Booker drove to Ina's house via the directions I'd gotten off MapQuest.

Liam called. "Where are you?" he demanded without preamble.

"Booker and I are taking a field trip." I explained the purpose of our outing. "How did it go with Garza?"

"He's dropping the charges. I have to hang around here for some paperwork and go before the judge to make it official."

"I'll give you a call after we talk to Ina."

"Can't you just go home?" he asked, exasperated.

"I have Booker with me. He's invincible."

"Yeah? Well tell him he's a dead man when I see him."

I intentionally didn't bother covering the mouthpiece. "Liam says thank you very much for taking me to see Ina."

"You're killing me, Finley," Liam said.

I smiled. "Just roll with it."

I hung up and then pointed to an upcoming turn. "Make this right. Hers should be the second house on the left."

As we turned the corner, I noted the professionally manicured lawns and the sizes of the homes. Still, Ina Lopez's house stood out because it had been customized with ramps leading from the driveway to the front door. There was a blue van parked in front with a metal grate attachment for a wheelchair.

Booker parked behind the van. "I'll go in with you," he said. Well, it was more like a directive than a statement.

As we exited the vehicle, I heard the hum of lawn mowers and could smell freshly cut grass carried on the gentle breeze. We walked up the ramp, Booker just behind me and to the right. I pressed the doorbell.

A woman I guessed was somewhere in her late fifties, wearing scrubs, answered the door.

"Mrs. Lopez?" I asked.

"No," she said with a shake of her head. Her hair was gray and pulled into a tight bun at the crown of her head. "I'll get her," she added, then stepped away from the partially opened door.

A pretty woman with exotically dark features and a cautious smile came to the door. "I'm Ina Lopez."

"I'm Finley Tanner," I said, offering her one of my cards. "And this is my assistant, Mr. Booker." Hope she bought that one. My assistant was dressed in camo slacks and a tight black T-shirt. He looked more like an army recruitment poster than any assistant.

"I'm sorry," Ina said with a slight Spanish accent. "Do I know you?"

She was dressed in shorts and a top and her long black hair fell nearly to her waist. "No. We're here about José."

Her eyes narrowed suspiciously. "What about José?"

"May we come in?" I asked.

She hesitated a minute, then swung the door wide.

We stepped into what should have been a living room but had been transformed into a hospital room. Along the far wall was a hospital bed. There was a frail-looking woman lying there connected to a breathing machine that made a whooshing sound at regular intervals. There were other machines as well, but I didn't know what they were for. The caregiver was seated next to the bed reading a book while the elderly woman slept. At least I hoped she was sleeping.

The house smelled of rubbing alcohol and antibacterial soap.

"Let's go into the kitchen, I don't want to disturb my mother."

Booker and I followed her down a wide hallway. The ceilings had to be at least fourteen feet high, and other than the wheelchair folded and parked near the knee wall separating the two rooms, it was a stunning home.

Ina showed us to the table in the kitchen across from the center island. The kitchen was well appointed—Sub-Zero fridge, state-of-the-art six-burner stove with a modern hood. The walls were white with red accent pieces everywhere. Two bar stools were askew and there were crumbs on the breakfast bar, indicating that at least two children lived in the home.

"What is it you want?" Ina asked.

"We want to find out who killed José. The man originally accused—"

"I know," she interrupted. "The charges were dropped this morning. It was on the news at noon."

"Right," I said. Now I had to think of a way to ask her about José without calling him a criminal. Even though they were divorced, I noticed several framed family photographs in the dining room. Many of them featured José, so even in divorce, he was still a part of her life and I didn't want to spook her.

"Are we keeping you from . . ." I hooked my thumb over my shoulder in the direction of the makeshift hospital room.

"My mother," she supplied. "She has Alzheimer's disease. End stage."

"I'm so sorry," I said in earnest.

Ina shifted in her seat. "It has been a difficult six years. She declined very quickly. The doctors say it won't be much longer."

"At least she gets to spend her last days with you and your family," I said.

"Maybe," she said with sadness in her voice. "Without José's help, I'm not sure I can afford to keep her here with me."

"José's help?" I prodded.

"From his second job. He loved my mother very much and has made sure she's gotten the best care even though she has no insurance."

"What was his second job?" I asked.

"He loaded containers for shipment. It was hard work and not always steady, but every penny he made he gave to me for Mama's care."

"What was the name of the company he worked for?"

"Southern Allied Cartage," she said. "Out at the Port of Palm Beach."

SA was whizzing through my head and it was everything I could do not to react. "So José was good to you?"

She nodded.

"Then why," I asked gently, "did you divorce?"

"José decided he didn't want to be married anymore. I

wanted us to go to counseling at the church, but he wouldn't go."

"When was that?"

She sighed heavily. "About six years ago, a little while after we found out Mama was sick."

"But you saw him regularly?" I asked.

Again she nodded. "He takes the kids when he isn't working weekends and he always paid his child support and gave me the envelope."

"What envelope?" I pressed.

"I guess it doesn't matter now," she said. "Southern Allied paid him in cash, under the table. The only thing he ever asked of me was that I pay in cash for all of Mama's expenses. I honored his wishes. Now I don't know what I'll do."

"Did José have life insurance?"

"He bought a policy when we were divorced. It's enough to put our children through college, but that's all."

"You have two children?" I asked, remembering my research.

"A boy, eight, and a girl about to turn seven. They're in school now."

"What school?"

"St. Mary's. José wanted them to have a good Catholic education. Now that he's gone I'm not sure if I can make that happen."

"A lot of Catholic schools have scholarship programs," I suggested. "I'm sure they'd be willing to work with you."

"That would be a relief." She got up and asked if either of us would care for a drink. We both declined. "You haven't told me why you are so curious about José."

"We want to find his killer," I told her as I brushed my hair away from my face.

"But why?" she pushed.

"My firm represents Mr. McGarrity. Now that he's been cleared, we'd like to do everything in our power to find the real killer."

"When Liam was arrested I was surprised. José was very protective of him."

"How so?"

She took a sip of water. "He never wanted me to let Liam know about his other job. José knew Liam would have to turn him in if the department ever found out he was working an under-the-table job."

"Do you know if any of the other men José worked with also worked at Southern Allied?"

"I think so. But José never said who and I didn't ask. I was just grateful that he made it possible for me to keep Mama at home."

I stood up. "We've taken up enough of your time," I said. "Thank you for speaking with us."

"Tell Liam I said hello and that I'm happy his troubles are over."

"I will," I promised.

"You thinking what I'm thinking?" Booker asked when we went outside.

I heard the squeal of tires but when I looked in that direction, the white sedan was already turning the corner. Probably some mother late to pick her kid up from school. "I'm thinking we may have found the right SA."

"We should call Liam," Booker said. I tried his number but it went directly to voice mail. "He must be in court," I said. "Let's go back to my place so I can see what I can dig up on this cartage company."

Booker and I got home just after four. I instantly went to my laptop and started searching for anything on Southern Allied.

"Anything?" Booker asked impatiently as my fingers whizzed over the keyboard.

"Shell corporations. A lot of DBAs, doing business as," I explained. "These guys are good," I said absently as I tracked the corporations through half of Europe. "Gotcha," I said triumphantly. "The trail ends in the Cayman Islands."

Perry Mason barked and then the doorbell rang. Booker went to the window. "What's the name of your alarm company?" he asked.

"Palm Beach Protection Services."

"Your alarm guy is here."

Booker opened the door and I heard a zapping noise; Booker crumpled in a heap on the floor. The dog lunged and then whimpered as the uniformed man shocked him with the Taser.

He looked at me with steely black eyes and said, "You can walk out or I can carry you."

Love is giving a person the power to hurt you
but trusting him not to.

twenty-two

I ran toward my bedroom, reaching the nightstand. I had my hand on the gun and was stuffing it in my purse when I felt a sharp pain in my side, followed by nothingness.

My body ached when I regained consciousness. It took me several seconds to realize I was in the back of a police cruiser. I was lying across the back bench seat with my hands secured behind my back. My mouth tasted of something metallic as fear and adrenaline surged through me.

It took me a few seconds but I finally got to a sitting position. A large metal grate and thick Plexiglas separated me from the driver. I kicked the seat. Hard.

"Calm down, we're almost there."

Almost where? I looked out the window and realized we were speeding along Interstate 95, headed toward Riviera Beach. I had a suspicion we were going to the port. I heard muffled pounding coming from the trunk. My first thought was Liam. Was he locked in there?

My second thought was that this was all my fault. If I hadn't insisted on going to see Ina Lopez, I wouldn't have stirred the hornet's nest and discovered Southern Allied. Tears filled my eyes, half from fear and half from frustration. I kicked the seat again and again, feeling completely helpless. Probably not a smart move. He could turn around and shoot me and no one would be any the wiser.

At each car we passed, I mouthed the words "Help me." My pleas were greeted with humor from the other drivers. Of course they'd find it funny for a person in custody to be asking for help. To them I was some lowlife being carted off to jail.

The patrol car turned down a deserted road, each side stacked high with cargo containers. It was like driving through a canyon. One I probably wouldn't come out of alive. The car stopped on gravel; I could hear the tiny pellets pinging against the undercarriage. The pounding from the trunk grew louder.

As soon as we were parked, two men came out of an aluminum warehouse. I recognized them both. One was Diego Ferrer, the other was Carlos Santiago. The driver was a mystery until he turned around and I saw his nameplate: CALDERONE. The one guy who had refused to come to the door.

They stood talking for a minute, then Calderone came to the back door while the other two went to the trunk. I was yanked out of the car so hard I thought he'd dislocated my shoulder in the process. I smelled diesel fuel and the briny scent of water. There wasn't another soul in sight and the sun was starting to set.

To my surprise, the person from the trunk was Booker. His hands were secured with zip ties and he was gagged. While I was sorry that being my babysitter had gotten him into this mess, I was relieved to know it wasn't Liam. At least he was safe.

My relief didn't last long. I was marched into the warehouse, my footfalls echoing in the nearly empty building. There was an old wooden desk in the middle of the space. In the center of the room was a single light fixture dangling from the ceiling, and just below the lamp, Liam was tied to one of three chairs. I took one look at him and had to fight back tears. He'd been beaten. Badly. His face was swollen. His lower lip was split and blood had dripped down the front of his shirt from a cut on his cheek.

While I was walking like a zombie, Booker was struggling the whole way. It took two of them to keep the large man from gaining his freedom.

I was unceremoniously dumped into one chair, then Calderone went back outside. I thought about running, but the sight of guns tucked into the waistbands of the men holding Booker kept me in place. I scooted my chair closer to Liam. He was breathing, but unconscious.

Calderone came back with my purse and dumped the contents on top of the desk. He then placed my gun on the pile and turned to give me a sarcastic wink. "She was packing," he told the others. They also seemed amused.

Packing? Was I in a bad Clint Eastwood film? No. This was real and Clint wasn't coming to save the day. Santiago and Ferrer secured Booker's ankles to the chair legs. I guess they didn't consider me much of a threat because other than the restraints on my hands, I was left untethered.

"Liam!" I whispered loudly.

"He's, um, napping," Calderone said with a malevolent smile.

Pleading sounded like a good idea. "You can let us go. We won't say anything to anyone."

"Yeah, right," Calderone shot back at me. "You're real good at keeping your mouth shut."

"I am," I insisted. "I won't tell anyone. Neither will they. I promise."

"Hey, Carlos!" he called. "She promised. Think we should let her go?"

"She'll be going, just not till the boss gets here."

That had to be Vasquez. He was the only one left.

"At least untie my hands," I said. They all looked at me as if I'd just spoken in tongues. "Seriously, what do you think I'll do? There's three of you and only one of me."

Calderone came toward me, sticking his hand in his pocket, and when he got very, very close to my face, he pinched the hilt of his knife and a very scary blade popped up.

"Don't make me regret this," he warned.

I rubbed my wrists and hands as the feeling returned. Pleading wasn't working. Time to go on the offensive. "People will miss me," I said. "If anything happens to me, it can easily be traced back to you."

"I don't think so," Calderone said. "Besides, it doesn't matter. No one will think anything of you disappearing."

"I have a mother. I have friends. People I talk to every day. My bosses are lawyers. They'll get suspicious."

"I don't think so," he taunted again.

"But you can't know that for sure. Booker made phone calls about you. People know Liam has been working on José's case. None of us can disappear without raising suspicions."

"But you can," came a familiar voice from behind me. "Of course, none of this would have been necessary if Deputy Calderone had carried out the plan without screwing up. First Lopez contacted Stan Cain, so we had to clean that up before Cain could do anything about it. Then he goes and calls Liam, and we knew José's conscience had gotten the better of him. José wanted out but that's not how it works.

"Calderone was sent to José's last week to make it look like a murder-suicide. Only he missed the shot at Liam."

I turned and saw ASA Garza walking toward me. He was dressed in a nice suit and tie and strolled as if he was taking a leisurely walk on the beach. "It was you!"

"You should have gone with your initial instincts," he said. "Once Liam searched Young's place, I had a feeling he'd find what we were looking for."

"And Deputy Young?"

"I'm afraid he's no longer with us."

"But there's blood on the boat. People will get concerned."

"All cleaned up and set adrift. The Coast Guard will assume he fell overboard," Garza said. "Any other details you want explained?"

"Yeah. Why are you such an asshole?"

His response was to slap me across the face. It stung so much tears came. Liam moaned then. "Don't worry," I whispered to him. "I'll get us out of this."

Garza shook his head and then backhanded me again. This

time he knocked me to the floor. Booker was struggling against his restraints and now a conscious Liam was doing the same thing.

I'd hit my head on the concrete, so I was literally seeing stars. I rolled over onto my back. "Didn't your mother ever tell you it isn't nice to hit girls?"

"My mother taught me to be pragmatic," Garza answered. He then turned to the three other men. "Two of you wait outside. I don't want to risk any company."

Ferrer and Santiago left. Calderone was standing next to Garza and, judging by the look on his face, he was enjoying watching me get my ass kicked. "What else has you concerned, Finley?"

"You dismissed the charges against Liam, so the police will continue their investigation. Liam can't just disappear."

"Good point," he said with a chuckle. "Only Liam is supposed to disappear."

"Why would you think that?"

"Because I worked out all the particulars with his lawyer today. Mr. Caprelli was in complete agreement with my plan."

"What plan?" Did I really want to know?

"As I told Mr. Caprelli, we've now linked José Lopez's murder to the Latin Bandits. The person who shot at you and Liam was a Latin Bandit."

"Since when?"

"Since he was given the contract by one of my associates. Unfortunately, he was killed by Deputy Santiago, so there won't be any investigation."

"You've thought of everything, huh?"

"Tony knows neither Liam nor I would walk away from our lives.

"If only you could have seen the look of understanding on his face," Garza said.

Ferrer came racing into the building. "Just heard over the radio. There are cops on the way here."

Thank God! "Guess you weren't as thorough as you thought," I told Garza.

He shrugged. "Minor inconvenience." He turned to Ferrer and Vasquez. "You two and Santiago get out of here. Calderone, call in your location. Tell them you heard shots fired inside the warehouse. Then come back here and do away with our friends. Then fire off some rounds so it looks like you were targeting someone. We'll find a Latin Bandit to pin it on later."

The four men jogged to the door and I knew my time was limited. I decided on a plan of action. I just didn't know if it would work.

I jumped up and head-butted Garza, knocking him to the floor. Then I ran to the desk and retrieved my gun. With unsteady hands, I trained it on him. But instead of looking afraid, he smiled up at me. "Unfortunately for you, Calderone removed the magazine."

Great! A gun with no bullets and Calderone would be back in seconds.

"Shoot, Finley!" Liam called from behind me.

I closed one eye and pulled the trigger. Instantly Garza reached for his chest, then fell to his knees, his expression a mixture of shock and fear.

"Get something sharp," Booker said. I went to the desk, shoving things around until I found my fingernail scissors. I cut Liam free and then he freed Booker. I heard the door open.

"Run!" Liam said as he grabbed my hand and pulled me in the direction of stacked boxes.

All three of us climbed down into the maze. I was sandwiched between Booker and Liam. "Now what?" I whispered.

Liam pulled my hand and we went to the right. I could hear Calderone's footsteps getting closer. There probably weren't more than four boxes between Calderone and us. Booker and Liam stopped and looked at each other. Then Liam held up three fingers. Then two, then one.

Together they pushed the load off the top and almost simultaneously I heard a man yelp. Booker and Liam went over the boxes and I heard a scuffle, then a gunshot. I couldn't reach the top of the boxes so I had to go back the way I'd come. I was quivering and so worried about Liam that I didn't even think of my own safety.

Turns out I didn't have to. Booker and Liam took turns punching Calderone in the face. Then the door burst open and a bunch of men in black gear came in holding assault rifles.

Garza was on the floor, writhing around in pain.

Calderone was taken into custody immediately. An ambulance came for Garza and I stood off to the side rubbing my arms. Liam came over and folded me into his embrace. "How did you know?" I asked.

"Know what?"

"That there was still a bullet in the gun?"

"I didn't. I was just hoping Calderone forgot to empty the chamber when he took out the magazine."

"That was quite a chance you took."

"Look on the bright side," Liam said as he stroked my hair. "You hit the target."

"I was aiming for his head," I admitted.

◆

"We are a pair," Liam said as he looked past me into the mirror and examined the wounds and welts on his face. Me? I'd gotten away with just a lump on my head and a small cut on my lip.

"C'mon, we have company."

He swatted me on the fanny as we left my bedroom after cleaning up. Tony, Becky, Liv, Jane, Booker, and Perry Mason were all seated in the living room with a bottle of champagne. Tony popped the cork and began to fill all the glasses. "To computers," he said as he raised his glass.

"To Becky," Liv added just before the ceremonial clink.

I sipped the champagne and savored the taste as the bubbles tickled my nose. I was very aware of the fact that Liam still had his hand on the center of my back. I guess we did have the kind of relationship that allows for public displays of affection. That warmed me more than the alcohol.

"It was genius," Becky said on a satisfied breath.

"What was?" I asked.

"When I told her you were going into witness protection, she told me I was nuts," Tony said.

"True," I agreed.

"So I came here and checked your Internet history," Becky explained. "That's how I found the name of Southern Allied."

"So that's why the cops came?"

Tony nodded. "I called a cop I know personally since we didn't know who all was involved in the conspiracy."

I went to Becky and gave her a hug. "Thank you."

"A good friend always knows to check your Internet history," she returned.

"Come, Perry," Liam said to the dog. Other than some singed fur, Perry Mason was none the worse for his experience. Liam petted the dog's head. I did, too. Perry was growing on me. Mainly because he stayed off the furniture.

We drank and laughed and ate the crackers and Brie Liv had brought along. She knows me well enough to know my house is BYOF—bring your own food. I was relaxed for the first time in days. And, if I did say so myself, I was proud of the way I'd handled danger. Though I don't think I'll turn into a gun-toting woman any time soon.

The celebration lasted until midnight. Booker was the first to leave. I gave him a hug, or tried to—I couldn't get my arms around his beefy body. I did kiss his cheek, and to my surprise, he blushed.

Tony left with the girls, leaving Liam and me alone. My chest tightened. What now? Do I ask him to stay over? Do I wait for him to ask? I needed a man manual.

We had a slightly awkward moment as he helped me load the dishwasher. It was such a domestic chore but it felt weird. *I* felt weird. And I couldn't stand the tension.

"We can watch the late news," I suggested.

He smiled and shook his head. "Not interested."

My insides felt coiled. "We could take Perry for a walk. He likes the beach."

"Perry is fine," he said as he stepped a fraction closer to me.

"Rent a movie?" I offered.

"Nope."

"Then what do you want to do?" I asked.

He slipped his arm around my waist and pulled me to him. He kissed my forehead, then his mouth slipped lower until he was placing feather-light kisses on my collarbone. "What do you want now?"

"You," I said, so breathless I wasn't sure I could get out more than one word.

He lifted his head and held my gaze. "For how long?"

"At least until I find out if you're drawer worthy."